MELOMANIACS

MELOMANIACS

BY

JAMES HUNEKER

Come, let us march against the powers of heaven,
And set black streamers in the firmament,
To signify the slaughter of the Gods.

Marlowe

NEW YORK
CHARLES SCRIBNER'S SONS
1902

Copyright, 1902, by
CHARLES SCRIBNER'S SONS

PUBLISHED, FEBRUARY, 1902

University Press:
JOHN WILSON AND SON, CAMBRIDGE, U.S.A.

TO

PHILIP HALE

CONTENTS

CONTENTS

MELOMANIACS

THE LORD'S PRAYER IN B

AT the close of the first day they brought Baruch into the great Hall of the Oblates, sometime called the Hall of the Unexpected. The young man walked with eyes downcast. Aloft in the vast spaces the swinging domes of light made more reddish his curly beard, deepened the hollows on either side of his sweetly pointed nose, and accented the determined corners of his firmly modelled lips. He was dressed in a simple tunic and wore no Talith; and as he slowly moved up the wide aisle the Grand Inquisitor, visibly annoyed by the resemblance, said to his famulus, "The heretic dares to imitate the Master." He crossed himself and shuddered.

Mendoza abated not his reserve as he drew near the long table before the Throne. Like a quarry that is at last hemmed in, the Jew was quickly surrounded by a half thousand black-robed monks. The silence — sick, profound, and awful — was punctuated by the low, sullen tapping of a drum. Its droning sound reminded the prisoner of life-blood dripping from some single pore; the tone was B, and its insistent, muffled,

funereal blow at rhythmic intervals would in time
have worn away rock. Mendoza felt a prevision
of his fate; being a musician he knew of music's
woes and warnings. And he lifted eyes for the
first time since his arrest in a gloomy, star-lit
street of Lisbon.

He saw bleached, shaven faces in a half circle;
they seemed like skulls fastened on black dum-
mies — so immobile their expression, so deadly
staring their eyes. The brilliant and festal
appearance of the scene oppressed him and
his eyeballs ached. Symphonies of light were
massed over the great high walls; glistening
and pendulous, they illuminated remote ceilings.
There was color and taunting gaiety in the
decoration; the lofty panels contained pictures
from the classic poets which seemed profane in
so sacred an edifice, and just over the Throne
gleamed the golden tubes of a mighty organ.
Then Baruch Mendoza's eyes, half blinded by
the strange glory of the place to which he had
been haled, encountered the joyful and ferocious
gaze of the Grand Inquisitor. Again echoed
dolefully the tap of the drum in the key of B,
and the prisoner shuddered.

A voice was heard: "Baruch Mendoza, thou
art before the Throne, and one of the humblest
of God's creatures asks thee to renounce thy
vile heresies." Baruch made no answer. The
voice again modulated high, its menace sweetly
hidden.

2

"Baruch Mendoza, dost thou renounce?" The drum counted two taps. Baruch did not reply. For the third time the voice issued from the lips of the Grand Inquisitor, as he drew the hood over his face.

"Baruch Mendoza, dog of a Jew, dog of a heretic, believer in no creed, wilt thou recant the evil words of thy unspeakable book, prostrate thyself before the altar of the Only God, and ask His forgiveness? Answer, Baruch Mendoza!"

The man thus interrogated wondered why the Hall of the Oblates was adorned with laughing Bacchantes, but he responded not. The drum tapped thrice, and there was a burst of choral music from the death-like monks; they chaunted the *Dies Iræ*, and the sonorous choir was antiphonally answered with anxious rectitude from the gallery, while the organ blazed out its frescoed tones. And Baruch knew that his death-hymn was being sung.

To him, a despiser of the vesture of things, to him the man with the spiritual inner eye, whose philosophy was hated and feared because of its subtle denial of the God in high heaven, to Baruch Mendoza the universe had seemed empty with an emptiness from which glared no divine Judge — his own people's Jahveh — no benignant sufferer appeared on the cross. He saw no future life except in the commingling of his substance with the elements; and for

3

this contumacious belief, and his timidly bold expression of it, he had been waylaid and apprehended in the gloomy star-lit street of Lisbon.

The single tap of the drum warned him; the singing had ceased. And this bitter idealist, this preacher of the hollowness of the real, wondered where were the sable trappings of woe, the hideous envisagement of them that are condemned with mortuary symbols in garbs of painted flame to the stake, faggot, axe, and headsman. None of these were visible, and the gentle spirit of the prisoner became ruffled, alarmed. He expected violence but instead they offered churchly music. Restless, his nerves fretted, he asked himself the reason. He did not fear death, for he despised life; he had no earthly ties; his life's philosophy had been fittingly enunciated; and he knew that even though a terrible death overtook him his seed had fallen on ripe soil. As he was a descendant from some older system that denied the will to live, so would he in turn beget disciples who would be beaten, burned and reviled by the great foe to liberty — the foe that strangled it before Egypt's theocracy, aye! before the day of sun-worshippers invoking their round, burning god, riding naked in the blue. Baruch pondered these things, and had almost lost his grasp on time and space when something jarred his consciousness.

4

THE LORD'S PRAYER IN B

It was the tap of the drum, sombre, dull, hollow and threatening; he shivered as he heard its percussive note, and with a start remembered that the *Dies Iræ* had been chaunted in the same key. Once more he wondered.

A light touch on the shoulder brought him realization. He stood almost alone; the monks were gliding down the great Hall of the Oblates and disappearing through a low arched door, the sole opening in the huge apartment. One remained, a black friar, absolutely hooded.

Baruch followed him. The pair noiselessly traversed the wonderful hall with its canopies of light, its airy arches, massive groinings and bewildering blur of color and fragrance; the air was thick and grateful with incense. Exactly in the middle of the hall there rested on the floor a black shadow, a curiously shaped shadow. It was a life-sized crucifix which Baruch had not seen before. To it he was led by the black friar, who motioned him to the floor; then this unbelieving Jew and atheist laid himself humbly down, and with outstretched arms awaited his end.

In few rapid movements the prisoner was chained to the cross; and with a penetratingly sweet smile the friar gave him a silent blessing, while Baruch's eyes followed the dazzling tracery on the ceiling, and caught a glimpse of the golden, gleaming organ tubes above the Throne of Judgment.

need they pray over him? Why did they not take him to his damp cell to rot or to be eaten by vermin? This blaze of light was unendurable; it penetrated his closed eyelids, painted burning visions on his brain, and the music — the accursed music — continued. Again the Lord's Prayer was solemnly intoned, and noticing the freshness of the voices he opened his eyes, counted ten cowled monks around him; and the key they sang was B, the mode major.

Another set, Baruch thought, as he remarked the stature of the singers, and sought oblivion. All that night and all next day he chased sleep, and the morning of the third day found him with half mad gaze, sleepless and frantic. When from deadly exhaustion he would half faint into stupor the hollow, sinister sound of the drum stunned his ears, while rich, churchly voices of men would intone " Pater noster, qui es in cœlis! " and always in the agonizing key of B.

This tone became a monstrous serpent that plunged its fangs into Baruch's brain and hissed one implacable tone, the tone B. The drum roared the same tone; the voices twined about the crucified Jew and beat back sleep, beat back death itself.

The evening of the fourth day Baruch Mendoza was more pallid than his robe; his eyes looked like twin stars, they so glittered, and the fire in them was hardly of this earth. His cheek-bones started through the skin; beard and hair hung in damp masses about the ghastly face and head ; his lips were parted in a contemptuous grin, and there was a strained, listening look on the countenance : he was listening for the key that was slaying him, and he saw it now, saw it in the flesh, a creeping, crawling, shapeless thing that slowly strangled his life. All his soul had flown to his ears, all his senses were lodged in the one sense of hearing, and as he heard again and again the Lord's Prayer in the key of B the words that compose it separated themselves from the tone and assumed an individual life. The awful power of the spoken word assailed him, and " Our Father who art in heaven" became for Baruch a divine gigantic cannibal, devouring the planets, the stars, the firmament, the cosmos, as he created them. The heavens were copper, and there gleamed and glared the glance of an eyeball burning like a sun, and so threatening that the spirit of the atheist was consumed as a scroll in the flame. He cried aloud, " If there is a God, let Him come from on high and save me ! " The drum sounded more fiercely, a monk moistened with water the tortured man's lips, and Baruch groaned when the cowled choir chaunted, " Pater noster, qui es in cœlis ! "

" Give us this day our daily bread." He asked himself if he had ever known hunger and thirst ; then other letters of fire came into his brain, but through the porches of his ears. " And forgive us our trespasses as we forgive those who trespass against us." Could he, he whispered to his soul — could he forgive these devils that sang like angels? He almost shivered in his attempt to smile; and loathing life heard with sardonic amusement: " Lead us not into temptation, but deliver us from evil! "

" Amen," groaned Baruch Mendoza. Again the drum boomed dolorously, and monkish voices intoned: " Pater noster, qui es in cœlis! "

There was no dawn, no eve in this brassy hell of music. The dripping monotone of voices, the dreary pelting of the drum never ceased; and the soul of the unbeliever was worn slowly away. The evening of the seventh day the Grand Inquisitor, standing at his side, noticed with horror the resemblance to the Master, and piously crossed himself.

Seeing the end was nigh, for there was thin froth on the shrivelled gums of the man, the mild-voiced Inquisitor made a sign to the black friar, and in a moment the music that had never ceased for six days was no longer heard, though the air continued to hum with the vibrations of the diabolical tone. The black friar knelt beside the dying one, and drawing an ivory crucifix from his habit held it to Mendoza's face. Baruch, aroused by the cessation of the torturing tonality, opened his eyes, which were as black as blood, saw the symbol of Christianity, and with a final effort forced from his cracked lips:

" Thou traitor ! " As he attempted to blaspheme the sacred image he died, despairingly invoking Adonai.

Then rolled forth in rich, triumphant tones the music of " Our Father who art in heaven," while the drum sonorously sounded in the key of B, and the mode was major.

A SON OF LISZT

It originated in the wicked vanity of Sir William Davenant himself, who, disdaining his honest but mean descent from the vintner, had the shameless impiety to deny his father and reproach the memory of his mother by claiming consanguinity with Shakespeare.

— REED'S SHAKESPEARE.

LITTLE HOLLAND was very dry.

Little Holland is a shapeless stretch of meadowland pierced by irregular canals through which sluggishly flows the water at high tide. Odd shaped houses are scattered about, one so near the river that its garden overflows in the full of the moon. Dotted around stand conical heaps of hay gleaned from this union of land and water. It is called Little Holland, for small schooners sail by under the very nose of your house, and the hired girl often forgets to serve the salad while flirting with the skipper of some sloop. But this August night Little Holland was very dry.

As we stood facing the river I curiously examined my host. His face was deeply lined by life which had carved a quarter hundred little wrinkles about his eyes and the corners of his mouth. His eyes were not true. They shifted too much. His thick, brown hair was thrown off his forehead in a most exuberantly artistic fashion. His nose jutted well into the outer world, and I had to confess that his profile was of a certainty striking. But his full face was disappointing. It was too narrow; its expression was that of a meagre soul, and his eyes were very close together. Yet I liked Piloti; he played the piano well, sang with no little feeling, painted neat water sketches and was a capital host.

A sliced cantaloupe moon, full of yellow radiance, arose as we listened to the melancholy fall of the water on the muddy flats, and I said to Piloti, " Come, let us go within; there you will play for me some tiny questioning Chopin prelude, and forget this dolorous night." . . . He had been staring hard at the moon when I aroused him. " As you will; let us go in-doors by all means, for this moon gives me the spleen." Then we moved slowly toward the house.

Piloti was a bachelor; an old woman kept house and he always addressed her in the Hungarian tongue. His wants were simple, but his pride was Lucifer's. By no means a virtuoso, he had the grand air, the grand style, and when he sat down to play one involuntarily stopped breathing. He had a habit of smiting the keyboard, and massive chords, clangorous harmonies inevitably preluded his performances. I knew some conservatory girls who easily could

outstrip Piloti technically, but there was something which differentiated his playing from that
of other pianists. Liszt he did very well.

When we came into the shabby drawing-room
I noticed a picture of the Abbé Liszt over the
grand piano, and as Piloti took a seat he threw
back his head; and my eyes which had rested a
moment on the portrait involuntarily returned
to it, so before I was aware of it I cried out,
"I say, Piloti, do you know that you look like
Liszt?" He blushed deeply, and gave me a
most curious glance.

"I have heard it said often," he replied, and
he crashed into the master's B minor Sonata,
"The Invitation to Hissing and Stamping," as
Gumprecht has christened it.

Piloti played the interesting work most vigorously. He hissed, he stamped and shook back
his locks in true Lisztian style. He rolled
off the chorale with redundant meaning, and
with huge, flamboyant strokes went through the
brilliant octave finale in B major. As he closed,
and I sat still, a sigh near at hand caused me to
turn, and then I saw the old housekeeper, her
arms folded, standing in a doorway. The moon-
light biliously smudged her face, and I noticed
her staring eyes. Piloti's attention was attracted
by my silence, and when he saw the woman he
uttered a harsh, crackling word. She instantly
retired. Turning to me, with a nervous laugh,
he explained:

" The old fool always is affected by moon-light and music."

We strolled out-of-doors, cigarettes in hand, and the rhythmic swish-swash of the river told that the tide was rising. The dried-up gullies and canals became silver-streaked with the in-coming spray, and it needed only a windmill to make the scene as Dutch as a Van Der Neer. Piloti was moody. Something worried him, but as I was not in a very receptive condition, I forbore questioning him. We walked over the closely cut grass until the water was reached. He stopped, tossed his cigarette away:

" I am the unhappiest man alive ! " At once I became sympathetic.

He looked at me fiercely: " Do you know who I am? Do you know the stock I spring from? Will you believe me if I tell you? Can I even trust you? " I soothed the excited mu-sician and begged him to confide in me. I was his nearest friend and he must be aware of my feelings. He became quieter at once; but never shall I forget the look on his face as he reverently took off his hat.

" I am the son of Franz Liszt, and I thank God for it ! "

" Amen ! " I fervently responded.

Then he told me his story. His mother was a Hungarian lady, nobly born. She had been an excellent pianist and studied with Liszt at Wei-mar and Buda-Pesth. When Piloti became old enough he was taught the piano, for which he had aptitude. With his mother he lived the years of his youth and early manhood in London. She always wore black, and after Liszt's death Piloti himself went into mourning. His mother sickened and died, leaving him nothing but sad memories. It sounded very wretched, and I hastened to console him as best I could. I reminded him of the nobility of his birth, and that it was greater to be the son of a genius than of a duke. "Look at Sir William Davenant," I said; "'O rare Sir William Davenant,' as his contemporaries called him. What an honor to have been Shakespeare's natural son!" But Piloti shook his head.

"I care little for the legitimacy of my birth; what worries me, oppresses me, makes me the most miserable man alive, is that I am not a second Liszt. Why can I not play like my father?"

I endeavored to explain that genius is seldom transmitted, and did not forget to compliment him on his musical abilities. "You know that you play Liszt well. That very sonata in B minor, it pleased me much." "But do I play it like a Friedheim?" he persisted. And I held my peace. . . .

Piloti was downcast and I proposed bed. He assented. It was late; the foolish-looking young topaz moon had retired; the sky was cloudy, and the water was rushing over Little Holland. We did not get indoors without wetting our feet. After drinking a parting glass I shook his hand heartily, bade him cheer up, and said that study would soon put him in the parterre of pianists. He looked gloomy, and nodded good-night. I went to my room. As the water was likely to invade the cellar and even the ground floor, the bedrooms were all on the second floor. I soon got to my bed, for I was tired, and the sadness of this strange household, the moaning of the river, the queer isolated feeling, as if I were alone far out at sea, all this depressed me, and I actually pulled the covers over my head like a frightened child during a thunderstorm.

I must have been sleeping some time when voices penetrated the dream-recesses of my brain. As I gradually emerged from darkened slumber I became conscious of Piloti's voice. It was pitched a trifle above a whisper, but I heard every word. He was talking savagely to some one, and the theme was the old one.

" It has gone far enough. I 'm sick of it, I tell you. I will kill myself in another week. Don't," he said in louder tones and with an imprecation — " don't tell me not to. You 've been doing that for years."

A long silence ensued; a woman's voice answered:

" My son, my son, you break my heart with your sorrow! Study if you would play like your father, study and be brave, be courageous!

16

All will come out right. Idle fretting will do no good."

It was the voice of the housekeeper, and she spoke in English. Piloti's mother! What family secret was I upon the point of discovering? I shivered as I lay in my bed, but could not have forborne listening though I should die for it. The voices resumed. They came from the room immediately back of mine:

"I tell you, mother, I know the worst. I may be the son of a genius, but I am nevertheless a mediocrity. It is killing me! it is killing me!" and the voice of this morose monomaniac broke into sobs.

The poor mother cried softly. "If I only had not been Liszt's son," Piloti muttered, "then I would not be so wretched, so cursed with ambitions. Alas! why was I ever told the truth?"

"Oh, my son, my son, forgive!" I heard the noise of one dropping on her knees. "Oh, my boy, my pride, my hope, forgive me — forgive the innocent imposture I've practised on you! My son, I never saw Liszt; you are — "

With an oath Piloti started up and asked in heavy, thick speech: "What's this, what's this, woman? Seek not to deceive me. What do you tell me? Never saw Liszt! Who, then, was my father? You must speak, if I have to drag the words from between your teeth."

"O God! O God!" she moaned, "I dare not tell you — it is too shameful — I never saw

Liszt — I heard much of him — I adored him, his music — I was vain, foolish, doting! I thought, perhaps, you might be a great pianist, and if you were told that Liszt was your father — your real father." . . .

"My real father — who was he? Quick, woman, speak!"

"He was Liszt's favorite piano-tuner," she whispered.

Dull silence reigned, and then I heard some one slowly descending the stairs. The outer door closed, and I rushed to the window. In the misty dawn I could see nothing but water. The house was completely hemmed in by a noiseless sheet of sullen dirty water. Not a soul was in sight, and almost believing that I had been the victim of a nightmare, I went back to my bed and fell asleep. I was awakened by loud halloas and rude poundings at my window. A man was looking in at me: "Hurry up, stranger; you have n't long to wait. The water is up to the top of the porch. Get your clothes on and come into my boat!"

It did not take me hours to obey this hint, and I stepped from the window to the deck of a schooner. The meadows had utterly disappeared. Nothing but water glistened in the sunlight. When I reached the mainland I looked back at the house. I could just descry the roof.

Little Holland was very wet.

A CHOPIN OF THE GUTTER

J'ai vu parfois au fond d'un théâtre banal
Qu'enflammait l'orchestre sonore
Une fée allumer dans un ciel infernal
Une miraculeuse aurore ;

J'ai vu parfois au fond d'un théâtre banal
Un être qui n'était que lumière, or et gaze,
Terrasser l'énorme Satan ;
Mais mon cœur que jamais ne visite l'extase,

Est un théâtre où l'on attend.
Toujours, toujours en vain l'être aux ailes gaze.
— Baudelaire.

They watched him until he turned the
corner of the Rue Puteaux and was lost to them.

He moved slowly, painfully, one leg striking
the pavement in syncopation, for it was sadly
crippled by disease. He twisted his thin head
only once as he went along the Batignolles. It
seemed to them that his half face was sneering
in the mist. Then the band passed up to the
warmer lights of the Clichy Quarter, where they
drank and argued art far into the night. They
one and all hated Wagner, adoring Chopin's
morbid music.

Minkiewicz walked up the lower side of the
little street called Puteaux until he reached a

stupid, overgrown building. It was numbered 5, and was a shabby sort of pension. The Pole painfully hobbled up the evil-smelling stairway, more crooked than a youth's counterpoint, and on the floor next to the top halted, breathing heavily. The weather was oppressive and he had talked too much to the young men at the brasserie.

" Ah, good boys all," he murmured, trying the door; " good lads, but no talent, no originality. Ah! " The door yielded and Minkiewicz was at home.

An upright piano, a bed, a shaky wash-stand and bureau, one feeble chair, music — pounds of it — filled the chamber lighted by one candle. The old man threw himself on the bed and sighed drearily. Then he went to the piano, lifted the lid and ran his fingers over the keyboard. He sighed again. He sat down on the chair and closed his eyes. He did not sleep, for he arose in a few moments, took off his coat, and lighted a cigarette in the flame of the candle. Minkiewicz again placed himself before the instrument and played, but with silent fingers. He executed the most intricate passages, yet the wind in the room was soundless. He sat in his shirt-sleeves, his hat on his head, playing a Chopin concerto in dumb profile, and the night wore on. . . .

He was awakened in the morning by the entrance of a grimy garçon who grinned and

put on the floor an oblong basket. Minkiewicz
stirred restlessly.

"The absinthe — you have not forgotten it?"
he questioned in a weak voice.

"Ah, no, sir; never, sir, do I forget the green
fairy for the great musician, sir," was the answer,
evidently a set one, its polite angles worn away
by daily usance.

The man grasped the proffered glass and
swallowed, choking, the absinthe. It did him
good, for he sat up in bed, his greasy, torn
nightgown huddled about him, and with long,
claw-like fingers he uncovered the scanty breakfast. When he had finished it he wiped his
mouth and hands on the counterpane:

"Charge it as usual."

The waiter packed up the dishes, bade a bon
jour, and with a mocking gesture left the room.
Minkiewicz always had his breakfasts charged.

At noon he crawled out of bed and dressed
at a grave tempo. He wore always the same
shirt, a woollen one, and his wardrobe knew no
change. It was faded, out of fashion by a full
half-century, and his only luxury a silk comforter
which he knotted loosely about his neck. He
had never worn a collar since Chopin's death.
It was two of the clock when he stumbled downstairs. At the doorway he met Bernard the
hunchback landlord.

"No money to-day, M. Minkiewicz? Well, I
suppose not — terribly hard times — no money.

Will you have a little glass with me?" The musician went into the dusky dining-room and crank a pony of brandy with the good-natured Alsatian; then he shambled down the Rue Puteaux into the Boulevard des Batignolles, and slowly aired himself.

"A great man, M. Minkiewicz; a poet, a pianist, a friend of M. Chopin — ah! I admire him much, much," explained Bernard to a neighbor. . . .

It was very wet. But the slop and swish of the rain did not prevent the brasserie of The Fallen Angels from being filled with noisy drinkers. In one corner sat Minkiewicz. He was drinking absinthe. About him clustered five or six good-looking young fellows. The chatter in the room was terrific, but this group of disciples heard all the master said. He scarcely spoke above a whisper, yet his voice cut the hot air sharply.

"You ask me, Henri, how well I knew Frédéric. I could ask you in turn how well did you know your mother? I was with him at Warsaw. I, too, studied under Elsner. I accompanied him on his first journey to Vienna. I was at his first concert. I trembled and cried as he played our first — his first concerto in F minor. I wrote — we wrote the one in E minor later. I proposed for the hand of Constance Gladowska for Frédéric, and he screamed when I brought back the answer. Ah! but I did not tell him that Constance, Constantia, had said, 'Sir Friend, why not let the little Chopin woo for himself?' and she threw back her head and smiled into my eyes. I could have killed her for that subtle look. Yes; I know she married an ordinary merchant. What cared I? I loved Frédéric, Frédéric only. I never left his side. When it rained, rained as it is raining to-night, he would tremble, and often beat me with his spider-like hands, but I did n't mind it, for I was stronger then.

"I went with him to Paris. It was I who secured for him from Prince Radziwill the invitation to the Rothschild's ball where he won his first triumph. I made him practise. I bore his horrible humors, his mad, irritating, capricious temper. I wrote down his music for him. Wrote it down, did I say? Why, I often composed it for him; yes, I, for he would sit and moon away at the piano, insanely wasting his ideas, while I would force him to repeat a phrase, repeat it, polish it, alter it and so on until the fabric of the composition was complete. Then, how I would toil, toil, prune and expand his feeble ideas! Mon Dieu! Frédéric was no reformer by nature, no pathbreaker in art; he was a sickly fellow, always coughing, always scolding, but he played charmingly. He had such fingers! and he knew all our national dances. The mazurek, the mazourk, the polonaise and the krakowiak. Ah! but then he had

no blood, no fire, no muscle, no vitality. He
was not a revolutionist. He did not discover
new forms; all he cared for was to mock the
Jews with their majufes, and play sugar-water
nocturnes.

" I was the artistic mate to this little Pole who
allowed that old man-woman to deceive him —
George Sand, of course. Ah! the old rascal,
how she hated me. She forbade me to enter
their hotel in the Cour d'Orléans, but I did —
Chopin would have died without me, the delicate little vampire! I was his nurse, his mother,
his big brother. I fought his fight with the
publishers, with the creditors. I wrote his polonaises, all — all I tell you — except those sickly
things in the keys of C sharp minor, F minor
and B flat minor. Pouf! don't tell me anything
about Chopin. He write a polonaise? He
write the scherzi, the ballades, the études? —
you make me enraged. I, I made them
all and he will get the credit for all time,
and I am glad of it, for I loved him as a
father."

The voice of Minkiewicz became strident as
he repeated his old story. Some of the clients
of The Fallen Angels stopped talking for a
moment; it was only that crazy Pole again with
his thrice-told tale.

Minkiewicz drank another absinthe.

" And were you then a poet as well as a composer? " timidly asked young Louis.

A CHOPIN OF THE GUTTER

"I was the greatest poet Poland ever had. Ask of Chopin's friends, or of his living pupils. Go ask Georges Mathias, the old professor of the Conservatoire, if Minkiewicz did not inspire Chopin. Who gave him the theme for his Revolutionary étude — the one in C minor?" Minkiewicz ran his left hand with velocity across the table. His disciples followed those marvellously agile fingers with the eyes of the hypnotic. . . .

"I was with Frédéric at Stuttgart. I first heard the news of the capture of Warsaw. Pale and with beating heart I ran to the hotel and told him all. He had an attack of hysteria; then I rushed to the piano and by chance struck out a phrase. It was in C sharp minor, and was almost identical with the theme of the C minor study. At once Chopin ceased his moaning and weeping and came over to the instrument. 'That's very pretty,' he said, and began making a running bass accompaniment. He was a born inventor of finger tricks; he took up the theme and gradually we fashioned the study as it now stands. But it was first written in C sharp minor. Frédéric suggested that it was too difficult for wealthy amateurs in that key, and changed it to C minor. More copies would be sold, he said. But he spoke no more of Warsaw after that. Why? Ah! don't ask me — the true artist, I suppose. Once that his grief is objectified, once that his sorrow is trans-

lated into tone, the first cause is quite forgotten,
— Art is so selfish, so beautiful, you know!

" I never left Frédéric but once; the odious
Sand woman, who smoked a pipe and swore like
a cab driver, smuggled the poor devil away to
Majorca. He came back a sick man; no wonder! You remember the de Musset episode.
The poet's mother even implored the old dragon
to take Alfred to Italy. He, too, was coughing
— all her friends coughed except Liszt, who
sneered at her blandishments — and Italy was
good for consumptives. De Musset went away
ailing; he returned a mere shadow. What
happened? Ah! I cannot say. Possibly his
eyes were opened by the things he saw — you
remember the young Italian physician — I think
his name was Pagello? It was the same with
Chopin. Without me he could not thrive.
Sand knew it and hated me. I was the sturdy
oak, Frédéric the tender ivy. I poured out my
heart's blood for him, poured it into his music.
He was a mere girl, I tell you — a sensitive,
slender, shrinking, peevish girl, a born prudish
spinster, and would shiver if any one looked at
him. Liszt always frightened him and he hated
Mendelssohn. He called Beethoven a sour old
Dutchman, and swore that he did not write
piano music. For the man who first brought
his name before the public, the big-hearted
German, Robert Schumann — here's to his
memory — Chopin had an intense dislike. He

confessed to me that Schumann was no composer, a talented improviser only. I think he was a bit jealous of the man's genius. But Freddie loved Mozart, loved his music so madly that it was my turn to become jealous.

"And fastidious! Bon Dieu! I tell you that he could not drink, and once Balzac told us a piquant story and Frédéric fainted. I remember well how Balzac stared and said in that great voice of his: ' Guard well thy little damsel, my good Minkiewicz, else he may yet be abducted by a tom-cat,' and then he laughed until the window-panes rattled. What a brute! . . .

"I gave my brain to Chopin. When he returned to me from that mad trip to the Balearic Islands I had not the heart to scold. He was pallid and even coughed in a whisper. He had no money; Sand was angry with him and went off to Nohant alone. I had no means, but I took twenty-four little piano preludes that I had made while Frédéric was away and sold them for ready money. You know them, all the world knows them. They say now that he wrote them whilst at Majorca, and tell fables about the rain-drop prelude in D flat. A pack of lies! I wrote them and at my old piano without strings, the same that I still have in the Rue Puteaux. But I sha'n't complain. I love him yet. What was mine was his — is his, even my music."

The group became uneasy. It was late. The rain had stopped, and through the open doors of The Fallen Angels could be seen the soft-starred sky, and melting in the distance were the lights of the Gare Saint-Lazare. It was close by the Quarter of Europe, and the women who walked the boulevard darted swift glances into the heated rooms of the brasserie.

Minkiewicz drank another absinthe — his last. There was no more money. The disciples had spent their all for the master whom they loved as they hated the name of Wagner. His slanting eyes — the eyes of the Calmuck — were bloodshot; his face was yellow-white. His long, white hair hung on his shoulders and there were bubbles about his lips.

" But I often despair. I loved Chopin's reputation too much ever to write a line of music after his death. Besides who would have believed me? Which one of you believes in his secret heart of hearts one word I have spoken to-night? It is difficult to make the world acknowledge that you are not an idiot; very difficult to shake its belief that Chopin was not a god. Alas! there are no more gods. You say I am a poet, yet how may a man be a poet if godless? I know that there is no God, yet I am unhappy longing after Him. I awake at the dawn and cry for God as children cry for their mother. Curse reason! curse the knowledge that has made a mockery of my old faiths! Frédéric died, and dying saw Christ. I look at the roaring river of azure overhead and see the cruel sky — nothing more. I tell you, my children, it has killed the poet in me, and it will kill the gods themselves when comes the crack of doom.

"I dream often of that time — that time John, the poet of Patmos, foretold in his Revelations: The time when the Sixth Seal was opened. Alas! when the Son of Man cometh out of the clouds and round about the throne are the four-winged beasts, what will he see?

"Nothing — nothing, I tell you.

"Unbelief will have killed the very soul of creation itself. And where once burned the eye of the Cosmos will be naught but a hideous emptiness.

"Hélas! mes enfants, I could drink one more absinthe; my soul grieves for my lost faith, my lost music, my lost Frédéric, my lost life." . . .

But they went away. It was past the hour of closing and the host was not in a humor for parleying.

"Ah! the old pig, the old blasphemer!" he said, shaking his head as he locked the doors.

They watched him until he turned the corner of the Rue Puteaux and was lost to them.

He moved slowly, painfully, one leg striking the pavement in syncopation, for it was sadly crippled by disease. He did not twist his thin head as he went along the Batignolles. Then the band passed once more up to the warmer lights of the Clichy Quarter and argued art far into the night.

They one and all hated Wagner, adoring Chopin's magic music.

THE PIPER OF DREAMS

The desert of my soul is peopled with black gods,
Huge blocks of wood;
Brave with gilded horns and shining gems,
The black and silent gods
Tower in the naked desert of my soul.

With eyes of wolves they watch me in the night;
With eyes like moons.
My gods are they; in each the evil grows,
The grandiose evil darkens over each
And each black god, silent
Under the iron skies, dreams
Of his omnipotence — the taciturn black gods!

And my flesh and my brain are underneath their feet;
I am the victim, and I perish
Under the weight of these nocturnal gods
And in the iron winds of their unceasing wrath.

I

IT was opera night, and the lights burned with
an official brilliancy that challenged the radiance
of the Café Monferino across the asphalt. There,
all was decorous gaiety; and the doubles of
Pilsner never vanished from the little round
metal tables that overflowed into the juncture
of the streets Gluck and Halévy. Among the

brasseries in Paris this the most desirable to
lovers of the Bohemian brew. The cooking,
Neapolitan and Viennese, perhaps explained the
presence, one June evening in the year 1930, of
tall, blond, blue-eyed Illowski, the notorious Russian symphonist. With several admirers he sat
sipping bocks and watched the motley waves of
the boulevard wash back strange men and women
— and again women.

Lenyard spoke first. Young and from New
England he was studying music in Paris.

"Master, why don't you compose a music
drama?" Illowski, gazing into the soft blur of
light and mist over the Place de l'Opéra, did
not answer. Scheff burst into laughter. The
one who had put the question became angry.
"Confound it! What have I said, Mr. Dutchman, that seems so funny to you?" Illowski
put out a long, thin hand, — a veritable flag of
truce: "Children, cease! I have written something better than a music drama. I told Scheff
about it before he left St. Petersburg last spring.
Don't be jealous, Lenyard. There is nothing in
the work that warrants publicity — yet. It is
merely a venture into an unfamiliar region,
nothing more. But how useless to write for a
public that still listens to Meyerbeer in the
musical catacombs across the street!"

Lenyard's lean, dark features relaxed. He
gazed smilingly at the fat and careless Scheff.
Then Illowski arose. It was late, he said, and

his head ached. He had been scoring all day — sufficient reason for early retirement. The others demurred, though meekly. If their sun set so early, how could they be expected to pass the night with any degree of pleasure? The composer saw all this; but he was sensibly selfish, and buttoning the long frock-coat which hung loosely on his attenuated frame shook hands with his disciples, called a carriage and drove away. Lenyard and Scheff stared after him and then faced the situation. There were many tell-tale porcelain tallies on the table to be settled, and neither had much money; so the manœuvring was an agreeable sight for the cynical waiter. Finally Lenyard, his national pride rising at the spectacle of the Austrian's penuriousness, paid the entire bill with a ten-franc piece.

Scheff sank back in his chair and grinningly inquired, " Say, my boy, I wonder if Illowski has enough money for his coachman when he reaches the mysterious, old dream-barn he calls home?" Lenyard slowly emptied his glass: "I don't know, you don't know, and, strictly speaking, we don't care. But I'd dearly like to see the score of his new work."

Scheff blinked with surprise. He, too, was thinking of the same dread matter. "What, in God's name, do you mean? Speak out. I've been frightened long enough. This Illowski is a terrible man, Scheff. Do you suspect the

3

stories are true, after all — ?" Then both men stood up, shook hands and said: " Neshevna will tell us. She knows." . . .

II

Pavel Illowski was a man for whom the visible world had never existed. Born a Malo-Russ, nursed on Little-Russian legends, a dreamer of soft dreams until more than a lad, he was given a musical education in Moscow, the White City — itself a dream of old Alexander Nevsky's days. Within sight of the Kremlin the slim and delicate youth fed upon the fatalistic writers of the nineteenth century. He knew Schopenhauer before he learned to pronounce German correctly; and the works of Bakounin, Herzen, Kropotkin became part of his cerebral tissue. Proudhon, Marx, and Ferdinand Lassalle taught him to hate wealth, property, power; and then he came across an old volume of Nietzsche in his uncle's library. The bent of the boy's genius was settled. He would be a composer — had he not, as a bare-headed child, run sobbing after Tschaïkowsky's coffin almost to the Alexander Nevsky Monastery in 1893 — but a composer who would mould the destinies of his nation, perhaps the destinies of all the world, a second Svarog. He early saw the power — insidious, subtle, dangerous power — that lurked in great art, saw that the art of the twentieth century, his century, was music. Only thirteen when the greatest of all musical Russians died, he read Nietzsche a year later; and these men were the two compelling forces of his life until the destructive poetry of the mad, red-haired Australian poet, Lingwood Evans, appeared. Illowski's philosophy of anarchy was now complete, his belief in a social, æsthetic, ethical regeneration of the world, fixed. Yet he was no militant reformer; he would bear no polemical banners, wave no red flags. A composer of music, he endeavored to impart to his work articulate, emotion-breeding and formidably dangerous qualities.

Deserting the vague and fugitive experimentings of Berlioz, Wagner, Liszt and Richard Strauss, Illowski modelled himself upon Tschaïkowsky. He read everything musical and poetical in type, and his first attempt, when nearly thirty, was a symphonic setting of a poem by a half-forgotten English poet, Robert Browning, " Childe Roland to the Dark Tower Came," and the music aroused hostile German criticism. Here is a young Russian, declared the critics, who ventures beyond Tschaïkowsky and Strauss in his attempts to make music say something. Was not the classic Richard Wagner a warning to all who endeavored to wring from music a message it possessed not? When Wagner saw that Beethoven — Ah, the sublime Beethoven! — could not do without the aid of the human voice in his Ninth Symphony, he fashioned his music drama accordingly. With the co-operation of pantomime, costume, color, lights, scenery, he invented a new art — patched and tinkered one, said his enemies, who thought him old-fashioned — and so " Der Ring," " Tristan und Isolde," " Die Meistersinger" and " Parsifal " were born. True classics in their devotion to form and freedom from the feverishness of the later men headed by Richard Strauss — why should any one seek to better them, to supplant them? Wagner had been the Mozart of his century. Down with the musical Tartars of the East who spiritually invaded Europe to rob her of peace, religion, aye, and morals!

Much censure of this kind was aimed at Illowski, who continued calmly. Admiring Richard Strauss, he saw that the man did not dare enough, that his effort to paint in tone the poetic heroes of the past century, himself included, was laudable; but Don Juan, Macbeth, quaint Till Eulenspiegel, fantastic Don Quixote were, after all, chiefly concerned with a moribund æstheticism. Illowski best liked the Strauss setting of "Also Sprach Zarathustra" because it approached his own darling project, though it neither touched the stars nor reached the earth. Besides, this music was too complicated. A new art must be evolved, not a synthesis of the old arts dreamed by Wagner, but an art consisting of music alone: an art for the twentieth century, a democratic art in which poet and tramp alike could revel. To the profoundest science must be united a clearness of exposition that only Raphael has. Even a peasant enjoys Velasquez. The Greeks fathomed this mystery: all Athens worshipped its marbles, and Phidias was crowned King of Emotions. Music alone lagged in the race, music, part speech, part painting, with a surging undertow of passion, music had been too long in the laboratories of the wise men. To free it from its Egyptian bondage, to make it the tongue of all life, the interpreter of the world's desire — Illowski dreamed the dreams of madmen.

Chopin, who divined this truth, went first to the people, later to Paris, and thenceforward he became the victim of the artificial. Beethoven was born too soon in a world grown gray under scholars' shackles. The symphony, like the Old Man of the Sea, weighed upon his mighty shoulders; music, he believed, must be formal to be understood. Illowski, in his many wanderings, pondered these things: saw Berlioz on the trail, in his efforts to formulate a science of instrumental timbres; saw Wagner captivated by the glow of the footlights; saw Liszt, audacious Liszt, led by Wagner, and tribute laid upon his genius by the Bayreuth man; saw Tschaïkowsky struggling away from the temptations of the music drama only to succumb to the symphonic poem — a new and vicious version of that old pitfall, the symphony; saw César Franck, the Belgian mystic, narrowly graze the truth in some of his chamber music, and then fall victim to the fascinations of the word; as if the word, spoken or sung, were other than a clog to the free wings of imaginative music! Illowski noted the struggles of these dreamers, noted Verdi swallowed by the maelstrom of the theatre; noted Richard Strauss and his hesitation at the final leap.

To the few in whom he confided, he admitted that Strauss had been his forerunner, having upset the notion that music must be beautiful to be music and seeing the real significance of the characteristic, the ugly. Had Strauss developed courage or gone to the far East when young — Illowski would shrug his high shoulders, gnaw his cigarette and exclaim, "Who knows?"

Tolstoy was right after all, this sage, who under cover of fiction preached the deadliest doctrines; doctrines that aimed at nothing less than the disequilibration of existing social conditions. Tolstoy had inveighed bitterly against all forms of artificial art. If the Moujik did not understand Beethoven, then all the worse for Beethoven; great art should have in it Mozart's sunny simplicities, without Mozart's elaborate technical methods. This Illowski believed. To unite the intimate soul-searching qualities of Chopin and exclude his alembicated art; to sweep with torrential puissance the feelings of the common people, whether Chinese or German, Esquimaux or French; to tell them things, things found neither in books nor in pictures nor in stone, neither above the earth nor in the waters below; to liberate them from the tyranny of laws and beliefs and commandments; to preach the new dispensation of Lingwood Evans — magnificent, brutal, and blood-loving — ah! if Illowski could but discover this hidden philosophers stone, this true Arcana of all wisdom, this emotional lever of Archimedes, why then the whole world would be his: his power would depose Pope and Emperor.   And again he dreamed the dreams of madmen — his mother had been nearly related to Dostoïewsky. . . .

Of what avail the seed-bearing Bach and his fugues — emotional mathematics, all of them! Of what avail the decorative efforts of tonal fresco painters, breeders of an hour's pleasure, soon forgotten in the grave's muddy disdain! Had not the stage lowered music to the position of a lascivious handmaiden? To the sound of cymbals, it postured for the weary debauchee. No; music must go back to its origins. The church fettered it in its service, knowing full well its good and evil. Before Christianity was, it had been a power in hieratic hands. Ancient Egyptian priests hypnotized the multitudes with a single silvery sound; and in the deepest Indian jungles inspired fakirs induced visions by the clapping of shells. Who knows how the

Grand Llama of Thibet decrees the destinies of millions! Music again, music in some other garb than we now sense it. Illowski groaned as he attacked this hermetic mystery. He had all the technique of contemporary art at his beck; but not that unique tone, the unique form, by which he might become master of the universe and gain spiritual dominion over mankind. Yet the secret, so fearfully guarded, had been transmitted through the ages. Certain favored ones must have known it, men who ruled the rulers of earth. Where could it be found? "The jealous gods have buried somewhere proofs of the origins of all things, but upon the shores of what ocean have they rolled the stone that hides them, O Macareus?" Thus echoed he the fatidical query of the French poet. . . .

Illowski left Europe. Some said he had gone to Asia, the mother of all religions, of all corruptions. He had been seen in China, and later stories were related of his attempts to enter the sacred city, Lhasa. He disappeared and many composers and critics were not sorry; his was a too commanding personality: he menaced modern art. Thus far church and state had not considered his individual existence; he was but one of the submerged units of Rurik's vast Slavic Empire which now almost traversed the Eastern hemisphere. So he was forgotten and a minor god arose in his place — a man who wrote pretty ballets, who declared that the end of music was to enthrall the senses; and his ballets were danced over Europe, while Illowski's name faded away. . . .

At the end of ten years he returned to St. Petersburg. Thinner, much older, his long, spidery arms, almost colorless blond hair and eroded features gave him the air of a cenobite who had escaped from some Scandinavian wilderness into life. His Oriental reserve, and evident dislike of all his former social habits, set the musical world wagging its head, recalling the latter days of Dostoïewsky. But Illowski was not mad: he simply awaited his opportunity. It came. The morning after his first concert he was awakened by fame knocking at his gate, the most horrible kind of fame. He was not called a madman by the critics, for his music could never have been the product of a crazy brain — he was pronounced an arch-enemy to mankind, because he told infamous secrets in his music, secrets that had lain buried in the shale of a vanished epoch. And, lest the world grow cold, he drove to its very soul the most hideous truths. A hypnotist, he conducted his orchestra through extraordinary and malevolent forests of tone. The audience went into the night, some sobbing, some beating the air like possessed ones, others frozen with terror. At the second concert the throngs were so dense that the authorities interfered. What poison was being disseminated in the air of a concert hall? What new device of the revolutionists? What deadly secret did this meagre, dreamy, harmless-looking Russian possess? The censors were alert. Critics were instructed by the heads of their journals to drive forth this musical anarchist; but criticism availed not. A week, and Illowski became the talk of Russia, a month, and Europe filled with strange rumors about him. Here was a magician who made the dead speak, the living dumb — what were the limits of his power? What his ultimate intention? Such a man might be converted into a political force would he but range himself on the right side of the throne. If not — why, then there was still Siberia and its weary stretches of snow!

When he reached Moscow rioting began in the streets. Leaving, he went with his dark-skinned Eastern musicians to the provinces. And the government trembled. Peasants threw aside spade, forgot vodka and rushed to his free concerts, given in canvas-covered booths; and the impetus communicated to this huge, weltering mass of slaving humanity, broke wave-like upon the remotest borders of the empire. The church became alarmed. Anti-Christ had been predicted for centuries, and latterly by the Second Adventists. Was Illowski the one at whose nod principalities and powers of earth should tremble and fall? Was he the prince of darkness himself? Was the liberation of the seven seals at hand — that awful time foretold by the mystic of Patmos? The Metropolitan of the Greek church did not long hesitate. A hierarchy that became endangered because a fanatic wielded hypnotic powers, must exert its prerogative. The aid of the secret police invoked, Illowski was hurried into Austria; but with him were his men, and he grimly laughed as he sat in a Viennese café and counted the victories of his first campaign.

"It has begun," he told his first violinist, a stolid fellow with black blood in his veins.

It had begun. After a concert in Vienna, Illowski was politely bidden to leave Austria. The unsettled political condition, the disaffection of Czech and Hungarian, were a few of the reasons given for this summary retirement. Yet Illowski's orchestra did not play the Rakoczy march! The clergy heard of his impieties; a report obtained credence that the Russian composer had written music for the black mass, most blasphemous of missal travesties. When he was told of this he smiled, for he did not aim at attacking mere sectarian beliefs; with Bakounin, he swore that there must be total destruction of all existing institutions, or — nothing!

He went to Germany believing the countrymen of Nietzsche would receive with joy this Overman from the East. There was no longer any Bayreuth — the first performance of " Parsifal " elsewhere had killed the place and the work. In Munich, the authorities forewarned, Illowski was arrested as a dangerous character and sent to Trieste. Thence he shipped to Genoa; and once in Italy, free. On the peninsula his progress was that of a trailing comet. The feminine madness first manifested itself there and swept the countryside with epidemic fury. Wherever he played the dancing mania set in, and the soldiery could not put it down by force of arms. Nietzsche's dancing philosopher, Zarathustra, was incarnated in Illowski's compositions. Like the nervous obsessions of mediæval times, this music set howling, leaping and writhing volatile Italians, until it began to assume the proportions of a new evangel, an hysterical hallucination that bade defiance to law, doctors, even the decencies of life. Terrible stories reached the Vatican, and when it was related that one of his symphonic pieces delineated Zarathustra's Cave with its sinister mockery of prelate and king, the hated Quirinal was approached for assistance, and Illowski vanished from Italy.

In the British Isles, the same wicked tales were told of him. He was denounced by priest and publican as a subverter of morals. No poet, no demagogue, had ever so interested the masses. Musicians of academic training held aloof. What had they in common with this charlatan who treated the abominable teachings of Walt Whitman symphonically? He could not be a respectable man, even if he were a sane. And then the unlettered tiller of the soil, drunken mechanic and gutter drab all loved his music. What kind of music was it thus to be understood by the ignorant?

The police thought otherwise. Illowski gathered crowds — that was sufficient to ban him, not as the church does, with bell, book and candle, but with stout oaken clubs. Forth he fared, and things came to such a pass that not a steamer dared convey him or his band to America. By this time the scientific reviews had taken him up as a sort of public Illusionist. Disciples of Charcot explained his scores — though not one had been published — while the neo-moralists gladly denounced him as a follower of the Master Immoralist, a sublimated emotional expression of the ethical nihilism of Friedrich Nietzsche. Others, more fanciful, saw in his advent and in his art an attempt to overturn nations, life itself, through the agency of corrupting beauty and by the arousing of illimitable desires. Color and music, sweetness and soft luxuries, declared these modern followers of Ambrose and Chrysostom, were the agencies of Satan in the undermining of morals. Pulpits thundered. The press sneered at the new Pied Piper of Hamelin, and poets sang of him. One Celtic bard named him " Master of the Still Stars and of the Flaming Door."

For women his music was as the moth's de sire. Wherever he went were women — women and children. Old legends were revived about the ancient gods. The great Pan was said to be abroad; rustling in the night air set young folk blushing. An emotional renascence swept like a torrid simoon over Europe. Those who had not heard, had not seen him, felt, nevertheless, Illowski's subtle influences in their bosoms. The fountains of democracy's great deeps were breaking up. Too long had smug comfort and utilitarianism ruled a world grown weary of debasing commerce. All things must have an end, even wealth; and to the wretched, to those in damp mines, to the downcast in exile and in prisons and to the muck of humanity his name became a beautiful, illuminated symbol. The charges of impiety were answered: " His music makes us dream." Music now became ruler of the universe, and the earth hummed tunes; yet Illowski's maddening music had been heard by few nations.

Humble, poor, asking nothing, always giving, he soon became a nightmare to the orthodox. He preached no heresies, promised no future rewards, nor warred he against church or kingdom. He only made music and things were not as before; some strange angel had passed that way filling men's souls with joy, beauty and bitterness. Duties, vows, beliefs fell away like snow in the sun; families, tribes, states grew restless, troops were called and churches never closed. A wave of belated paganism rolled over the world; thinkers and steersmen of great political and religious organizations became genuinely alarmed. So had come the downfall of the classical world: a simple apparition in a far away Jewish province, and the Cæsars fell supine — their empires cracked like mirrors! To imprison Illowski meant danger; to kill him would deify him, for in the blood of martyrs blossom the seeds of mighty religions. Far better if he go to Paris — Paris, the cradle and the tomb of illusions. There this restless demagogue might find his dreams stilled in the scarlet negations and frivolous philosophies of the town; thus the germ-plasm of a new religion, of a new race, perhaps of a new world, be drowned in the drowsy green of a little glass.

Illowski, this Spirit that Denied, this new Mephisto of music, did not balk his evil wishers.

" Paris, why not? She refused to understand Berlioz, flouted Wagner, and mocked Rodin's marble egotisms, the ferocious, white stillness of his Balzac! Perhaps Paris will give me, if not a welcome, at least repose. I am tired."

To Paris he went and excepting a few cynical paragraphs received no attention. The Conservatoire, the Académie de Musique did not welcome officially this gifted son of the Neva; the authorities blandly ignored him, though the police were instructed that if he attempted to play in front of churches, address mobs or build barricades, he must be confined. Paris had no idea of Illowski's real meaning; Paris, even in the twentieth century, always hears the news of the world last; besides, she conceives no other conquest save one that has for its object the several decayed thrones within her gates. Illowski was not molested and his men, despite their strange garb and complexion, went about freely. The Russian composer of ballets was just then the mode.

Some clever caricatures appeared of Illowski representing him as a musical Napoleon, cocked hat, sleek white horse and all. Another gave him the goat's beard of Brother Jonathan, with the baton of a Yankee band-master; and then it was assured that the much advertised composer was a joking American masquerading as a Slav, possibly the vender of some new religious cure born in the fanatical bake-ovens of Western America. "Faust" alternated with "Les Huguenots" at the Opéra, Pilsner beer was on tap at the Café Monferino — why worry over exotic stories told of this visitor's abnormal musical powers? And little did any one surmise that he had just given a symphonic setting to Lingwood Evans's insurrectionary poem with its ghastly refrain: "I hear the grinding of the swords, and He shall come — " Thus did Paris unwittingly harbor the poet, philosopher, composer and pontiff of the new dispensation — Pavel Illowski. And Lenyard with Scheff was hastening to Auteuil to see Neshevna, whose other name was never known.

III

Lenyard disliked Neshevna before he saw her; when they met he made no attempt to conceal his hatred. He again told himself this, as with Scheff he pursued the gravel path leading to the porter's lodge of Illowski's house. In Auteuil it overlooked the Seine which flowed a snake of sunny silver between its green-ribbed banks. Together the pair entered, mounted a low flight of steps and rang the private bell. Neshevna opened the door. In the flood of a westering sun the accents of her fluid Slavic face and her mannish head set upon narrow shoulders — all the disagreeable qualities of the woman — were exaggerated by this bath of clear light. Her hard gaze softened when she saw Scheff. She spoke to him, not noticing the other:

"The master is not at home." Lenyard contradicted her: "He is; the concierge said so."

"The concierge lies; but come in. I will see."

Following her they reached the music room, which was bare of instruments, pictures, furniture, all save a tall desk upon which lay a heap of music paper. Neshevna made a loping dart to the desk — she was like a wolf in her movements — and threw a handkerchief over it. Lenyard watched her curiously. Scheff gave one of his good-natured yawns and then laughed:

"Neshevna, we come to ask!"

"What?" she gravely inquired. There was a lithe alertness in the woman that puzzled Lenyard. Scheff lounged on the window-sill. "Now, Neshevna, be a good girl! Don't forget Moscow or your old adorer."

She answered him with sarcastic emphasis: "You fat fool, you and your clerical friend there, what do you both want spying upon Illowski like police?" Her voice became shrill as she rapidly uttered these questions, her green eyes seemed shot with blood. "If you think I'll tell either of you anything concerning the new music —"

"That's all we are here to learn."

"All? Imbeciles! As if you or your American could understand Illowski and his message!"

"What message?" Lenyard's grave face was not in the least discomposed by the Cossack passion of the woman. "What message has Illowski? I've heard queer stories, and cannot credit them. You are in his confidence. Tell us, we ask in humility, what message can any man's music have but the revelation of beauty?"

Lenyard's diplomatic question did not fail of its mark. Neshevna pushed back her flamboyant gray hair and walked about the room.

"Mummies!" she suddenly cried. "As if beauty will content a new generation fed on something besides the sweetmeats and pap of your pretty, meaningless music! Why, man, can't you see that all the arts are dead — save music? Don't you know that painting, litera- ture, creeds — aye, and the kingdoms are dying for want of new blood, new ideas? Music alone is a vital force, an instrument for rescuing the world from its moral and spiritual decay. Nietzsche was a potent force in the nineteenth century, but not understood. They condemned him to a living death. Lingwood Evans, poet, prophet, is now too old to enforce his message — it is Illowski, Illowski alone who shall be the destructive Messiah of the new millennial. ' He cometh not to save; not peace, but blood!'"

The fire of fanaticism was in her eyes, in her speech. She grasped Lenyard by the elbow: "You, you should serve the master. Scheff is too fond of pleasure to do anything great. He is to give the signal — that's glory enough for him. But you, discontented American, have the stuff in you to make a martyr. We need martyrs. You hate me? Good! But you must worship Illowski. Art gives place to life, and in Illowski's music is the new life. He will sweep the globe from pole to pole, for all men understand his tones. Other gods have but prepared the way for him. No more misery, no more promises unfulfilled by the rulers of body and soul — only music, music like the air, the tides, the mountains, the moon, sun, and stars! Your old-fashioned melody and learning, your school-boy rules of counterpoint — all these Illowski ignores."

Lenyard eagerly interrupted her: "You say that he does away with melody, themes, harmony — how does he replace them, and how does he treat the human voice?" Neshevna let his arm fall and went slowly to the tall desk. She leaned against it, her hand upon her square chin. Scheff still gazed out upon the lawn where splashed a small, movable fountain. To Lenyard the air seemed as if charged with electric questionings. His head throbbed.

"You ask me something I dare not tell. Even Scheff, who knows some things, dares not tell. If Illowski's discovery — which is based on the great natural laws of heat, light, gravitation, electricity — if this discovery were placed in the hands of fools, the world would perish. Music has been so long the plaything of sensuality, the theatre for idle men and women, that its real greatness is forgotten. In Illowski's hands it is a moral force. He comes to destroy that he may rebuild. He accomplishes it with the raw elements themselves. Remember — 'I hear the grinding of the swords, and He shall come — !'" Neshevna made a nervous gesture and disappeared through a door near the tall desk covered with music-paper — the desk whereon Illowski plotted the ruin of civilization.

"Now since you have seen the dread laboratory, don't hang around that desk; there's nothing there you can understand. The music-paper is covered with electrical and chemical formulæ, not notes. I've seen them. Lenyard, let's go back to Paris and dine, like sensible men, — which we are not." Scheff dragged his friend out of the house, for the other was in a stupor. Neshevna's words cleaved his very soul. The American, the puritan in him, swiftly rose to her eloquent exhortation. All life was corrupt, he had been taught; art was corrupt, a snare, a delusion. Yet — was all its appalling power, its sensuous grandeur to be wasted in the service of the world, the flesh, the devil? Lenyard paused. " Oh, come on, Len. Why do you bother your excitable, sick heart with that lunatic's prophecies? Illowski is a big man, a very big man; but he is mad, mad! His theories of the decomposition of tone — he only imitates the old painter-impressionist of long ago — and his affected simplicity — why, he is after the big public, that's all. As to your question about what part the human voice plays in his scheme, I may tell you now that he does n't care a farthing for it except as color. He uses the voice as he would use any instrumental combination, and he mixes his colors so wonderfully that he sometimes polarizes them — they no longer have any hue or scent. He should have been a painter not a composer. He makes panoramas, psychological panoramas, not music."

"You heard them, saw them?"

"Yes," said Scheff, sourly. "Some of the early ones, and I had brain fever for months afterward."

"Yet," challenged Lenyard, "you deny his powers?"

"I don't know what he has written recently," was the sullen answer, "but if the newspapers are to be believed, he is crazy. Music all color, no rhythm, no themes, and then his preaching of Nietzsche — it's all wrong, all wrong, my boy. Art was made for joy. When it is anything else, it's a dangerous explosive. Chemically separate certain natural elements and they rush together with a thunder-clap. That's what Illowski has done. It isn't art. It's science — the science of dangerous sounds. He discovered that sound-vibrations rule the universe, that they may be turned into a musical Roentgen ray. He presents this in a condensed art, an electric form — "

"But the means, man, the methods, the instruments, the form?" Lenyard's voice was tense with excitement. The phlegmatic Scheff noticed this and soothingly said:

"The means? Why, dear boy, he just hypnotizes people, and promises them bank accounts and angel-wings. That's how he does the trick. Here's the tramcar. Jump in. I'm dying of thirst. To the Monferino!" . . .

Paris laughed when Illowski announced the performance of his new orchestral drama named

"Nietzsche." The newspapers printed columns about the composer and his strange career. A disused monster music-hall, near the Moulin Rouge on Montmartre, was to be the scene of the concert and the place was at once christened "Théâtre du Tarnhelm"—for a story had leaked out about the ebon darkness in which the Russian's music was played. This was surpassing the almost forgotten Richard Wagner. Concerts in the dark must be indeed spirituelle. The wits giggled over their jokes; and when the kiosks and bare walls were covered by placards bearing the names of "Illowski—'Nietzsche,'" with a threatening sword beneath them, the excitement became real. Satirical songs were sung in the cafés chantants, and several fashionable clerics wove the name of Illowski into their Sunday preachments. In a week he was popular, two a mystery, three a necessity. The authorities maintained a dignified silence—and watched. Politics, Bourbonism, Napoleonism, Boulangerism ere this had crept in unawares sporting strange disguises. Perhaps Illowski was a friend of the Vatican, of the Czar; perhaps a destructive, bomb-throwing Nihilist, for the indomitable revolutionists still waged war against the law. Might not this music be the signal for a dangerous uprising of some sort? . . .

Lenyard was asked to sit in a box with Neshevna that last night. Scheff refused to join them; he swore that he was tired of music and would remain in town. The woman smiled as he said this, then she handed him a letter, made a little motion — "the signal."

It was on the esplanade that Neshevna and Lenyard stood. The young man, weary with vigils, his face furrowed by curiosity, regarded the city below them as it lay swimming in the waves of a sinking sun. He saw the crosses of La Trinité as molten copper, then dusk and dwindle in the shadows. The twilight seemed to prefigure the fading of the human race. Neshevna walked with this dreamer to the rear of the theatre — the theatre of the Tarnhelm, that was to darken all civilization. He asked for Illowski, but she did not reply; she, too, was steeped in dreams. And all the streets were thick with men and women tumbling up to the top.

"We sit in a second-tier box," she presently said. "If you get tired, or — annoyed, you may go out on the balcony and look down upon the lights of Paris, though I fear it will be a dark night. There is no moon," she added, her voice dropping to a mumble. . . .

They sat in a dark box that last night. The auditorium, vast and silent with the breath-catching silence of thousands, lay below them; but their eyes were glued upon a rosy light beginning to break over the space where was the stage. It spread, deepened, until it fairly hummed with scarlet tones. Gradually emerging from this cruel crimson the image of a huge sword became visible. Neshevna touched Lenyard's hand.

" The symbol of his power ! " she crooned.

Blending with the color of the light a musical tone made itself seen, heard, felt. Lenyard shuddered. At last, the new dispensation was about to be revealed, the new gospel preached. It was a single vibratile tone, and was uttered by a trumpet. Was it a trumpet? It pealed with the peal of bells shimmering high in heaven. No occidental instrument had ever such a golden, conquering tone. It was the tone of one who foretold the coming, and was full of invincible faith and sweetness. Lenyard closed his eyes. That a single tone could so thrill his nerves he would have denied. This, then, was the secret. For the first time in the Christian world, the beauties of tonal timbres were made audible — almost visible ; the quality appealed to the eye, the inner eye. Was not the tinted music so cunningly merged as to impinge first on the optic nerve? Had the East, the Hindus and the Chinese, known of this purely material fact for ages, and guarded it in esoteric silence? Here was music based on simple, natural sounds, the sounds of birds and air, the subtle sounds of silk. For centuries Europe had been on the wrong track with its melodic experimenting, its complex of har-

monies. Illowski was indeed the saviour of
music — and Neshevna, her great, green, luminous eyes upon him, held Lenyard's hand.

The sound grew in volume, grew less silken,
and more threatening, while the light faded
into mute, misty music like the purring of cats.
A swelling roar assaulted their ears; nameless
creeping things seemed to fill the tone. Yet it
was in one tonality; there was no harmony, no
melody. The man's quick ear detected many
new, rich timbres, as if made by strange instruments. He also recognized interior rhythms,
the result of color rather than articulate movement. Then came silence, a silence that shouted
cruelly across the gulfs of blackness, a silence
so profound as to be appalling. Sound, rhythm,
silence — the material from which is fashioned
the creative stuff of the universe! Lenyard became restless; but the grip on his fingers tight-
ened. He felt the oppressive dread that precedes
the flight of a nightmare; the dread that mankind knows when sunk in shallow, horrid sleep.
A low, frightened wail mounted out of the
darkness wherein massed the people. Another
tone usurped the ear, pierced the eyes. It
was a blinding beam of tone, higher and more
undulating. His heart harshly ticking like a
clock, he viewed, as in a vision, the march of
the nations, the crash of falling theocracies, of
dying dynasties. On a stony platform, vast and
crowded, he knelt in sackcloth and ashes; the

heavens thundered over the weeping millions of Nineveh; and the Lord of Hosts would not be appeased. Stretching to the clouds were black, basaltic battlements, and above them reared white terraced palaces, as swans that strain their throats to the sky. The day of wrath was come. And amid the granitic clashing of the elements, Lenyard saw the mighty East resolving into dust. Neshevna pressed his hand.

By the waters of Babylon he wandered, and found himself at the base of a rude little hill. The shock of the quaking earth, the silent passing of the sheeted dead, and the rush of affrighted multitudes told him that another cosmic tragedy was at hand. In a flare of lightning he saw silhouetted against an angry sky three crosses at the top of the sad little hill. He reeled away, his heart almost bursting, when Neshevna grasped him. " You saw the death of the gods ! " she hoarsely whispered.

He could not answer, for the music showed him a thunder-blasted shore fringing a bituminous sea. This sea stirred not, while the air above it was frozen in salty silence. Faint, thin light came up through the waters, and Lenyard caught a glimpse in the deeps below of sparkling pinnacles and bulbous domes of gold; a dead sea rolled over the dead cities of the bitter plain. He trembled as Neshevna said, with a grinding sob, " That was the death of life."

Lenyard's sombre soul modulated to another dream — the last. Suffocating and vague, the stillness waxed and ran over the troubled edges of eternity. The Plain, gloomy and implacable, was illuminated on its anonymous horizon by one rift of naked, leering light. Over its illimitable surface surged and shivered women, white, dazzling, numberless. As waves that, lap on lap, sweep fiercely across the sky-line, as bisons that furiously charge upon grassy wastes, " as the rill that runs from Bulicamé to be portioned out among the sinful women," these hordes of savage creatures rose and fell in their mad flight across the Plain. No sudden little river, no harsh accent of knoll or hill, broke the immeasurable whiteness of bared breast and ivoried shoulder. It was a white whirl of women, a ferocious vortex of terrified women. Lenyard saw the petrified fear upon the faces of them that went into the Pit; and he descried the cruel and looming figure of Illowski piping to them as they went into the Pit. The maelstrom of faces turned to their dream-master; faces blanched by regret, sunned by crime, beaming with sin; faces rusted by vain virtue; wan, weary faces, and the triumphant regard of those who loved — all gazed at the Piper as vertiginously they boiled by. The world of women passed at his feet radiant, guilty, white, glittering and powerless. Lenyard felt the inertia of sickness seize him when he saw the capital expression upon these futile faces — the expression of insurgent souls that see for the last time their conqueror. Not a sign made these mystic brides, not a sound; and, as in the blazing music they dashed despairingly down the gulf of time, Lenyard was left with eyes strained, pulses jangled, lonely and hopeless. He shivered, and his heart halted. . . .

"This is the death of love," shouted Neshevna. But Lenyard heard her not; nor did he hear the noise of the people beneath — the veritable booming of primordial gorilla-men. And now a corrosive shaft of tone rived the building as though its walls had been of gauze and went hissing towards Paris, in shape a menacing sword. Like the clattering of tumbrils in narrow, stony streets men and women trampled upon each other, fleeing from the accursed altar of this arch-priest of Beelzebub — Illowski. They over-streamed the sides of Montmartre, as ants washed away by water. And the howling of them was heard by the watchers in the doomed city below.

Neshevna, her arm clutched by Lenyard's icy fingers, shook him violently, and tried to release herself. Finding this impossible she dragged her silent burden out upon the crumpling balcony.

Paris was draped in flaming clouds — the blood-red smoke of mad torches. Tongues of fire twined about the towers of Notre Dame;

where the Opéra once stood yawned a black-ened hole. The air was shocked by fulminate blasts — the signals of the careless Scheff.

And the woman, her mouth filled with exult-ant laughter, screamed, "Thou hast conquered, O Pavel Illowski!"

AN EMOTIONAL ACROBAT

They were tears which he drummed.
— HEINE.

PERHAPS you think because I play upon an instrument of percussion I admire that other percussive machine of wood and wire, the piano, or consider the tympanum an inferior instrument?

You were never more mistaken, for I despise the piano as a shallow compromise between the harp, tympani and those Eastern tinkling instruments of crystal and glass, or dulcimers and cymbalom. It has no character, no individuality of its own. It is deplorable in conjunction with an orchestra, for its harsh, hard, unmalleable tone never blends with other instruments. It is a selfish instrument and it makes selfish artists of those who devote a lifetime to it.

Bah! I hate you and your pianos. Compare it to the tympani? Never, never! It is false, insincere, and smirks and simpers if even a silly school girl sits before it. It takes on the color of any composer's ideas, and submits like a slave to the whims of any virtuoso. I am disgusted. Here am I, an old kettle-drum-

63

mer — as you say in your barbarous English —
poor, unknown, forced to earn a beggarly living
by strumming dance tunes in a variety hall on a
hated piano, and often accompanying singers,
acrobats, and all the riffraff of a vaudeville,
where a mist of vulgarity hangs like a dirty
pearl cloud over all. I don't look at my music
any more. I know what is wanted. I have
rhythmic talent. I conduct myself, although
there is a butter-faced leader waving a silly
stick at us while I sit in my den, half under the
stage, and thrum and think, and blink and
thrum.

And what do you suppose I do with my
mornings — for I have to rehearse every afternoon with odious people who splash their
draggled lives with feeble, sick music — ? I stay
in my attic room and play upon my tympani,
my beloved children. I have three of them,
and I play all sorts of scores, from the wonderful first measures of Beethoven's Fifth, to
Saint-Saëns' Arabian music. Ah! those men
understand my instrument. It is no instrument
of percussion to them. It has a soul. It is
the heart of the orchestra. Its rhythmic throb
is the pulse of musical life. What are your
strings, your scratching, rasping strings! What
signifies the blare of your brass, or the bilious
bleating of your wood-wind! I am the centre,
the life giver. From me the circulation of
warm, musical blood emanates. I stand at the

back of the orchestra as high as the conductor. Ah! he knows it; he looks at me first. How about the Fifth Symphony? You now sneer no longer. It is I who outline with mystic taps the framework of the story. Wagner, great, glorious, glowing Wagner! — I kiss his memory — he appreciated the tympani and their noble mission in music. . . .

Yes, I am an educated man, but music snared me away from a worldly career. Music and — a woman; but never mind that part of it. Do you know Hunding's motif in "Die Walküre"? Ha! ha! I will give it to you. Listen! Is it not beautiful? The stern, acrid warrior approaches. And Wagner gave it to me, to the tympani. Am I crazy, am I arrogant, to feel as I do about my darling dwarf children? Look at their beloved bellies, so smooth, so elastic, so resonant! A tiny tap and I set vibrating millions of delicate, ethereal sounds, the timbre of which to my ears has color, form, substance, nuance, and thrills me even to my old marrow. Is it not delicious — that warm, velvety, dull percussion? Is it not delicious, I say? How it shimmers and senses about me! You have heard of drummed tears? I can make you weep, if I will, with a few melancholy, muffled strokes. The drum is the epitome of life. Sound is life. The cave-men bruised stones together and heard the first music.

I know your Herbert Spencer thinks dif-

ferently, but bah! what does he know about
tympani? Chopin would have been a great
tympanist if he had not wasted his life foolishly
at the piano. When he merely drummed with
his fingers on the table, Balzac said, he made
music, so exquisitely sensitive was his touch.
Ah me! what a tympanist was lost to the world.
What shading, what delicacy, what sunlight and
shadow he would have made flit across my little
darlings on their tripods! No wonder I hate
the piano; and yet, hideous mockery of fate! I
play upon an old grand to earn my bread and
wine. I can't play with an orchestra — it is
torture for me. They do not understand me;
the big noisy boors do not understand rhythm
or nuance. They play so loud that I cannot be
heard, and I will never stoop to noisy banging.
How I hate these orchestral players! How
they scratch and blow like pigs and boasters!
When I did play with them they made fun of
my red hair and delicate touch. The leader
could not understand me, and kept on yelling
" Forte, Forte." It was in the Fifth of Beethoven,
and I became angry and called out in my poor
German (ah! I hate German, it hurts my teeth):
" *Nein, so klopft das Schicksal nicht an die
Pforte.*" You remember Beethoven's words!

Well, everybody laughed at me, and I got
mad and covered up my instruments and went
home. Jackass! he wanted me to bang out that
wonderful intimation of fate as though it were

the milkman knocking at the door. I am a poet, and play upon the tympani; the conductor and the orchestra are boors. But I do injustice to one of them. He was an Alsatian, and spoke bad French. But he was an excellent bassoon player. He often called on me and we played duets for bassoon and tympani, and then read Amiel's journal aloud and wept. Oh! he had a sensitive soul, that bassoon player. He died of the cholera, and now I am alone. . . .

After my failure as an orchestral player I gave a concert in this city, and played my concerto for seven drums and wood-wind orchestra. The critics laughed me to distraction. Instead of listening to the innumerable rhythms and marvellous variety of nuances I offered them, they mocked my agile behavior and my curiously colored hair. Even my confrères envied and reviled me. I have genius, so am hated and despised. Oh, the pity of it all! They couldn't hear the tenderness, the fairy-like sobbing made by my wrists, but listened with admiration to the tinkling of a piano, with its hard, unchangeable tone. Oh, the stupidity of it all! . . .

But time will have its revenge. I will not stir a finger either. When I die the world of tone will realize that a great man has passed away, after a wretched, neglected life. I have composed a symphony, and for nothing but *Tympani!* Don't smile, because I have explored the most fantastic regions of rhythm, hitherto

undreamed.   Tone, timbre, intensity, rhythm,
variety in color, all, all will be in it; and how
much more subtly expressed than by your
modern orchestra, with its blare, blow, bang and
scratch.   And what great thoughts I have expressed !   I have gone beyond Berlioz, Wagner
and Richard Strauss.   I have discovered rhythms,
Asiatic in origin, that will plunge you into midnight woe; rhythms rescued from the Greeks of
old, that will drive you into panting dance;
rhythms that will make drunkards of sober men,
warriors of cowards, harlots of angels.   I can
intoxicate, dazzle, burn, madden you.   Why?
Because all music is rhythm.   It is the skeleton,
the structure of life, love, the cosmos.   God !
how I will exult, even if my skin crackles in
hell-fire, when the children of the earth listen to
my Tympani Symphony, and go crazy with its
tappings ! . . .

I have led a shiftless, uneventful life, yet I
envy no one, for I am the genius of a new art —
but stay a moment !   An uneventful life, did I
say?   Alas! my life has been one long, desperate effort to forget her, to forget my love,
my wife.   My God ! I can see her face now,
when she flashed across my sight at a provincial
circus.   It was in France.   I was a young man
drum-mad, and went to the circus to beguile my
time, for I couldn't practise all day.   Then I
saw her — " Mlle. Léontine, the Aërial Virtuoso
of the Century," the playbills called her.   She

68

was fair and slim, and Heaven had smiled into her eyes.

I am a poet, you see. Her hair was the color of tender wheat and her feet twinkled star-wise when she walked. She was my first, my only love, my life, my wife. She loved me, she told me so soon after we became acquainted, and I believed her; I believe her now, some-times, when I strike softly the skins of my dear little drum children. We soon married. There were no impediments on my side; my parents were dead and I had a little ready money. I gave it all to her. She took it and bought diamonds.

"They were so handy in case of hard luck," she said, and smiled. I smiled, too, and kissed her.

I kissed her very often, and was so desperately in love with her that I joined the circus and played the drums there; hush! don't tell it to any one — and the side-drums at that. I would have even played the piano for her, so frantically did I adore her. I was very proud of my wife, my Léontine. She did a tremendous act on the trapeze. She swung and made a flying leap across the tent and caught a bar, and every time I gave a tap on the big drum just as she grasped the trapeze. Oh! it would have made your blood shiver to see her slight figure hurtling through space and landing safely with my rhyth-mic accompaniment. And how people cheered, and what crowds flocked to view the spectacle!

In some towns the authorities made us use nets; then the crowds were not nearly so large. People like risks. The human animal is happy if it smells blood. Léontine noticed the decreased attendance when the safety nets were used, and begged the manager to dispense with them.

He often did so, for he loved money as much as she loved fame. She was perfectly fearless and laughed at my misgivings, so we usually did the act without nets. . . .

We had reached Rouen in our wanderings through the provinces, and I mooned about the old town, sauntering through the cathedral, plunged in a reverie, for I was happy, happy all the time. Léontine was so good, so amiable, so true. She associated with none of the women of the circus and with none of the men, except the manager and myself.

The manager reared her; she had been a foundling. She told me this at the beginning of our intimacy. We often played games of picking out the handsomest houses and châteaux we passed, pretending that her parents lived in them. She was very jolly, was my little Léontine, and remained with me nearly all the time, except when practising her difficult feats; this she did in company with the manager, who attended to the ropes and necessary tackling. He was a charming fellow, and very obliging.

One day I was sitting half-asleep in the spring sunshine, with my back to one of the tents, awaiting Léontine's return. She was, as usual, rehearsing, and I, composing and dreaming. Suddenly a laugh aroused me, and I heard a woman's voice:

"But the young idiot never will discover them; he is too blind and too fond of drumming."

I tuned up my ears. Another woman answered in a regretful tone:

"See what it is to be fascinating like Léontine; she gets all the boy's money, and has the manager besides. She must earn a pretty penny." . . .

I sat perfectly cold and still for several moments, then managed to wriggle away. I can give you no account of my feelings now, so many years have passed; besides, I don't think I felt at all. Every day I became more and more thoughtful, and Léontine and the manager rallied me on my silence. . . .

At last I made up my mind that it was time to act. We went to Lille and gave there our usual display. I had not seen Léontine all day, and when the evening came I sent a message telling her I was not hungry and would not be home for supper. I could be a hypocrite no longer.

In the evening the regular performance began. I was in a gay humor, and the men in the orchestra laughed at my wit, saying that I was more like my old self. My wife's aërial act came last on the bill, being the event of the show. What a brilliant house we had! I still can smell the sawdust, the orange peel, see the myriad of faces and hear the crack of the ring-masters' whips, the cries of the clowns and the crash of the music. . . .

"She comes, Léontine comes!" shrilled a thousand throats.

Into the ring she dashed on a milk-white horse, and, throwing off her drapery, stood bowing.

What a graceful figure she had, and how lovely she looked as she clambered aloft to her giddy perch! Breathlessly every one saw her make preparations for the flight through the air. The band became silent; all necks were strained as she swung lightly to and fro in space, increasing the speed to gain necessary momentum for the final launch.

Off she darted, like a thunderbolt — bang! went my drum — a moment too soon. The false unaccustomed rhythm shook her nerves and she tumbled with her face toward me.

There were no nets. . . .

Later I sought the manager. He was in his room, his head thrust beneath pillows. I tapped him on the shoulder; he shuddered when he saw me. "'T is you who should wear black," I said. . . .

ISOLDE'S MOTHER

Kennst du der Mutter Künste nicht?
— TRISTAN UND ISOLDE.

I

"I'D rather see her in her grave than as Isolde!" Mrs. Fridolin tightly closed her large, soft eyes, adding intensity to a declaration made for the enlightenment of her companion in a German railway carriage. The young woman laughed disagreeably.

"I mean what I say, Miss Bredd; and when you know as much about the profession as I do — when you are an older woman — you will see I am right. Meg — I should say Margaret — shall never sing Isolde with *my* permission. Apart from the dreadfully immoral situation, just think of the costume in the garden scene, that chiton of cheese-cloth! And these Wagnerites pretend to turn up their nose at 'Faust'! I once told dear, old M. Gounod, when Meg was in Paris with Parchesi, his music was positively decent compared — "

The train, which had been travelling at a dangerous pace for Germany, slackened speed, and the clatter in the compartment ahead caused the two women to crane their heads out of the window.

"Bayreuth!" cried the younger theatrically, "Bayreuth, the Mecca of the true Wagnerite." Mrs. Fridolin gazed at her, at the neat American belted serge suit, the straw sailor hat, the demure mouse colored hair, the calm, insolent eyes — eyes that bored like a gimlet. "Oh, you love Wagner?" The girl hesitated, then answered in the broadest burr of the Middle West, "Well, you see, I have n't heard much of him, except when the Thomas Orchestra came over to our place from Chicago. So I ain't going to say whether I like him or not till I hear him. But I 've written lots about the 'Ring' — " "Without hearing it? How very American!" — "And I 'm a warm admirer of your daughter. Madame Fridolina always seemed to me to be a great Wagner singer. Now *she* can sing the Liebestod better than any of the German women — "

"Thank you, my dear; one never goes to Bayreuth for the singing."

"I know that; but as it 's my first trip over here I mean to make the most of it. I am a journalist, you know, and I 'll write lots home about Wagner and Fridolina."

"Thanks again, my dear young lady. I 'm sure you will tell the truth. Margaret was refused the Brünnhilde at the last moment by Madame Cosima — that 's Mrs. Wagner, you know — and she had to content herself with Fricka in 'Rheingold,' and Gutrune in 'Götterdämmerung,' two odious parts. But what can she do? The Brünnhilde is Gulbranson. She is a great favorite in Bayreuth, and has kept her figure, while poor Meg — wait till you see her!"

The train rounded the curve and, leaving behind the strange looking theatre, surely a hieratic symbol of Wagner's power, entered the station full of gabbling, curious people — Bayreuth at last.

II

The atelier was on the ground floor at the end of a German garden full of angular desolations. It was a large, bare, dusty apartment, the glare of the August sun tempered by green shades nearly obscuring the big window facing the north. A young woman sat high on a revolving platform. She was very fat. As the sculptor fixed her with his slow glance he saw that her head, a pretty head, was too small for her monstrous bulk; her profile, pure Greek, the eyes ox-like, the cups full of feeling, with heavy accents beneath them. Her face, almost slim, had planes eloquent with surface meanings upon the cheeks and chin, while the mouth, sweet for a large woman, revealed amiability quite in accord with the expression of the eyes.

These were the glory of her countenance, these and her resonant black hair. Isolate this head from the shoulders, from all the gross connotations of the frame, and the trick would be done. So thought the sculptor, as the problem posed itself clearly; then he saw her figure and doubted.

"I *am* hopeless, am I not, Herr Arthmann?" Her voice was so frankly appealing, so rich in comic intention, that he sat down and laughed. She eagerly joined in: "And yet my waist is not so large as Mitwindt's. We always call her Bagpipes. She is absurd. And such a chest — ! Why, I'm a mere child. Anyhow, all Germans like big singers, and all the German Wagner singers are big women, are they not, Herr Arthmann? There was Alboni and Parepa-Rosa — I know they were not Wagner singers; but they were awful all the same — and just look at the Schnorrs, Materna, Rosa Sucher, poor Klafsky and — "

"My dear young friend," interrupted the sculptor as he took up a pointer and approached a miniature head in clay which stood upon a stand, "my dear" — he did not say "friend" the second time — "I remarked nothing about your figure being too large for the stage. I was trying to get it into harmony your magnificent shoulders and antique head. That's all." His intonation was caressing, the speech of a cultivated man, and his accent slightly Scandinavian;

at times his voice seemed to her as sweetly staccato as a mandolin. He gazed with all his vibrating artistic soul into the girl's humid blue eyes; half frightened she looked down at her pretty, dimpled hands — the hands of a baby despite their gladiatorial size.

"How you do flatter! All foreigners flatter American girls, don't they? Now you know you don't think my shoulders magnificent, do you? And my waist — O! Herr Arthmann, what shall I do with my waist? As Brünnhilde, I'm all right to move about in loose draperies, but as Fricka, as Gutrune — Gutrune who falls fainting beside Siegfried's bier! How must I look on my back? Oh, dear! and I diet, never drink water at meals, walk half the day and seldom touch a potato. And you know what that means in Germany! There are times when to see a potato, merely hearing the word mentioned, brings tears to my eyes. And yet I get no thinner — just look at me!"

He did. Her figure was gigantic. She weighed much over two hundred pounds, though the mighty trussing to which she subjected herself, and a discreet manner of dressing made her seem smaller. Arthmann was critical, and did not disguise the impossibility of the task. He had determined on a head and bust, something heroic after the manner of a sturdy Brünnhilde. The preparations were made, the skeleton, framework of lead pipe for the clay, with

77

crossbar for shoulders and wooden "butter-flies" in position. On the floor were water-buckets, wet cloths and a vast amount of wet clay — clay to catch the fleshly exterior, clay to imprison the soul — perhaps, of Fridolina. But nothing had been done except a tiny wax model, a likeness full of spirit, slightly encouraging to the perplexed artist. The girl was beautiful; eyes, hair, teeth, coloring — all enticed him as man. As sculptor the shapeless, hopeless figure was a thing for sack-like garments, not for candid clay or the illuminating commentary of marble. She drew a silk shawl closer about her bare shoulders.

"And Isolde — what shall I do? Frau Cosima says that I may sing it two summers from now; but then she promised me Brünnhilde two years ago after I had successfully sung Elsa. I know every note of 'Tristan,' for I've had over a thousand piano rehearsals, and Herr Siegfried and Caspar Dennett both say that in time it will be my great rôle." "Who was it you mentioned besides the Prince Imperial?" — they always call Siegfried Wagner the Prince Imperial or the Heir Apparent in Bayreuth — "Mr. Dennett. He is the celebrated young American con-ductor — the only American that ever con-ducted in Bayreuth. You saw him the other night at Sammett's garden. Don't you remem-ber the smooth faced, very good-looking young man? — you ought to model him. He was with

Siegfried when he spoke to me." "And you say that he admires your Isolde?" persisted Arthmann, pulling at his short reddish beard. "Why, of course! Did n't he play the piano accompaniments?" "Was his wife always with you?" "Now, Herr Arthmann, you are a regular gossipy German. Certainly she was n't. We in America don't need chaperons like your Ibsen women — are you really Norwegian or Polish? Is your name, Wenceslaus, Bohemian or Polish? Besides, here I am alone in your studio in Bayreuth, the most scandal-mongering town I ever heard of. My mother would object very much to this sort of thing, and I 'm sure we are very proper." "Oh, very," replied the sculptor; "when do you expect your mother? To-morrow, is it not?"

The girl nodded. Tired of talking, she watched with cool nervousness the movements of the young man; watched his graceful figure, admirable poses; his long, brown fingers smoothing and puttering in the clay; his sharply etched profile, so melancholy, insincere. "And this Dennett?" he resumed. She opened her little mouth. "Please don't yawn, Fridolina," he begged. "I was n't yawning, only trying to laugh. Dennett is on your mind. He seems to worry you. Don't be jealous — Wenceslaus; he is an awful flirt and once frightened me to death by chasing me around the dressing-room at the opera till I was out of breath and black and blue from pushing the chairs and tables in his way. And what do you suppose he gave as an excuse? Why, he just said he was exercising me to reduce my figure, and had n't the remotest notion of kissing me. Oh, no, he had n't, had he?" She pealed with laughter, her companion regarding her with tense lips. "No one but a Yankee girl would have thought of telling such a story." "Why, is it improper?" She was all anxiety. "No, not improper, but heartless, simply heartless. You have never loved, Margaret Fridolina," he said, harshly. "Call me Meg, Wenceslaus, but not when mamma is present," was her simple answer. He threw down his wooden modelling spatula.

"Oh, this is too much," he angrily exclaimed: "you tell me of men who chase you"—"a man Wenceslaus," she corrected him earnestly—"you tell me all this and you know I love you; without your love I shall throw up sculpture and go to sea as a sailor. Meg, Meg, have you no heart?" "Why, you little boy, what have I said to offend you? Why are you so cynical when I know you to be so sentimental?" Her voice was arch, an intimate voice with liquid inflections. He began pacing the chilly floor of the studio.

"Let us be frank. I 've only known you two months, since the day we accidentally met, leaving Paris for Bayreuth. You have written your mother nothing of our engagement—

well, provisional engagement, if you will — and
you insist on sticking to the operatic stage. I
loathe it, and I confess to you that I am sick
with jealousy when I see you near that lanky,
ill-favored German tenor Burgmann." " What,
poor, big me ! " she interjected, in teasing accents. " Yes, you, Fridolina. I can quite sym-
pathize with what you tell me of your mother's
dislike for the rôle of Isolde. You are not temperamentally suited to it; it is horrible to think
of you in that second act." " How horrible ?
My figure, you mean ? " " Yes, your figure,
too, would be absurd." He was brutal now.
" And you have n't the passion to make anything of the music. You 've never loved, never
will, passionately — " " But I 'll sing Isolde
all the same," she cried. " Not with my permission." " Then without you and your permission." She hastily arose and was about to
step down from her pedestal when the door
opened.

" Mother ! Why, mamma, you said you
were n't coming until Sunday." Mrs. Fridolin
could not see very well in the heavy shadows
after the blinding sunlight without. " What are
you doing here, Margaret, and of all things
alone up there on a throne ! Is this a rehearsal
for the opera ? " " I 'm not alone, mother.
This is Wenceslaus — Mr. Wenceslaus Arthmann, the sculptor, mamma, and he is doing
me in clay. Look at it; is n't it sweet ? Mr.

6

Arthmann, this is my mother — and who is the young lady, mamma?" "Oh, I forgot. I was so confused and put out not finding you at the station I drove at once to Villa Wahnfried — " "Villa Wahnfried!" echoed two voices in dismayed unison. "Yes, to Frau Cosima, and she directed me here." "She directed you here?" "Yes, why shouldn't she? Is there anything wrong in that?" asked the stately, high-nosed lady with the gray pompadour, beginning to peer about suspiciously. "Oh, no, mamma, but how did Frau Cosima know that I was here?" "I don't know, child," was the testy answer. "Come, get down and let me introduce you to my charming travelling friend, Miss Bredd." "Miss Saïs Bredd," put in the Western girl; "I was named Saïs after my father visited Egypt, but my friends call me Louie." — "And Miss Bredd, this is Mister — " "Arthmann, madame," said the sculptor. They all shook hands after the singer had released her mother from a huge, cavernous hug. "But Meg, Meg, where is your chaperon?" Fridolina looked at the young man: "Why, mamma, it was the *Hausfrau* who let you in, of course." Miss Bredd smiled cynically.

III

Up the Via Dolorosa toiled a Sunday mob from many nations. The long, nebulous avenue, framed on either side by dull trees, was dusty with the heels of the faithful ones; and the murmur of voices in divers tongues recalled the cluttering sea on a misty beach. Never swerving, without haste or rest, went the intrepid band of melomaniacs speaking of the singers, the weather and prices until the summit was reached. There the first division broke ranks and charged upon the caravansary which still stood the attacks of thirsty multitudes after two decades. Lucky ones grasped Schoppen of beer and Rhine wine hemmed in by an army of expectant throats, for the time was at hand when would sound Donner's motive from the balcony: music made by brass instruments warning the elect that "Rheingold" was about to unfold its lovely fable of water, wood and wind.

Mrs. Fridolin went to the theatre and longed with mother's eyes for the curtains to part and discover Fricka. She took her seat unconcernedly; she was not an admirer of Wagner, educated as she had been in the florid garden of Italian song. The darkness at first oppressed her. When from mystic space welled those elemental sounds, not mere music, but the sighing, droning, rhythmic swish of the waters, this woman knew that something strange and terrible was about to enter into her consciousness. The river Rhine calmly, majestically stole over her senses; she forgot Bellini, Donizetti, even Gounod and soon she was with the Rhine

Daughters, with Alberich. . . . Her heart
seemed to stop. All sense of identity vanished at a wave of Wagner's wand, as is absorbed the *ego* by the shining mirror of the
hypnotist. This, then, was the real Wagner — a
Wagner who attacked simultaneously the senses,
vanquished the strongest brain; a Wagner who
wept, wooed, sang and surged, ravished the
soul until it was brought lacerated and captive
to the feet of the victorious master magician.
The eye was promise-crammed, the ears sealed
with bliss, and she felt the wet of the waters.
She breathed hard as Alberich scaled the slimy
steeps; and the curves described by the three
swimming mermaids filled her with the joy of
the dance, the free ecstatic movements of free
things in the waves. The filching of the Rheingold, the hoarse shout of laughter from Alberich's love-foresworn lips, and the terrified cries
of the luckless watchers were as real as life.
Walhall did not confuse her, for now she caught
clues to the meaning of the mighty epic. Wotan
and Fricka — ah, Meg did not look so stout, and
how lovely her voice sounded! — Loki, mis-
chief-making, diplomatic Loki; the giants, Fafner
and Fasolt; Freia, and foolish, maimed, malicious Mime — these were not mere papier-maché,
but fascinating deities. She saw the gnomes'
underworld, saw the ring, the snake and the
tarnhelm; she heard the Nibelungs' anvil chorus
— so different from Verdi's — saw the giants

quarrelling over their booty; and the sonorous rainbow seemed to bridge the way to a fairer land. As the Walhall march died in her ears she found herself outside on the dusky, picturesque esplanade and forgot all about Meg, remembering her only as Fricka. With the others she slowly trod the path that had been pressed by the feet of art's martyrs. Mrs. Fridolin then gave tongue to her whirring brain:

"Oh! the magic of it all," she gasped.

"I'm afraid I rather agree with Nordau, Mrs. Fridolin — the whole affair reminds me of a tank-drama I once saw in Chicago." It was the cool voice of Miss Bredd that sounded in the hot, humming lane punctuated by vague, tall trees. . . .

Mrs. Fridolin and her party went to Sammett's for dinner that evening. This garden, once Angermann's and made famous by Wagner, is still a magnet. The Americans listened calmly to furious disputes, in a half-dozen tongues, over the performance to the crashing of dishes and the huddling of glasses always full, always empty. Arthmann ordered the entire menu, knowing well that it would reach them after much delay in the inevitable guise of veal and potatoes. The women were in no hurry, but the sculptor was. He drummed on the table, he made angry faces at his neighbors — contented looking Germans who whistled themes from " Rheingold "— and when Herr Sammett saluted his guests with a crazy trombone and crazier perversion of the Donner motive, Arthmann jumped up and excused himself. The two hours and a half in the theatre had made him nervous, restless, and he went away saying that he would be back presently. Mrs. Fridolin was annoyed. It did not seem proper for three ladies to remain unaccompanied in a public garden, even if that garden was in Bayreuth. Suppose some of her New York friends should happen by! . . . "I wonder where he has gone? I don't admire your new friend, Margaret. He seems very careless," she grumbled.

"Wenceslaus!"—Mrs. Fridolin looked narrowly at her daughter—"Mr. Arthmann, then, will be back soon. Like all sculptors he hates to be cooped up long." "I guess he's gone to get a drink at the bar," suggested the practical Miss Bredd. "How did you like my Fricka—oh, here's Mr. Dennett—Caspar, Caspar come over here, here!" The big girl stood up in elephantine eagerness, and a jaunty, handsome young man, with a shaven face and an important chin, slowly made his way through the press of people to the Fridolin table. It was Caspar Dennett, the conductor. After a formal presentation to the tall, thin Mrs. Fridolin, the young American musician settled himself for a talk and began by asking how they liked his conducting. He had been praised by the Prince Imperial himself—praise sufficient for any self-doubting

soul! Thank heaven, *he* had no doubt of his
vocation! It was Miss Bredd who answered
him:

"I enjoyed your conducting immensely, Mr.
Dennett, simply because I couldn't see you
work those long arms of yours. . . . I wrote
lots about you when you visited the West with
your band. I never cared for your Wagner
readings." He stared at her reproachfully and
she stared in return. Then he murmured, "I'm
really very sorry I didn't please you, Miss Bredd.
I didn't know that you were a newspaper woman." "Journalist, if you please!" "I beg your
pardon, journalist. I'm so sorry that Mrs. Dennett is visiting relations in England. She would
have been delighted to call on you;" — Miss
Bredd's expression became disagreeable — "and
now, Mrs. Fridolin, what do you think of your
daughter, your daughter Fricka Fridolina, as we
call her? Won't she be a superb Isolde some
day?" "I hope not, Mr. Dennett," austerely replied the mother. Margaret grasped his hands
gratefully, crying aloud, "You dear! Is n't he
a dear, mamma? Only think of your daughter as Isolde. Ah! there comes the deserter.
You thoughtless man!"

The sculptor bowed stiffly when presented,
and the two men sat on either side of Miss
Fridolin, far away from each other.

"Mr. Arthmann," fluted the singer — she was
all dignity now — "Mr. Dennett thinks I'm quite

ready for Isolde." "You said that to me this afternoon," he answered in a rude manner. The conductor glanced at him and then at Margaret. She was blushing. "What I meant," said Dennett, quickly turning the stream his way, "What I meant was that Miss Fridolina knows the score, and being temperamentally suited to the rôle—" "Temperamentally," sneered Arthmann. "Yes, that's what I said," snapped the other man, who had become surprisingly pugnacious—Fridolina was pressing his foot with heavy approval—"temperamentally." "You know Caspar"—the brows of the mother and sculptor were thunderous—"you know that Mr. Arthmann is a very clever sculptor, and is a great reader of faces and character. Now he says, that I have no dramatic talent, no temperament, and ought to—" "Get married," boomed in Arthmann with his most Norwegian accent. The bomb exploded. "I'd rather see her"—"in her grave, Mrs. Fridolin"—"Oh, you wicked, sarcastic Louie Bredd. No, not in her grave, but even as Isolde. Yes, I admit that I am converted to Wagnerism. Wagner's music is better for some singers than marriage. Prima donnas have no business to be married. If their husbands are not wholly worthless—and there are few exceptions—they are apt to be ninnies and spongers on their wives' salaries." Then she related the story of Wilski, who was a Miss Willies from Rochester. She married a novelist, a young man with the brightest possible prospects imaginable. What happened? He never wrote a story after his marriage in which he did n't make his wife the heroine, so much so that all the magazine editors and publishers refused his stuff, sending it back with the polite comment, Too much Wilski!

"That's nothing," interrupted Louie. "She ought to have been happy with such a worshipping husband. I know of a great singer, the greatest singer alive — Frutto " — they all groaned — " the *greatest*, I say. Well, she married a lazy French count. Not once, but a hundred times she has returned home after a concert only to find her husband playing cards with her maid. She raised a row, but what was the use? She told me that she 'd rather have him at home with the servant playing poker than at the opera where he was once seen to bet on the cards turned up by Calvé in the third act of ' Carmen.' I 've written the thing for my paper and I mean to turn it into a short story some day." Every one had tales to relate of the meanness, rapacity, dissipation and extravagance of the prima donna's husband from Adelina Patti to Mitwindt, the German singer who regularly committed her husband to jail at the beginning of her season, only releasing him when September came, for then her money was earned and banked.

"But what has this to do with me?" peevishly asked Fridolina, who was tired and sleepy. "If ever I marry it must be a man who will let me sing Isolde. Most foreign husbands hide their wives away like a dog its bone." She beamed on Wenceslaus. "Then you will never marry a foreign husband," returned the sculptor, irritably.

IV

"You must know, Mr. Arthmann, that my girl is a spoilt child, as innocent as a baby, and has everything to learn about the ways of the world. Remember, too, that I first posed her voice, taught her all she knew of her art before she went to Parchesi. What you ask — taking into consideration that we, that *I*, hardly know you — is rather premature, is it not?" They were walking in the cool morning down the green alleys of the Hofgarten, where the sculptor had asked Mrs. Fridolin for her daughter. He was mortified as he pushed his crisp beard from side to side. He felt that he had been far from proposing marriage to this large young woman's mother; something must have driven him to such a crazy action. Was it Caspar Dennett and his classic profile that had angered him into the confession? Nonsense! The conductor was a married man with a family. Despite her easy, unaffected manner, Margaret Fridolin was no fool; she ever observed the

ultimate proprieties, and being dangerously un-
romantic would be the last woman in the world
to throw herself away. But this foolish mania
about Isolde. What of that? It was absurd to
consider such a thing. . . . Her mother would
never tolerate the attempt —

"Don't you think my judgment in this
matter is just, Mr. Arthmann?" Mrs. Fridolin
was blandly observing him. He asked her pardon for his inattention; he had been dreaming
of a possible happiness! She was very amiable.
"And you know, of course, that Margaret has
prospects" — he did not, and was all ears —
"if she will only leave the operatic stage. Her
career will be a brilliant one despite her figure,
Mr. Arthmann; but there is a more brilliant
social career awaiting her if she follows her
uncle's advice and marries. My brother is a
rich man, and my daughter may be his heiress.
Never as a singer — Job is prejudiced against
the stage — and never if she marries a foreigner." "But I shall become a citizen of the
United States, madame." "Where were you
born?" "Bergen; my mother was from Warsaw," he moodily replied. "It might as well
be Asia Minor. We are a stubborn family, sir,
from the hills of New Hampshire. We never
give in. Come, let us go back to the Hotel
Sonne, and do you forget this foolish dream.
Margaret may never leave the stage, but I'm
certain that she will never marry *you*." She

smiled at him, the thousand little wrinkles in her face making a sort of reticulated map from which stared two large, blue eyes — Margaret's eyes, grown wiser and colder. . . . " Now after that news I 'll marry her if I have to run away with her ! " — resolved the sculptor when he reached his bleak claustral atelier, and studied the model of her head. And how to keep that man Dennett from spoiling the broth, he wondered. . . .

In the afternoon Arthmann wrote Margaret a letter. " Margaret, my darling Margaret, what is the matter? Have I offended you by asking your mother for you? Why did you not see me this morning? The atelier is wintry without you — the cold clay, corpse-like, is waiting to revive in your presence. Oh! how lovely is the garden, how sad my soul! I sit and think of Verlaine's ' It rains in my heart as it rains in the town.' Why won't you see me? You are mine — you swore it. My sweet girl, whose heart is as fragrant as new-mown hay " — the artist pondered well this comparison before he put it on paper; it evoked visions of hay bales. " Darling, you must see me to-morrow. To the studio you must come. You know that we have planned to go to America in October. Only think, sweetheart, what joy then! The sky is aflame with love. We walk slowly under the few soft, autumn, prairie stars; your hand is in mine, we are married! You see I am a poet for your sake. I beg for a reply hot from your heart. Wenceslaus." . . .

He despatched this declaration containing several minor inaccuracies. It was late when he received a reply. "All right, Wenceslaus. But have I *now* the temperament to sing Isolde?" It was unsigned. Arthmann cursed in a tongue that sounded singularly like pure English.

V

That night, much against his desire, he dressed and went to a reception at the Villa Wahnfried. As this worker in silent clay disliked musical people, the buzz and fuss made him miserable. He did not meet Fridolina, though he saw Miss Bredd arm-in-arm with Cosima, Queen Regent of Bayreuth. The American girl was eloquently exposing her theories of how Wagner should be sung and Arthmann, disgusted, moved away. He only remembered Caspar Dennett when in the street. That gentleman was not present either; and as the unhappy lover walked down the moonlit Lisztstrasse he fancied he recognized the couple he sought. Could it be! He rushed after the pair to be mocked by the slamming of a gate, he knew not on what lonely street. . . .

The next afternoon the duel began. Fridolina did not return for a sitting as he had hoped; instead came an invitation for a drive to the

Hermitage. It was Mrs. Fridolin who sent it.
Strange! Arthmann was surprised at this re-
newal of friendly ties after his gentle dismissal
in the Hofgarten. But he dressed in his most
effective clothes and, shining with hope, reached
the Hotel Sonne; two open carriages stood before its arched doorway. Presently the others
came downstairs and the day became gray for
the sculptor. Caspar Dennett, looking like a
trim Antinous with a fashionable tailor, smiled
upon all, especially Miss Bredd. Mrs. Fridolin
alone did not seem at ease. She was very
friendly with Arthmann, but would not allow
him in her carriage. "No," she protested, "you
two men must keep Margaret company. I'll
ride with my bright little Louie and listen to
her anti-Wagner blasphemies." She spoke as
if she had fought under the Wagner banner
from the beginning.

Margaret sat alone on the back seat. Although she grimaced at her mother's suggestion, she was in high spirits, exploding over every
trivial incident of the journey. Arthmann, as
he faced her, told himself that he had never seen
her so giggling and commonplace, so unlike an
artist, so bourgeois, so fat. He noticed, too,
that her lovely eyes expanded with the same
expression, whether art or eating was mentioned. He hardly uttered a word, for the
others discussed "Tristan und Isolde" until he
hated Wagner's name. She was through with

her work at Bayreuth and Frau Cosima had promised her Isolde — positively. She meant to undergo a severe *Kur* at Marienbad and then return to the United States. Mr. Grau had also promised her Isolde; while Jean de Reszké — dear, wonderful Jean vowed that he would sing Tristan to no other Isolde during his American tournée! So it was settled. All she needed was her mother's consent — and that would not be a difficult matter to compass. Had she not always wheedled the mater into her schemes, even when Uncle Job opposed her? She would never marry, never — anyhow not until she had sung Isolde — and then only a Wagner-loving husband.

"And the temperament, the missing link — how about that?" asked Arthmann sourly; he imagined that Dennett was exchanging secret signals with her. She bubbled over with wrath. "Temperament! I have temperament enough despite my size. If I have n't any I know where to find it. There is no sacrifice I'd not make to get it. Art for art is my theory. First art and then — the other things." She shrugged her massive shoulders in high bad humor. Arthmann gloomily reflected that Dennett's phrases at the Sammett Garden were being echoed. Mrs. Fridolin continually urged her driver to keep his carriage abreast of the other. It made the party more sociable, she declared, although to the sculptor it seemed as if she wished to watch Margaret closely. She had never seemed so suspicious. They reached the Hermitage.

Going home a fine rain set in; the hoods of the carriage were raised, and the excursion ended flatly. At the hotel, Arthmann did not attempt to go in. Mrs. Fridolin said she had a headache, Miss Bredd must write articles about Villa Wahnfried, while Dennett disappeared with Margaret. The drizzle turned into a downpour, and the artist, savage with the world and himself, sought a neighboring café and drank till dawn. . . .

He called at the hotel the following afternoon. The ladies had gone away. How gone away? The portier could not tell. Enraged as he saw his rich dream vanishing, Arthmann moved about the streets with lagging, desperate steps. He returned to the hotel several times during the afternoon — at no time was he very far from it — but the window-blinds were always drawn in the Fridolin apartment and he began to despair. It was near sunset when his *Hausfrau*, the disappearing chaperon, ran to him red-faced. A letter for Herr Arthmann! It was from her: "I've gone in search of that temperament. *Auf Wiedersehen.* Isolde." Nothing more. In puzzled fury he went back to the hotel. Yes, Madame Fridolin and the young lady were now at home. He went to the second landing and without knocking pushed open the door.

It was a house storm-riven. Trunks bulged, though only half-packed, their contents straggling over the sides. The beds were not made, and a strong odor of valerian and camphor flooded the air. On a couch lay Mrs. Fridolin, her face covered with a handkerchief, while near hovered Miss Bredd in her most brilliant and oracular attitude. She was speaking too loudly as he entered: "There is no use of worrying yourself sick about Meg, Mrs. Fridolin. She's gone for a time — that's all. When she finds out what an idiotically useless sacrifice she has made for art and is a failure as Isolde — she can no more sing the part than a sick cat — she will run home to her mammy quick enough."

"Oh, this terrible artistic temperament!" groaned the mother apologetically. The girl made a cautious movement and waved Arthmann out of the room. Into the hall she followed, soft-footed, but resolute. He was gaunt with chagrin. "Where is she?" — he began, but was sternly checked:

"If you had only flattered her more, and married her before her mother arrived, this thing would n't have happened."

"What thing?" he thundered.

"There! don't be an ox and make a stupid noise," she admonished. "Why, Meg — she is so dead set on getting that artistic temperament, that artistic thrill you raved about, that she has eloped."

"Eloped!" he feebly repeated, and sat down on a trunk in the hallway. To her keen, unbiassed vision Arthmann seemed more shocked than sorrowful. Then, returning to Isolde's mother, she was not surprised to find her up and in capital humor, studying the railway guide.

"He believes the fib — just as Dennett did!" Miss Bredd exclaimed, triumphantly; and for the first time that day Mrs. Fridolin smiled.

THE RIM OF FINER ISSUES

I

THERE seemed to be a fitting dispensation in the marriage of Arthur Vibert and Ellenora Bishop. She was a plain looking girl of twenty-four — even her enemies admitted her plainness — but she had brains; and the absence of money was more than compensated by her love for literature. It had been settled by her friends that she would do wonderful things when she had her way. Therefore her union with Arthur Vibert was voted " singularly auspicious." He had just returned from Germany after winning much notice by his talent for composition. What could be more natural than the marriage of these two gifted persons?

Miss Bishop had published some things — rhapsodic prose-poems, weak in syntax but strong in the quality miscalled imagination. Her pen name was George Bishop: following the example of the three Georges so dear to the believer in sexless literature — George Sand, George Eliot and George Egerton. She greatly admired the latter.

Ellenora was a large young woman of more brawn than tissue; she had style and decision, though little amiability. Ugly she was; yet, after the bloom of her ugliness wore off, you admired perforce the full iron-colored eyes alive with power, and wondered why nature in dowering her with a big brain had not made for her a more refined mouth. The upper part of her face was often illuminated; the lower narrowly escaped coarseness; and a head of rusty red hair gave a total impression of strenuous brilliancy, of keen abiding vitality. A self-willed New York girl who had never undergone the chastening influence of discipline or rigorously ordered study — she averred that it would attenuate the individuality of her style; avowedly despising the classics, she was a modern of moderns in her tastes.

She had nerves rather than heart, but did not approve of revealing her vagaries in diary form. Adoring Guy de Maupassant, she heartily disliked Marie Bashkirtseff. The Frenchman's almost Greek-like fashion of regarding life in profile, his etching of its silver-tipped angles, made an irresistible appeal to her; and she vainly endeavored to catch his crisp, restrained style, his masterly sense of form. In the secrecy of her study she read Ouida and asked herself why this woman had not gone farther, and won first honors in the race. Her favorite heroines were Ibsen's Nora, Rebecca and Hedda. Then, bitten by the emancipation craze, she was fast developing into one of the "shrieking sisterhood" when Arthur Vibert came from Berlin.

A Frenchman has said that the moment a woman occupies her thoughts with a man, art ceases for her. The night Ellenora Bishop met the young pianist in my atelier, I saw that she was interested. Arthur came to me with letters from several German critics. I liked the slender, blue-eyed young fellow who was not a day over twenty-one. His was a true American type tempered by Continental culture. Oval-faced, fair-haired, of a rather dreamy disposition and with a certain austerity of manner, he was the fastidious puritan — a puritan expanded by artistic influences. Strangely enough he had temperament, and set to music Heine and Verlaine. A genuine talent, I felt assured, and congratulated myself on my new discovery; I was fond of finding lions, and my Sunday evenings were seldom without some specimen that roared, if somewhat gently, yet audibly enough, for my visitors. When Arthur Vibert was introduced to Ellenora Bishop, I recognized the immediate impact of the girl's brusque personality upon his sensitized nature.

She was a devoted admirer of Wagner, and that was bond enough to set reverberating other chords of sympathy in the pair. I do not assert in cold blood that the girl deliberately set herself to charm the boyish-looking composer, but there was certainly a basking allurement in her gaze when her eyes brushed his. With her complicated personality he could not cope — that was only too evident; and so I watched the little comedy with considerable interest, and not without misgiving.

Arthur fell in love without hesitation, and though Ellenora felt desperately superior to him — you saw that — she could not escape the bright, immediate response of his face. The implicated interest of her bearing — though she never lost her head — his unconcealed adoration, soon brought the affair to the altar — or rather to a civil ceremony, for the bride was an agnostic, priding herself on her abstention from established religious forms.

Her clear, rather dry nature had always been a source of study to me. What could she have in common with the romantic and decidedly shy youth? She was older, more experienced — plain girls have experiences as well as favored ones — and she was not fond of matrimony with poverty as an obbligato. Arthur had prospects of pupils, his compositions sold at a respectable rate, but the couple had little money to spare; nevertheless, people argued their marriage a capital idea — from such a union of rich talents surely something must result. Look at the Brownings, the Shelleys, the Schumanns, not to mention George Eliot and her man Lewes!

They were married. I was best man, and

realized what a menstruum is music — what curious trafficking it causes, what opposites it intertwines. And the overture being finished the real curtain arose, as it does on all who mate. . . .

I did not see much of the Viberts that winter. I cared not at all for society and they had moved to Harlem; so I lost two stars of my studio receptions. But I occasionally heard they were getting on famously. Arthur was composing a piano concerto, and Ellenora engaged upon a novel — a novel, I was told, that would lay bare to its rotten roots the social fabric; and knowing the girl's inherent fund of bitter cleverness I awaited the new-born polemic with gentle impatience. I hoped, however, like the foolish inexperienced old bachelor I am, that her feminine asperity would be tempered by the suavities of married life.

One afternoon late in March Arthur Vibert dropped in as I was putting the finishing touches on my portrait of Mrs. Beacon. He looked weary and his eyes were heavily circled.

" Hello, my boy! and how is your wife, and how is that wonderful concerto we've all been hearing about?"

He shrugged his shoulders and asked for a cigarette.

" Shall I play you some bits of it?" he queried in a gloomy way. I was all eagerness, and presently he was absently preluding at my piano.

There was little vigor in his touch, and I recalled his rambling wits by crying, "The concerto, let's have it!"

Arthur pulled himself together and began. He was very modern in musical matters and I liked the dynamic power of his opening. The first subject was more massive than musical and was built on the architectonics of Liszt and Tschaïkowsky. There was blood in the idea, plenty of nervous fibre, and I dropped my brushes and palette as the unfolding of the work began with a logical severity and a sense of form unusual in so young a mind.

This first movement interested me; I almost conjured up the rich instrumentation and when it ended I was warm in my congratulations.

Arthur moodily wiped his brow and looked indifferent.

"And now for the second movement. My boy, you always had a marked gift for the lyrical. Give us your romanza — the romanza, I should say, born of your good lady!"

He answered me shortly: "There is no romance, I've substituted for it a scherzo. You know that's what Saint-Saëns and all the fellows are doing nowadays, Scharwenka too."

I fancied that there was a shade of eager anxiety in his explanation, but I said nothing and listened.

The scherzo — or what is called the scherzo since Beethoven and Schumann — was too heavy, inelastic in its tread, to dispel the blue-devils. It was conspicuous for its absence of upspringing delicacy, light, arch merriment. It was the sad, bitter joking of a man upon whose soul life has graven pain and remorse, and before the trio was reached I found myself watching the young composer's face. I knew that, like all modern music students, he had absorbed in Germany some of that scholastic pessimism we encounter in the Brahms music, but I had hoped that a mere fashion of the day would not poison the springs of this fresh personality.

Yet here I was confronted with a painful confession that life had brought the lad more than its quantum of spiritual and physical hardship; he was telling me all this in his music, for his was too subjective a talent to ape the artificial, grand, objective manner.

Without waiting for comment he plunged into his last movement which proved to be a series of ingenious variations — a prolonged passacaglia — in which the grace and dexterity of his melodic invention, contrapuntal skill and symmetrical sense were gratifyingly present.

I was in no flattering vein when I told him he had made a big jump in his work.

"But, Arthur, why so much in the Brahms manner? Has your wife turned your love of Shelley to Browning worship?" I jestingly concluded.

" My wife, if she wishes, can turn Shelley into slush," he answered bitterly. This shocked me. I felt like putting questions, but how could I? Had I not been one of the many who advised the fellow to marry Ellenora Bishop? Had we not all fancied that in her strength was his security, his hope for future artistic triumphs?

He went on as his fingers snatched at fugitive harmonic experimentings: "It 's not all right up town. I wish that you would run up some night. You 've not seen Ellenora for months, and perhaps you could induce her to put the brake on." I was puzzled. Putting the brake on a woman is always a risky experiment, especially if she happens to be wedded. Besides, what did he mean?

" I mean," he replied to my tentative look of inquiry, " that Ellenora is going down-hill with her artistic theories of literature, and I mean that she has made our house a devilish unpleasant place to live in."

I hastily promised to call in a few days, and after seeing him to the door, and bidding him cheer up, I returned to the portrait of Mrs. Beacon, and felt savage at the noisiness of color and monotony of tonal values in the picture.

" Good Lord, why will artists marry? " I irritably asked of my subject in the frame. Her sleek Knickerbocker smile further angered me, and I went to my club and drank coffee until long after midnight.

II

If, as her friends asserted, Ellenora Vibert's ugliness had softened I did not notice it. She was one of those few women in the world that marriage had not improved. Her eyes were colder, more secret; her jaw crueller, her lips wider and harder at the edges. She welcomed me with distinguished loftiness, and I soon felt the unpleasant key in which the household tune was being played. It was amiable enough, this flat near Mount Morris Park in Harlem. The Viberts had taste, and their music-room was charming in its reticent scheme of decoration — a Steinway grand piano, a low crowded bookcase with a Rodin cast, a superb mezzotint of Leonardo's Monna Lisa after Calmatta, revealing the admirable poise of sweetly folded hands — surely the most wonderful hands ever painted — while the polished floor, comforting couches and open fireplace proclaimed this apartment as the composition of refined people.

I am alive to the harmonies of domestic interiors, and I sensed the dissonance in the lives of these two.

Soon we three warmed the cold air of restraint and fell to discussing life, art, literature, friends, and even ourselves. I could not withhold my admiration for Ellenora's cleverness. She was transposed to a coarser key, and there was a suggestion of the overblown in her figure; but her tongue was sharp, and she wore the air of a woman who was mistress of her mansion. Presently Arthur relapsed into silence, lounged and smoked in the corner, while Mrs. Vibert expounded her ideas of literary form, and finally confessed that she had given up the notion of a novel.

"You see, the novel is overdone to-day. The short story ended with de Maupassant. The only hope we have, we few who take our art seriously, is to compress the short story within a page and distil into it the vivid impression of a moment, a lifetime, an eternity." She looked intellectually triumphant. I interposed a mild objection.

"This form, my dear lady, is it a fitting vehicle for so much weight of expression? I admire, as do you, the sonnet, but I can never be brought to believe that Milton could have compressed 'Paradise Lost' within a sonnet."

"Then all the worse for Milton," she tartly replied. "Look at the Chopin prelude. Will you contradict me if I say that in one prelude this composer crowds the experience of a lifetime? When he expands his idea into the sonata form how diffuse, how garrulous he becomes!"

I ventured to remark that Chopin had no special talent for the sonata form.

"The sonata form is dead," the lady asserted. "Am I not right, Arthur?"

"Yes, my dear," came from Arthur. I fully understood his depression.

"No," she continued, magnificently, "it is this blind adherence to older forms that crushes all originality to-day. There is Arthur with his sonata form — as if Wagner did not create his own form!"

"But I am no Wagner," interrupted her husband.

"Indeed, you are not," said Mrs. Vibert rather viciously. "If you were we wouldn't be in Harlem. You men to-day lack the initiative. The way must be shown you by woman; yes, by poor, crushed woman — woman who has no originality according to your Schopenhauer; woman whose sensations, not being of coarse enough fibre to be measured by the rude emotion-weighing machine of Lombroso, are therefore adjudged of less delicacy than man's. What fools your scientific men be!"

Mrs. Vibert was a bit pedantic, but she could talk to the point when aroused.

"You discredit the idea of compressing an epic into a sonnet, a sonata into a prelude; well, I've attempted something of the sort, and even if you laugh I'll stick to my argument. I've attempted to tell the biological history of the cosmos in a single page. . . . I begin with the unicellular protozoa and finally reach humanity; and to give it dramatic interest I trace a germ-cell from eternity until the now, and you shall hear its history this moment." She stopped for breath, and I wondered if Mrs. Somerville or George Eliot had ever talked in this astounding fashion. I was certain that she must have read Iamblichus and Porphyry. Arthur on his couch groaned.

" Mock if you please," Ellenora's strong face flushed, " but women will yet touch the rim of finer issues. Paul Goddard, who is a critic I respect, told me I had struck the right note of modernity in my prose poem." I winced at the " note of modernity," and could not help seeing the color mount to Arthur's brow when the man's name was mentioned.

"And pray who is Mr. Paul Goddard?" I asked while Mrs. Vibert was absent in search of her manuscript. Arthur replied indifferently, " Oh, a rich young man who went to Bayreuth last summer and poses as a Wagnerite ever since! He also plays the piano!"

Arthur's tone was sarcastic; he did not like Paul Goddard and his critical attentions to his wife. The poor lad looked so disheartened, so crushed by the rigid intellectual atmosphere about him, that I put no further question and was glad when Mrs. Vibert returned with her prose poem.

She read it to us and it was called

FRUSTRATE

O the misty plaint of the Unconceived! O crystal incuriousness of the monad! The faint swarming toward the light and the rending of the sphere of hope, frustrate, inutile. I am the seed called Life; I am he, I am she. We walk, swim, totter, and blend. Through the ages I lay in the vast basin of Time; I am called by Fate into the Now. On pulsing terraces, under a moon blood-red, I dreamed of the mighty confluence. About me were my kinsfolk. Full of dumb pain we pleasured our centuries with anticipation; we watched as we gamed away the hours. From Asiatic plateaus we swept to Nilotic slime. We roamed in primeval forests, vast and arboreally sublime, or sported with the behemoth and listened to the serpent's sinuous irony; we chattered with the sacred apes and mouthed at the moon; and in the Long Ago wore the carapace and danced forthright figures on coprolitic sands — sands stretching into the bosom of the earth, sands woven of windy reaches hemming the sun. . . . We lay with the grains of corn in Egyptian granaries, and saw them fructify under the smile of the sphinx; we buzzed in the ambient atmosphere, gaudy dragon-flies or whirling motes in full cry chased by humming-birds. Then from some cold crag we launched with wings of fire-breathing pestilence and fell fathoms under sea to war with lizard-fish and narwhal. For us the supreme surrender, the joy of the expected. . . . With cynical glance we saw the Buddha give way to other gods. We watched protoplasmically the birth of planets and the confusion of creation. We saw hornéd monsters become gentle ruminants, and heard the scream of the pterodactyl on the tree-tops dwindle to child's laughter. We heard, we saw, we felt, we knew. Yet hoped we on; every monad has his day. . . . One by one the billions disintegrated and floated into formal life. And we watched and waited. Our evolution had been the latest delayed; until heartsick with longing many of my brethren wished for annihilation. . . .

At last I was alone, save one. The time of my fruition was not afar. O! for the moment when I should realize my dreams. . . . I saw this last one swept away, swept down the vistas toward life, the thunderous surge singing in her ears. O! that my time would come. At last, after vague alarms, I was summoned. . . .

The hour had struck; eternity was left behind, eternity loomed ahead, implacable, furrowed with Time's scars. I hastened to the only one in the Cosmos. I tarried not as I ran in the race. Moments were precious; a second meant æons; and crashing into the light— Alas! I was too late. . . . Of what avail my travail, my countless, cruel preparations? O Chance! O Fate! I am one of the silent multitude of the Frustrate. . . .

When she had finished reading this strange study in evolution she awaited criticism, but with the air of an armed warrior.

"Really, Mrs. Vibert, I am overwhelmed," I

managed to stammer. "Only the most delicate symbolism may dare to express such a theme." I felt that this was very vague — but what could I say?

She regarded me sternly. Arthur, catching what I had uttered at random, burst in:

"There, Ellenora, I am sure he is right! You leave nothing to the imagination. Now a subtile veiled idealism — " He was not allowed to finish.

"Veiled idealism indeed!" she angrily cried. "You composers dare to say all manner of wickedness in your music, but it is idealized by tone, is n't it? What else is music but a sort of sensuous algebra? Or a vast shadow-picture of the emotions? . . . Why can't language have the same privilege? Why must it be bridled because the world speaks it?"

"Just because of that reason, dear madame," I soothingly said; "because reticence is art's brightest crown; because Zola never gives us a real human document and Flaubert does; and the difference is a difference of method. Flaubert is magnificently naked, but his nakedness implicates nothing that is — "

"As usual you men enter the zone of silence when a woman's work is mentioned. I did not attempt a monument in the frozen manner of your Flaubert. Mr. Goddard believes — " There was a crash of music from the piano as Arthur endeavored to change the conversation.

His wife's fine indifference was tantalizing, also instructive.

"Mr. Goddard believes with Nietzsche that individualism is the only salvation of the race. My husband, Mr. Vibert, believes in altruism, self-sacrifice and all the old-fashioned flummery of out-worn creeds."

"I wonder if Mr. Vibert has heard of Nietzsche's ' Thou goest to women ? Remember thy whip'?" I meekly questioned. Ellenora looked at her husband and shrugged her shoulders; then picking up her manuscript she left the room with the tread of a soldier, laughing all the while.

"An exasperating girl!" I mused, as Vibert, after some graceful swallow-like flights on the keyboard, finally played that most dolorously delicious of Chopin's nocturnes, the one in C sharp minor.

That night in my studio I did not rejoice over my bachelorhood, for I felt genuinely sad at the absence of agreeable modulations in the married life of my two friends.

I thought about the thing for the next month, with the conclusion that people had to work out their own salvation, and resolved not to visit the Viberts again. It was too painful an experience; and yet I could see that Vibert cared for his wife in a weak sort of a way. But she was too overpowering for him and her robust, intellectual nature needed Nietzsche's whip — a stronger, more passionate will than her own. It was simply a case of mismating, and no good would result from the union.

Later I felt as if I had been selfish and priggish, and resolved to visit the home in Harlem and try to arrange matters. I am not sure whether it was curiosity rather than a laudable benevolence that prompted this resolve. However, one hot afternoon in May, Arthur Vibert entered my room and throwing himself in an easy-chair gave me the news.

" She 's left me, old man, she 's gone off with Paul Goddard." . . .

I came dangerously near swearing.

" Oh, it 's no use of your trying to say consoling things. She 's gone for good. I was never strong enough to hold her, and so it 's come to this disgraceful smash."

I looked eagerly at Arthur to discover overmastering sorrow; there was little. Indeed he looked relieved; his life for nearly a year must have been a trial and yet I mentally confessed to some disappointment at his want of deep feeling. I saw that he was chagrined, angry, but not really heart-hurt. Lucky chap! he was only twenty-two and had all his life before him. I asked for explanations.

" Oh, Ellenora always said that I never understood her; that I never could help her to reach the rim of finer issues. I suppose this fellow

Goddard will. At least she thinks so, else she would n't have left me. She said no family could stand two prima-donnas at the same time: as if I ever posed, or pretended to be as brilliant as she! No, she stifled me, and I feel now as if I might compose that romanza for my concerto."

I consoled the young pianist; told him that this blow was intended as a lesson in self-control; that he must not be downcast, but turn to his music as a consolation; and a whole string of such platitudes. When he left me I asked myself if Ellenora was not right, after all. Could she have reached that visionary rim of finer issues — of which she always prated — with this man, talented though he was, yet a slender reed shaken by the wind of her will? Besides, his chin was too small.

He could not master her nature. Would she be happy with Paul Goddard, that bright-winged butterfly of æstheticism? I doubted it. Perhaps the feminine, receptive composer was intended to be her saving complement in life. Perhaps she unconsciously cared for Arthur Vibert; and arguing the question as dispassionately as I could my eyes fell upon "Thus Spake Zarathustra," and opening the fat unwieldly volume I read:

"Is it not better to fall into the hands of a murderer than into the dreams of an ardent woman?"

"Pooh!" I sneered. "Nietzsche was a rank woman-hater;" then I began my work on Mrs. Beacon's portrait, the fashionable Mrs. Beacon, and tried to forget all about the finer issues and the satisfied sterility of its ideals.

AN IBSEN GIRL

I

As Ellenora Vibert quietly descended the stairs of the apartment house in Harlem where she had lived with her husband until this hot morning in May, she wondered at her courage. She was taking a tremendous step, and one that she hoped would not be a backward one. She was leaving Arthur Vibert after a brief year of marriage for another man. Yet her pulse fluttered not, and before she reached the open doorway a mocking humor possessed her.

Her active brain pictured herself in the person of Ibsen's Nora Helmer. But Nora left children behind, and deserted them in hot blood; no woman could be cold after such a night in the Doll's House — the champagne, the tarantella, the letter and the scene with Torvold! No, she was not quite Nora Helmer; and Paul, her young husband, was hardly a Scandinavian bureaucrat. When Ellenora faced the cutting sunshine and saw Mount Morris Park, green and sweet, she stopped and pressed a hand to her hip. It was a characteristic pose, and the first inspiration of the soft air gave her peace and hardihood.

"I've been penned behind the bars too long," she thought. Arthur's selfish, artistic absorption in his musical work and needless indifference to the development of her own gifts must count no longer.

She was free, and she meant to remain so as long as she lived.

Then she went to the elevated railroad and entered a down-town train, left it at Cortlandt Street, reached the Pennsylvania depot before midday, and in the waiting-room met Paul Goddard. A few minutes later they were on the Philadelphia train. The second chapter of Ellenora Vibert's life began — and most happily.

II

Paul Goddard, after he had returned from Bayreuth, gave his musical friends much pain by his indifference to old tastes. His mother, Mrs. Goddard of Madison Square, was not needlessly alarmed. She told her friends that Paul always had been a butterfly, sipping at many pretty arts. She included among these fine arts, girls. Paul's devotion to golf and a certain rich young woman gave her fine maternal satisfaction. "He stays away from that odious Bohemian crowd, and as long as he does that I am satisfied. Paul is too much of a gentleman to make a good musician."

During the winter she saw little of her son. His bachelor dinners were pronounced models, but the musical mob he let alone. " Paul must be going in for something stunning," they said at his club, and when he took off his moustache there was a protest.

The young man was not pervious to ridicule. He had found something new and as he was fond of experimenting and put his soul into all he did, was generally rewarded for his earnestness. He met Mrs. Arthur Vibert at the reception of a portrait-painter, and her type being new to him, resolved to study it.

Presently he went to the art galleries with the lady, and to all the piano recitals he could bid her. He called several times and admired her husband greatly; but she snubbed this admiration and he consoled himself by admiring instead the intellect of the wife.

" I suppose," she confided to him one February afternoon at Sherry's, " I suppose you think I am not a proper wife because I don't sit home at his feet and worship my young genius? "

Paul looked at her strong, ugly face and deep iron-colored eyes, and smiled ironically.

" You don't go in for that sort of thing, I suppose. If you did love him would you acknowledge it to any one, even to yourself — or to me? "

Ellenora flushed slightly and put down her glass.

"My dear man, when you know me better you won't ask such a question. I always say what I mean."

"And I don't." They fell to fugitive thinking.

"What poet wrote 'the bright disorder of the stars is solved by music'?"

"I never read modern verse."

"Yes, but this is not as modern as that cornet-virtuoso Kipling, or as ancient as Tennyson, if you must know."

"What has it to do with you? You are all that I am interested in — at the present." Paul smiled.

"Don't flatter me, Mr. Goddard. I hate it. It's a cheap trick of the enemy. Flatter a woman, tell her that she is unlike her sex, repeat to her your wonderment at her masculine intellect, and see how meekly she lowers her standard and becomes your bondslave."

"Hello! you have been through the mill," said Paul, brightly. "If I thought that it would do any good, be of any use, I would mentally plump on my knees and say to you that Ellenora Vibert is unlike any woman I ever met." Ellenora half rose from the table, looking sarcastically at him.

"My dear Mr. Goddard, don't make fun. You have hurt me more than I dare tell you. I fancied that you were a friend, the true sort." She was all steel and glitter now. Paul openly admired her.

"Mrs. Vibert, I beg your pardon. Please forget what I said. I do enjoy your companionship, and you know I am not a lady-killer. Tell me that you forgive me, and we will talk about that lovely line you quoted from — ? "

"Coventry Patmore, a dead poet. He it was that spoke of Wagner as a musical impostor, and of the grinning woman in every canvas of Leonardo da Vinci. I enjoy his 'Angel in the House' so much, because it shows me the sort of a woman I am not and the sort of a woman we modern women are trying to outlive. . . . Yes, 'the bright disorder of the stars is solved by music,' he sings; and I remember reading somewhere in Henry James that music is a solvent. But it's false — false in my case. Mr. Vibert is, as you know, a talented young man. Well, his music bores me. He is said to have genius, yet his music never sounds as if it had any fire in it; it is as cold as salt. Why should I be solved by his music? "

Ellenora upset her glass and laughed. Paul joined in at a respectful pace. The woman was beyond him. He gave her a long glance and she returned it, but not ardently; only curiosity was in her insistent gaze.

"Ah! Youth is an alley ambuscaded by stars," he proclaimed. The phrase had cost him midnight labor.

"Don't try to be epigrammatic," she retorted, "it does n't suit your mental complexion. I 'll be glad, then, when my youth has passed. It's a time of turmoil during which one can't really think clearly. Give me cool old age."

" And the future? "

" I leave that to the licensed victuallers of eternity." Paul experienced a thrill. The woman's audacity was boundless. Did she believe in anything? . . .

" I wonder why your husband does not give you the love he puts into his music."

" He has not suffered enough yet. You know what George Moore says about the ' sadness of life being the joy of art! ' . . . Besides, Arthur is only half a man if he can't give it to both. Where is your masculine objectivity, then? " she retorted.

" Lord, what a woman! ' Masculine objectivity,' and I suppose ' feminine subjectivity ' too. I never met such a blue-stocking. Do you remember how John Ruskin abused those odious terms ' objective ' and ' subjective '? " Paul asked.

" I can't read Ruskin. He is all landscape decoration; besides, he believes in the biblical attitude of woman. Put a woman on the mantelpiece and call her luscious, poetic names and then see how soon she 'll hop down when another man simply cries ' I love you.' If a man wishes to spoil a woman successfully let him idealize her."

" Poor Ruskin! There are some men in this world too fine for women." Paul sighed, and slily watched Ellenora as she cracked almonds with her strong white fingers.

"Fine fiddlesticks!" she ejaculated. "Don't get sentimental, Mr. Goddard, or else I'll think you have a heart. You are trying to flirt with me. I know you are. Take me away from this place and let us walk, walk! Heavens! I'd like to walk to the Battery and smell the sea!"

Paul discreetly stopped, and the pair started up Fifth Avenue. The day was a fair one; the sky was stuffed with plumy clouds and the rich colors of a reverberating sunset. The two healthy beings sniffed the crisp air, talked of themselves as only selfish young people can, and at Fifty-ninth street, Ellenora becoming tired, waited for a cross-town car — she expected some people at her house in the evening, and must be home early. Paul was bidden, but declined; then without savor of affection they said good-by.

The man went slowly down the avenue thinking: "Of all the women I've met, this is the most perverse, heartless, daring." He recalled his Bayreuth experiences, and analyzed Ellenora. Her supple, robust figure attracted his senses; her face was interesting; she had brains, uncommon brains. What would she become? Not a poet, not a novelist. Perhaps a literary critic, like Sainte-Beuve with shining Monday morning reviews. Perhaps — yes, perhaps a critic, a writer of bizarre prose-poems; she has personal style, she is herself, and no one else.

"That's it," said Paul, half aloud; "she has style, and I admire style above everything." He resolved on meeting Ellenora as often as he could. . . .

The following month he saw much of Arthur Vibert's wife, and found himself a fool in her strong grasp. The girl had such baffling contrasts of character, such slippery moods, such abundant fantasy that the young man — volatility itself — lost his footing, his fine sense of honor and made love to this sphinx of the inkpot, was mocked and flouted but never entirely driven from her presence. More than any other woman, Ellenora enjoyed the conquest of man. She mastered Paul as she had mastered Arthur, easily; but there was more of the man of the world, more of the animal in the amateur, and the silkiness of her husband, at first an amusement, finally angered her.

Vibert knew that his wife saw Paul much too often for his own edification, but only protested once, and so feebly that she laughed at him.

"Arthur," she said, taking him by his slender shoulders, "why don't you come home some night in a jealous rage and beat me? Perhaps then I might love you. As it is, Mr. Goddard only amuses me; besides, I read him my new stories, otherwise I don't care an iota for him."

He lifted his eyebrows, went to the piano and played the last movement of his new concerto, played it with all the fire he could master, his face white, muscles angry, a timid man transformed.

"Why don't you beat me instead of the piano, dear?" she cried out mockingly; "some women, they say, can be subdued in that fashion." He rushed from the room. . . .

April was closing when Vibert, summoned to Washington, gave a piano recital there, and Ellenora went down-town to dinner with Goddard. She was looking well, her spring hat and new gown were very becoming. As they sat at Martin's eating strawberries, Paul approved of her exceedingly. He had been drinking, and the burgundy and champagne at dinner made him reckless.

"See here, Ellenora Vibert, where is all this going to end? I'm not a bad fellow, but I swear I'm only human, and if you are leading me on to make a worse ass of myself than usual, why, then, I quit."

She regarded him coolly. "It will end when I choose and where I choose. It is my own affair, Paul, and if you feel cowardly qualms, go home like a good boy to your mamma and tell her what a naughty woman I am."

He sobered at once and reaching across the narrow dining-table took her wrist in both of his hands and forced her to listen.

" You disdainful woman ! I 'll not be mastered by you any longer — "

" That means," interrupted Ellenora coolly, " do as you wish, and not as I please."

Paul, his vanity wounded, asked the waiter for his reckoning. His patience was worn away.

" Paul, don't be silly," she cried, her eyes sparkling. " Now order a carriage and we 'll take a ride in the park and talk the matter over. I 'm afraid the fool's fever is in your blood ; the open air may do it good. Oh ! the eternal nonsense of youth. Call a carriage, Paul ! — April Paul ! ". . .

III

Life in Philadelphia runs on oiled wheels. After the huge clatter of New York, there is something mellow and human about the drowsy hum of Chestnut Street, the genteel reaches of Walnut, and the neat frontage of Spruce Street. Ellenora, so quick to notice her surroundings, was at first bored, then amused, at last lulled by the intimate life of her new home. She had never been abroad, but declared that London, out-of-the-way London, must be something like this. The fine, disdainful air of Locust Street, the curiously constrained attitude of the brick houses on the side streets — as if deferentially listening to the back-view remarks of their

statelier neighbors, the brown-stone fronts — all
these things she amused herself telling Paul,
playfully begging him not to confront her
with the oft-quoted pathetic fallacy of Ruskin.
Had n't Dickens, she asked, discerned human
expression in door-knockers, and on the faces
of lean, lonely, twilight-haunted warehouses?

She was gay for the first time in her restless
dissatisfied life. By some strange alchemy she
and Paul were able to precipitate and blend the
sum total of their content, and the summer was
passed in peace. At first they went to a hotel,
but fearing the publicity, rented under an assumed name a suite in the second storey of
a pretty little house near South Rittenhouse
Square. Here in the cheerful morning-room
Ellenora wrote, and Paul smoked or trifled at the
keyboard. They were perfectly self-possessed
as to the situation. When tired of the bond it
should be severed. This young woman and this
young man had no illusion about love — the
word did not enter into their life scheme.
Theirs was a pact which depended for continu-
ance entirely upon its agreeable quality. And
there was nothing cynical in all this; rather the
ready acceptance of the tie's fallibility mingled
with a little curiosity how the affair would turn
out.

It was not yet November when Paul stopped
in the middle of a Chopin mazurka:

"Ellenora, have you heard from Vibert?"

She looked up from the writing-desk.

" How could I ?   He does n't know where we are."

" And I fancy he does n't care."   Paul whistled a lively lilt.   His manner seemed offensive. She flushed and scowled.   He moved about the room still whistling and made much noise. Ellenora regarded him intently.

" Getting bored, Paul ?   Better go to New York and your club," she amiably suggested.

" If you don't care," and straightway he began making preparations for the journey.   In a quarter of an hour he was ready, and with joy upon his handsome face kissed Ellenora fervently and went away to the Broad Street station.   Then she did something surprising.   She threw herself upon a couch and wept until she was hysterical.

" I 'm a nice sort of a fool, after all," she reflected, as she wiped her face with a cool handkerchief and proceeded to let her hair down for a good, comfortable brushing.   " I 'm a fool, a fool, to cry about this vain, selfish fellow.   Paul has no heart.   Poor little Arthur !   If he had been more of a man, less of a conceited boy. Yet conceit may fetch him through, after all. Dear me, I wonder what the poor boy did when he got the news."

Ellenora laughed riotously.   The silliness of the situation burned her sense of the incongruous.   There she stood opposite the mirror with her tears hardly dry, and yet she was thinking of the man she had deserted! It was absurd after all, this hurly-burly of men and women. Then she began to wonder when Paul would return. The day seemed very long; in the evening she walked in Rittenhouse Square and watched Trinity Church until its brown façade faded in the dusk. She expected Paul back at midnight, and sat up reading. She did n't love him, she told herself, but felt lonely and wished he would come. To be sure, she recalled with her morbidly keen memory that Howells had said: "There is no happy life for woman — the advantage that the world offers her is her choice in self-sacrifice." At two hours past the usual time, she went to bed and slept uneasily until dawn, when she reached out her hand and awoke with a start. . . .

The next night he came back slightly the worse for a pleasant time. He was too tired to answer questions. In the morning he told her that Vibert announced a concert in Carnegie Hall, the programme made up of his own compositions.

"His own compositions?" Ellenora indignantly queried. "He has nothing but the piano concerto, an overture he wrote in Germany, and some songs." She was very much disturbed. Paul noticed it and teased her.

"Oh, yes, he has; read this: "

"Mr. Arthur Vibert, a talented young composer, pupil of Saint-Saëns and Brahms, will give an instrumental concert at Carnegie Hall, November 10th, the programme of which will be devoted entirely to his own compositions. Mr. Vibert, who is an excellent pianist, will play his new piano concerto; a group of his charming songs will be heard; an overture, one of his first works, and a new symphonic poem will comprise this unusually interesting musical scheme. Mr. Vibert will have the valuable assistance of Herr Anton Seidl and his famous orchestra."

" I will go to New York and hear that symphonic poem." She spoke in her most aggressive manner.

"Well, why not?" replied Paul flippantly. "Only you will see a lot of people you know, and would that be pleasant?"

"You need n't go to the concert, you can meet me afterward, and we'll go home together."

Paul yawned, and went out for his afternoon stroll. . . . Ellenora passed the intervening days in a flame of expectancy. She conjectured all sorts of reasons for the concert. Why should Arthur give it so early in the season? Where did he get the money for the orchestra? Perhaps that old, stupid, busybody, portrait-painting friend of his had advanced it. But when did he compose the symphonic poem? He had said absolutely nothing about it to her; and she was surprised, irritated, a little proud that he had finished something of symphonic proportions.

She knew Arthur too well to suppose that he would offer a metropolitan audience scamped workmanship. Anyhow, she would go over even if she had to face an army of questioning friends.

Vibert! How singularly that name looked now. It was a prettier, more compact name than Goddard. But of course she was n't Mrs. Goddard, she was Mrs. Vibert, and would be until her husband saw fit to divorce her. Would he do that soon? Then she walked about furiously, drank tea, and groaned — she was ennuied beyond description. . . .

Paul had the habit of going to New York every other week, and she raised no objection as his frivolous manner was very trying during sultry days; when he was away she could abandon herself to her day-dreams without fear of interruption. She thought hard, and her strong head often was puzzled by the cloud of contradictory witnesses her memory raised. But she cried no more at his absence. . . .

It was quite gaily that she took her seat beside him in the drawing-room car of the train and impatiently awaited the first sight of the salt meadows before Jersey City is reached.

" Ah! the sea,'" she cried enthusiastically, and Paul smiled indulgently.

"You are lyrical, after all, Ellenora," he remarked in his most critical manner. " Presently you will be calling aloud 'Thalatta, Thalatta!' like some dithyrhambic Greek of old."

"Smell the ocean, Paul," urged Ellenora, who looked years younger and almost handsome. Paul's comment was not original but it was sound: "You are a born New York girl and no mistake." He took her to luncheon when they reached the city and in the afternoon she went to a few old familiar shops, felt buoyant, and told herself that she would never consent to live in Philadelphia, as inelastic as brass. Alone she had a hasty dinner at the hotel — Paul had gone to dine with his mother — and noted in the paper that there was no postponement of the Vibert concert. The evening was cool and clear, and with a singular sensation of lightness in her head she went up to the hall in a noisy Broadway car. . . .

Her heart beat so violently that she feared she was about to be ill; intense excitement warned her she must be calmer. All this fever and tremor were new to her, their novelty alarmed and interested her. Accustomed since childhood to time the very pulse-beats of her soul, this analytical woman was astounded when she felt forces at work within her — forces that seemed beyond control of her strong will. She did not dare to sit downstairs, so secured a seat in the top gallery, meeting none of Arthur's musical acquaintances. She eagerly read the programme. How odd "Vibert" seemed on it! She almost expected to see her own name follow her husband's. Arthur Vibert and

Ellenora, his wife, will play his own — their own — concerto for piano and orchestra!

She laughed at her conceit, but her laugh sounded so thin and miserable that she was frightened. . . .

Again she looked at the programme. After the concerto overture "Adonaïs" — Vibert loved Shelley and Keats — came the piano concerto, a group of songs — the singer's name an unfamiliar one — and finally the symphonic poem. The symphonic poem! What did she see, or were her eyes blurred?

"Symphonic Poem 'The Zone of the Shadow'. For explanatory text see the other side." Sick and trembling she turned the page and read "The Argument of this Symphonic Poem is by Ellenora Vibert."

THE ZONE OF THE SHADOW

To the harsh sacrificial tones of curious shells wrought from conch let us worship our blazing parent planet! We stripe our bodies with ochre and woad, lamenting the decline of our god under the rim of the horizon. O! sweet lost days when we danced in the sun and drank his sudden rays. O! dread hour of the Shadow, the Shadow whose silent wings drape the world in gray, the Shadow that sleeps. Our souls slink behind our shields; our women and children hide in the caves; the time is near, and night is our day. Softly, with feet of moss, the Shadow stalks out of the South. The brilliant eye of the Sun is blotted over, and with a remorseless mantle of mist the silvery cusp of the new moon is enfolded. Follow fast the stars, the little brethren of the sky; and like a huge bolster of fog the Shadow scales the ramparts of the dawn. We are lost in the blur of doom, and the long sleep of the missing months is heavy upon our eyelids. We rail not at the coward Sun-God who fled fearing the Shadow, but creep noiselessly to the caves. Our shields are cast aside, unloosed are our stone hatchets, and the fire lags low on the hearth. Without, the Shadow has swallowed the earth; the cry of our hounds stilled as by the hand of snow. The Shadow rolls into our caves; our brain is benumbed by its caresses; it closes the porches of the ear, and gently strikes down our warring members. Supine, routed we rest; and above all, above the universe, is the silence of the Shadow.

" Arthur has had his revenge," she murmured, and of a sudden went sick; the house was black about her as she almost swooned. . . . The old pride kept her up, and she looked about the thinly filled galleries; the concert commenced; she listened indifferently to the overture. When Vibert came on the stage and bowed, she noticed that he seemed rather worn but he was active and played with more power and brilliancy than she ever before recalled. He was very masterful, and that was a new note in his music. And when the songs came, he led out a pretty, slim girl, and with evident satisfaction accompanied her at the piano. The three songs were charming. She remembered them. But who was this soprano? Arthur was evidently interested in her; the orchestra watched the pair sympathetically.

So the elopement had not killed him! Indeed he seemed to have thriven artistically since her desertion! Ellenora sat in the black gulf called despair, devoured by vain regrets. Was it the man or his music she regretted? At last the Symphonic Poem! The strong Gothic head of Anton Seidl was seen, and the music began. . . .

The natural bent of Arthur for the mystic, the supernatural, was understood by his wife. Here was frosty music, dazzling music, in which the spangled North, with its iridescent auroras, its snow-driven soundless seas and its arctic cold, were imagined by this woman. She quickly discerned the Sun theme and the theme of the Shadow, and alternately blushed and wept at the wonderfully sympathetic tonal transposition of her idea. That this slight thing should have trapped his fantasy surprised her. After she had written it, it had seemed remote, all too white, a " Symphonie en Blanc Majeur " — as Théophile Gautier would have called it — besides devoid of human interest. But Arthur had interwoven a human strand of melody, a scarlet skein of emotion, primal withal, yet an attempt to catch the under emotions of the icebound Esquimaux surprised in their zone of silence by the sleep of the Shadow, the long night of their dreary winter. And the composer had succeeded surprisingly well. What boreal epic had he read into Ellenora's little prose poem, the only thing of hers that he had ever pretended to admire! She was amazed, stunned. She wondered how all this emotional richness could have been tapped. Had she left him too soon, or had her departure developed some richer artistic vein? She tortured her brain and heart. After a big tonal climax followed by the lugubrious monologue of a bassoon the work closed.

There was much applause, and she saw her husband come out again and again bowing. Finally he appeared with the young singer. Ellenora left the hall and feebly felt her way to the street. As she expected, Paul was not in sight, so she called a carriage, and getting into it she saw Arthur drive by with his pretty soprano.

IV

How she reached the train and Philadelphia she hardly remembered. She was miserably sick at soul, miserably mortified. Her foolish air-castles vanished, and in their stead she saw the brutal reality. She had deserted a young genius for a fashionable dilettante. In time she might have learned to care for Arthur —

but how was she to know this? He was so backward, such a colorless companion! . . . She almost disliked the man who had taken her away from him; yet six months ago Ellenora would have resented the notion that a mere man could have led her. Besides there was another woman in the muddle now! . . . In her disgust she longed for her own zone of silence. In her heart she called Ibsen and Nora Helmer delusive guides; her chief intellectual staff had failed her and she began to see Torvold Helmer's troubles in a different light. Perhaps when Nora reached the street that terrible night, she thought of her children — perhaps Helmer was watching her from the Doll's House window — perhaps — perhaps Arthur — then she remembered the young singer and bitterness filled her mouth. . . .

When Paul came back, twenty-four hours later, she turned a disagreeable regard upon him.

"Why did n't you stay away longer?" she demanded inconsistently.

"My dear girl, I searched for you at Carnegie Hall that night, but I suppose I must have come too late; so yesterday I went yachting and had a jolly time."

Ellenora fell to reproaching Paul violently for his cruel neglect. Did n't he know that she was ailing and needed him? He answered maliciously: "I fancied that your trip might upset your nerves. I am really beginning to believe you care more for your young composer than you do for me. Ellenora Vibert, sentimental-ist! — what a joke."

He smiled at his wit. . . .

"Leave me, leave me, and don't come here again! . . . I have a right to care for any man I please."

"Ah! Ibsen encore," said Paul, tauntingly.

"No, not Ibsen," she replied in a weak voice, "only a free woman — free even to admire the man whose name I bear," she added, her tem-per sinking to a sheer monotone.

"Free?" he sarcastically echoed. The shock of their voices filled the room. Paul angrily stared out of the window at the thin trees in dusty Rittenhouse Square, wondering when the woman would stop her tiresome reproaches. Ellenora's violent agitation affected her; and the man, his selfish sensibilities aroused by the most unheroic sight in the world, slowly de-scended the staircase, grumbling as he put on his hat. . . .

Too cerebral to endure the philandering Paul, Ellenora Vibert is still in Philadelphia. She has little hope that her husband will ever make any sign. . . . After a time her restless mind and need of money drove her into journalism. To-day she successfully edits the Woman's Page of a Sunday newspaper, and her reading of an essay on Ibsen's Heroines before the Twenty-first Century Club was declared a positive achievement. Ellenora, who dislikes Nietzsche more than ever, calls herself Mrs. Bishop. Her pen name is now Nora Helmer.

TANNHÄUSER'S CHOICE

I

" AND you say they met him this afternoon?" . . . "Yes, met him in broad daylight
coming from the house of that odious woman."
"Well, I never would have believed it!"
"That accounts for his mysterious absence
from the clubs and drawing-rooms. Henry
Tannhäuser is not the style of man to miss
London in the season, unless there is a big
attraction elsewhere." . . . The air was heavy
with flowers, and in the windows opening on the
balcony were thronged smartly dressed folk;
it was May and the weather warm. The Landgrave's musicale had been anticipated eagerly
by all music-lovers in town; Wartburg, the large
house on the hill, hardly could hold the invited. . . .

The evening was young when Mrs. Minne,
charming and a widow, stood with her pretty nun-
like face inclined to the tall, black Mr. Biterolf,
the basso of the opera. She had been sonnetted
until her perfectly arched eyebrows were famous. Her air of well-bred and conventual calm
never had been known to desert her; and her
high, light, colorless soprano had something in
it of the sexless timbre of the boy chorister.

With her blond hair pressed meekly to her shapely head she was the delight and despair of poets, painters and musicians, for she turned an impassable cheek to their pleadings. Mrs. Minne would never remarry; and it was her large income that made water the mouth of the impecunious artistic tribe. . . .

Just now she seemed interested in Karl Biterolf, but even his vanity did not lead him to hope. They resumed their conversation, while about them the crush became greater, and the lights burned more brilliantly. In the whirl of chatter and conventional compliment stood Elizabeth Landgrave, the niece of the host, receiving her uncle's guests. Mrs. Minne regarded her, a sweet, unpleasant smile playing about her thinly carved lips.

" Yet the men rave over her, Mr. Biterolf. Is it not so? What chance has a passée woman with such a pure, delicate slip of a girl? And she sings so well. I wonder if she intends going on the stage? " Her companion leaned over and whispered something.

" No, no, I 'll never believe it. What? Henry Tannhäuser in love with that girl! Jamais, jamais ! "

" But I tell you it 's so, and her refusal sent him after — well, that other one." Biterolf looked wise.

" You mean to tell me that he could forget her for an old woman? Stop, I know you are going to say that the Holda is as fascinating as Diana of Poitiers and has a trick of making boys, young enough to be her grandsons, fall madly in love with her. I know all that is said in her favor. No one knows who she is, where she came from, or her age. She's fifty if she's a day, and she makes up in the morning." Mrs. Minne paused for breath. Both women moved in the inner musical set of fashionable London and both captained rival camps. Mrs. Minne was voted a saint and Mrs. Holda a sinner — a fascinating one . . . There was a little feeling in the widow's usually placid voice when she again questioned Biterolf.

" I always fancied that Eschenbach, that man with the baritone voice, son of the rich brewer — you know him of course? — I always fancied that he was making up to our pretty young innocent over yonder."

Biterolf gazed in amusement at his companion. Her veiled, sarcastic tone was not lost on him; he felt that he had to measure his words with this lily-like creature.

" Oh, yes; Wolfram Eschenbach? Certainly, I know him. He sings very well for an amateur. I believe he is to sing this evening. Let us go out on the balcony; it's very warm." " I intend remaining here, for I shall not miss a trick in the game to-night and if, as you say, that silly Tannhäuser was seen leaving the Holda's house this afternoon — " " Yes, with young Walter Vogelweide, and they were quarrelling — " "Drinking, I suppose?" "No; Henry was very much depressed, and when Eschenbach asked him where he had been so long — " "What a fool question for a man in love with Elizabeth Landgrave," interposed Mrs. Minne, tartly. "Henry answered that he didn't know, and he wished he were in the Thames." "And a good place for him, say I." The lady put up her lorgnon and bowed amiably to Miss Landgrave, who was talking eagerly to her uncle. . . .

The elder Landgrave was as fond of hunting as of music, and sedulously fostered the cultivation of his niece's voice. As she stood beside him, her slender figure was almost as tall as his. Her eyes were large in the cup and they went violet in the sunlight; at night they seemed lustrously black. She was in virginal white this evening, and her delicately modelled head was turned toward the door. Her uncle spoke slowly to her.

"He promised to come." Elizabeth flushed. "Whether he does or not, I shall sing; besides, his rudeness is unbearable. Uncle, dear, what can I say to a man who goes away for a month without vouchsafing me a word of excuse?"

Her uncle coughed insinuatingly in his beard. He was a widower.

"Hadn't we better begin, uncle? Go out on the balcony and stop that noisy gypsy band.

I hate Hungarian music." . . . She carried herself with dignity, and Mr. Landgrave admired the pretty curves of her face and wondered what would happen when her careless lover arrived. Soon the crowd drifted in from the balcony and the great music-room, its solemn oak walls and ceilings blazing with light, was jammed. Near the concert-grand gathered a group of music makers, in which Wolfram Eschenbach's golden beard and melancholy eyes were at once singled out by sentimental damsels. He had long been the by-word of match-making mammas because of his devotion to a hopeless cause. Elizabeth Landgrave admired his good qualities, but her heart was held by that rake, *vaurien* and man about town, dashing Harry Tannhäuser; and as Wolfram bent over Miss Landgrave her uncle could not help regretting that girls were so obstinate.

A crashing of chords announced that the hour had arrived. After the " Tannhäuser " overture, Elizabeth Landgrave arose to sing. Instantly there was a stillness. She looked very fair in her clinging gown, and as her powerful, well modulated soprano uttered the invocation to the Wartburg " Dich, theure Halle, grüss ich wieder," the thrill of excitement was intensified by the appearance of Henry Tannhäuser in the doorway at the lower end of the room. If Elizabeth saw him her voice did not reveal emotion, and she gave, with rhetorical emphasis, "Froh grüss ich dich, geliebter Raum."

"He looks pretty well knocked out, doesn't he?" whispered Biterolf to Mrs. Minne. She curled her lip. She had long set her heart on Tannhäuser, but since he preferred to sing the praises of Mrs. Holda, she slaked her feelings by cutting up his character in slices and serving them to her friends with a saintly smile.

"Poor old Harry," went on Biterolf in his clumsy fashion. "Your poor old Harry had better keep away from his Venus," snapped the other; "he looks as if he'd been going the pace too fast." Every one looked curiously at the popular tenor. He stood the inspection very well, though his clean-shaven face was slightly haggard, his eyes sunken and bloodshot. But he was such good style, as the women remarked, and his bearing, as ever, gallant.

Elizabeth ended with "Sei mir gegrüsst," and there was a volley of handclapping. Tannhäuser made his way to the piano. His attitude was anything but penitent; the girl did not stir a muscle. He shook hands. Then he complimented her singing. She bowed her head stiffly. Tannhäuser smiled ironically.

"I suppose I ought to do the conventional operatic thing," he murmured — "cry aloud, 'Let me kneel forever here.'" She regarded him coldly. "You might find it rather embarrassing before this crowd. Do you ever sing any more?" He was slightly confused. "Let us sing the duo in the second act; you know it," she curtly said, "and stop the mob's gaping. Mrs. Minne over there is straining her eyes out." "She cannot say that I ever sang her praises," laughed Tannhäuser, and as he faced the audience with Elizabeth there was a hum which modulated gradually into noisy applause.

The pair began "Gepriesen sei die Stunde, gepriesen sei die Macht," and Mr. Landgrave looked on gloomily as the voices melted in lyric ecstasy. Henry's voice was heroic, like himself, and his friend Wolfram felt a glow when its thrilling top tones rang out so pure, so clear. What a voice, what a man! If he would only take care of himself, he thought and looked at Elizabeth's spiritual face wondering if she knew — if she knew of the other woman who was making Henry forget his better self!

The duo ceased and congratulations were heaped upon the singers. . . .

"How do you manage to keep it up, old man?" asked Biterolf while Mrs. Minne engaged Elizabeth.

Tannhäuser smiled. "You old grim wolf, Biterolf, you cling to the notion that a singer must lead the life of an anchorite to preserve his voice. I enjoy life. I am not a monk, but a tenor — " "Yes, but not a professional one!" "No; therefore I'm happy. If I had to sing to order, I'd jump into the river." "That's what you said this afternoon," replied Biterolf, knowingly.

Henry's face grew dark. "You've said nothing, have you? That's a good fellow. I assure you, Karl, I'm in the very devil of a fix. I've got rid of Holda, but no one can tell how long. She's a terror." "Why don't you travel?" "I have, I swear I have, but she has a trick of finding where my luggage goes and then turns up at Pau or Paris as if I expected her. She's a witch! That's what she is."

"She is Venus," said Biterolf moodily. "Aha! you've been hard hit, too? I believe she does come from the Hollow Hill. Her cavern must be full of dead men's bones, trophies of her conquests. I think I've escaped this time." Tannhäuser's face grew radiant. "Don't be too sure, she may turn up here to-night." "Good Lord, man, she's not invited, I hope." "I don't know why not — she goes with the best people. Take a tip from me, Harry. Don't waste any more time with her for Eschenbach may cut you out. He's very fond of Elizabeth, and you'd better cut short that duet over there now; Mrs. Minne is not fond of you." "Nonsense!" said Tannhäuser, but he lounged over toward the two women and his big frame was noted by all the girls in the room.

Tannhäuser had a very taking way with him. His eyes were sky-blue and his hair old gold. He was a terrific sportsman and when not making love was singing. From his Teutonic ancestry he had inherited a taste for music which desultory study in a German university town, combined with a musical ear, had improved. He had been told by managers that if he would work hard he could make a sensation, but Henry was lazy and Henry was rich, so he sang, shot big game and flirted his years away. Then he met Mrs. Holda, of Berg Street, Piccadilly.

The women were not looking at each other with loving eyes when he drew near. Elizabeth turned to him, her face aglow: " Let us walk a bit before Mr. Eschenbach sings." Her manner was almost seductive. Mrs. Minne sneered slightly and waved her fan condescendingly at the two as they moved slowly up the room. " There go the biggest pair of fools in all Christendom," she remarked to Biterolf; " why, she will believe everything he tells her. She would n't listen to my advice." Biterolf shook his head. When Tannhäuser and Elizabeth returned both looked supremely happy.

" That woman has actually been abusing you, Harry." He pressed her arm reassuringly. Wolfram Eschenbach began to sing " Blick' ich umher in diesem edlen Kreise," and once more silence fell upon the bored crowd. Sympathy was in his tones and he sang tenderly, lovingly.

Elizabeth listened unmoved. She now had eyes for Tannhäuser only, and she laughed aloud when he proposed to follow Wolfram with a solo.

"Do," she said enthusiastically, "it will stir them all up." Although this number was not down on the program, Tannhäuser was welcomed as he went to the piano. Wolfram seemed uneasy and once looked fixedly at Elizabeth. Then he walked out on the balcony as if seeking some one, and Mrs. Minne nudged her stolid neighbor. "Mark my words, there's trouble brewing," she declared.

By this time Tannhäuser was in his best form. He seemed to have regained all his usual elasticity, for Berg Street, with its depressing memories, had completely vanished. He expanded his chest and sang, his victorious blue eyes fastened on Elizabeth. He sang the song of Venus, "Dir, Göttin der Liebe," and all the old passion came into his voice; when he uttered "Zieht in den Berg der Venus ein" he was transported, his surroundings melted and once more he was gazing at the glorious woman, his Venus, his Holda. The audience was completely shaken out of its fashionable immobility, and "superb," "bravo," "magnificent," "encore," "bis," were heard on all sides. Elizabeth alone remained mute. Her skin was the pallor of ivory, and into her glance came the look of a lovely fawn run down by the hounds.

"He'd better pack his traps and make a pilgrimage to Rome," remarked Mrs. Minne with malice in her secular eyes as Tannhäuser strode to the balcony. Wolfram, looking anxious, went to Elizabeth and led her to her uncle; then the supper signal sounded and the buzz and struggle became tremendous.

Mrs. Minne disappeared. Ten minutes later she was at Miss Landgrave's side, and presently the pair left the table, slowly forced a passage through the mob of hungry and thirsty humans and reached the balcony.

The night was rich with May odors, but the place seemed deserted. Plucking at the girl's sleeve, her companion pointed to a couple that stood looking into the garden, the arm of the man passed about the waist of the woman. Even in the starlight Elizabeth recognized the exquisite head and turned to leave; the woman with her was bent on seeing the game. In sharp staccato she said, "What a relief after that hot supper-room!" and the others turned. Elizabeth did not pause a moment. She went to Tannhäuser's companion and said:

"My dear Mrs. Holda, where have you been hiding to-night? I fear you missed the music and I fear now you will miss the supper; do let us go in." . . .

Five minutes later Mrs. Holda left with Tannhäuser in her brougham, telling the coachman to drive to Berg Street.

II

The drawing-room was delicious that May afternoon — the next after the musicale at Landgrave's. Henry was indolently disposed, and on a broad divan, heaped with Persian pillows, he stretched his big limbs like a guardsman in a Ouida novel. The dark woman near watched him closely, and as he seemed inclined to silence she did not force the conversation.

"Shall we drive, Venus?" he nonchalantly asked. "Just as you please. We may meet your saint with the insipid eyes in the park." "Good heavens!" he testily answered, "why do you forever drag in that girl's name? She's nothing to me." Mrs. Holda went to the window and he lazily noticed her perfect figure, her raven hair and black eyes. She was a stunner after all, and didn't look a day over twenty-eight. How did she manage to preserve the illusion of youth? She turned to him, and he saw the contour of a face Oriental, with eyes that allured and a mouth that invited. A desirable but dangerous woman, and he fell to thinking of the other, of her air of girlhood, her innocence of poise, her calm of breeding that nothing disturbed. Like a good pose in the saddle, nothing could ever unseat the equanimity of Elizabeth. Mrs. Holda grew distasteful for the moment and her voice sounded metallic.

"When you cease your perverse mooning, Harry Tannhäuser, when you make up your mind once and for all which woman you intend to choose, when you decide between Elizabeth Landgrave and Venus Holda, I shall be most happy. As it is now I am"— Just then two cards were handed her by a footman, and after looking at them she laughed a mellow laugh. Tannhäuser sat up and asked her the news.

"I laugh because the situation is so funny," she said; "here are your two friends come to visit you and perhaps attempt your rescue from the Venusberg. Oh! for a Wagner now! What appropriate music he could set to this situation." She gave him the cards, and to his consternation he read the names of Elizabeth Landgrave and Wolfram Eschenbach. He started up in savage humor and was for going to the reception room. Quite calmly Mrs. Holda bade him stay where he was.

"They did not ask for you, Harry, dear; stay here and be a good boy, and I'll tell you all about it when they've gone." Her laughter was resilient as she descended the staircase, but to the young man it seemed sinister. He felt that hope had abandoned him when he entered the Berg Street house, and now Elizabeth's presence, instead of relieving his dull remorse, increased it. She was under the same roof with him, yet he could not go to her. . . .

Tannhäuser paced the parquetry almost hid-

den by Bokhara rugs, trying to forget the girl.
Stopping before an elaborate ebony and gold
lectern, he found a volume in vellum, opened
and in it he read: "Livre des grandes Mer-
veilles d'amour, escript en Latin et en françoys
par Maistre Antoine Gaget 1530." "Has love
its marvels?" pondered the disquieted young
man. Turning over the title-page he came
upon these words in sweet old English:

"Then lamented he weeping: Alas, most unhappy and accursed sinner that I am, in that I
shall never see the clemency and mercy of my
God. Now will I go forth and hide myself
within Mount Horsel, imploring my sweet lady
Venus for favor and loving mercy, for willingly
would I be forever condemned to hell for her
love. Here endeth all my deeds of arms and
my sweet singing. Alas, that my lady's face
and her eyes were too beautiful, and that in an
unfortunate moment I saw them. Then went
he forth sighing and returned to her, and dwelt
sadly in the presence of his lady, filled with
a surpassing love. And afterwards it came to
pass that one day the pope saw many red and
white flowers and leaf-buds spring forth from
his baton, and all without bloomed anew. So
that he feared greatly, and being much moved
thereby was filled with great pity for the chevalier who had gone forth hopeless like unto a man
forever damned and miserable. And straightway sent he numberless messengers to him to

bring him back, saying that he should receive
grace and absolution from God, for this his
great sin of love. But never more was he seen;
for the poor chevalier dwelt forever near unto
Venus, that most high and mighty Goddess, in
the bosom of the amorous mountain." . . .

Mrs. Holda was delightful as she welcomed
her visitors. " The drawing-room was not
empty," she said; "a friend, an old friend, a bit
of a bore, you know; " and they must just stay
downstairs, it was more cozy, more intimate.
Elizabeth, whose face was quite rosy from walking, studied the woman with the Egyptian profile and glorious hair, and wondered if she ever
told the truth. Wolfram alone seemed uneasy.
He could not get into the swing of conversation; he was in his watchful mood. He looked
at the portières as if every moment he expected
some one to appear. The musicale was discussed and Miss Landgrave's singing praised.
Wolfram rather awkwardly attempted to introduce Tannhäuser's name, but was snubbed by
Elizabeth.

" Now, my dear Mrs. Holda, I've come to
tell you some news; promise me, I beg of
you, promise me not to divulge it. We are
engaged, Wolfram and I, and you being such an
old friend I came to you first." The girl's pure
face was the picture of nubile candor, and her
eyes met fairly the shock of the other's quick
glance.

"How lovely, how perfectly lovely it all is, and how I appreciate your confidence," sang Mrs. Holda, in purring accents. "How glad Henry Tannhäuser will be to hear that his two best friends are to be married. I must tell — tell him this afternoon."

"Oh!" cried Elizabeth, lightly, "but your promise, have you forgotten it?" The other laughed in her face.

"We go to Rome, to make what dear Mrs. Minne calls the pilgrimage," declared the girl unflinchingly.

"Then I hope the Wagner miracle will take place again," mockingly answered Mrs. Holda, and after a few more sentences the visitors went away. Venus burst into her drawing-room holding her sides, almost choking. "Harry, Harry, Harry Tannhäuser, I shall die. They're engaged to be married. They came to tell me, to tell me, knowing that you were upstairs. Oh, that deceitful virgin with her sly airs! I understood her. She fancied that she would put me out of countenance. She and that sheep of a brewer's son, Eschenbach. They're engaged, I tell you, and going to Rome on their wedding trip — their pilgrimage she called it. Oh, these affected Wagnerites! You had better go, too, Mr. Tannhäuser; perhaps the miracle might be renewed and your staff of faith grow green with the leaves of repentance. Oh, Harry, what a lark it all is!"

He sat on the couch and stared at her as she rolled about on a divan, gripped by malicious laughter. . . . Engaged! Elizabeth Landgrave engaged to be married! And a few hours ago she told him she loved him, could never love another — and now! What had happened in such a brief time to make her change her mind? Engaged to Wolfram Eschenbach, dear, old stupid Wolfram, who had loved her with a dog's love for years, even when she flouted him. Wolfram, his best friend, slow Wolfram, with his poetizing, his fondness for German singing societies, his songs to evening stars; Eschenbach, the brewer's son, to cut him out, cut out brilliant Harry Tannhäuser! It was incredible, it was monstrous! . . . He slowly went to the window. The street was empty, and only his desperate thoughts made noise as they clattered through his hollow head. Her voice roused him. "You can take the pitcher too often to the well, Harry dear, and you drove once too often to Berg Street. Elizabeth, sensible girl, instead of dying, takes the best man she could possibly find; a better man than you, Harry, and she couldn't resist letting me know it. So, silly old boy, better give up your Wartburg ambitions, your pilgrimage to Rome, and stay here in the Venusberg. I know I'm old, but, after all, am I not your Venus?" In the soft light of an early evening in May the face of Mrs. Holda seemed impossibly charming. . . .

THE RED–HEADED PIANO PLAYER

THE two young men left the trolley car that carried them from Bath Beach to the West End of Coney Island, and walked slowly up the Broad Avenue of Confusing Noises, smoked and gazed about them with the independent air that notes among a million the man from New York. And as they walked they talked in crisp sentences, laughing at the seller of opulent Frankfurter sausages and nodding pleasantly to the lovely ladies in short, spangled skirts, who, with beckoning glances, sought their eyes. The air reverberated with an August evening's heat and seemed sweating. Its odor modulated from sea-brine to Barren Island, and the wind hummed. The clatter was striking; ardent whistling of peanut steam-roasters, vicious brass bands, hideous harps, wheezing organs, hoarse shoutings and the patient, monotonous cry of the fakirs and photographers were all blended in a dense, huge symphony; while the mouse-colored dust churned by the wheels of blackguard beach-wagons blurred a hard, blue sky from which pricked a soft, hanging star. An operatic sun had just set with all the majestic tranquillity of a fiery hen; and the two friends felt laconically gay. "Let's eat here," suggested the red-haired one.

"Not on your life," answered the other, a stout, cynical blond; "you get nothing but sauerkraut that is n't sour and dog-meat sausage. I'm for a good square meal at Manhattan or Sheepshead Bay."

"Yes, but Billy, there's more fun here, and heavens knows I'm dead tired." The young fellow's accents were those of an irritable, hungry human animal, and his big chum gave in. . . .

They searched the sandy street for a comfortable beer place, and after passing dime-museums, unearthly looking dives, amateur breweries, low gin mills and ambitious establishments, the pair paused opposite a green, shy park of grass and dwarf trees, and listened.

"Piano playing, and not bad," cried Billy. They both hung over the rustic palings and heard bits of Chopin's Military Polonaise, interrupted by laughter and the rattling of crockery.

"I'm for going in, Billy," and they read the sign which announced a good dinner, with music, for fifty cents. They followed the artificial lane to a large summer cottage, about which were bunched drooping willows and, finding all the tables occupied, went inside.

A long room furnished for dining, gaudy pictures on the walls, and at one end upon a raised platform a grand piano. The place was full; and the tobacco-smoke, chatter and calls of the waiters disconcerted the two boys. Just then the piano sounded. Chopin again, and curious to know who possessed such a touch at Coney Island, the friends found a table to the right of the keyboard and sat down. As they did, they looked at the pianist and both exclaimed:

" Paderewski or his ghost! " The fellow wore a shock of lemon-tinted hair after the manner of the Polish virtuoso, but his face was shaven clean.

" Harry, he looks like a lost soul," said Billy, who was rather plain spoken in his judgments.

" Let's give him a drink," whispered Harry, and he called a waiter. "Whiskey," said the waiter after a question had been put, and presently the piano player was bowing to them as he threw the liquor into his large mouth. Then the Chopin study in C minor was recommenced and half-finished and the two music lovers forgot their dinner. A waiter spoke to them twice; the manager, seeing that music was hurting trade, went to the piano and coughed. The pianist instantly stopped, and a dinner was ordered by Harry. Billy looked around him with a trained eye. He noticed that the women were all sunburned and wore much glittering jewelry; the men looked like countrymen and were timid in the use of the fork. When the music began they stopped eating and their companions ordered fresh drinks. Billy could have sworn that he saw one woman crying. But as soon as the music ceased conversation began, and the rattle of dishes was deafening.

"I say, Harry, this is a queer go. There's something funny about this place and this piano. It upsets all my theories of piano music. When the piano begins here the audience forgets to eat, and its passion mounts to its ears. Not like the West End at all, is it?" Harry was busy with his soup. He was sentimental, and the sight of kindred hair — the hue beloved of Paderewski — roused his sympathies.

"By George, Billy, that fellow's an artist. Just look at his expression. There's a story in him, and I'm going to get it. It may be news."

They chatted, and asked the pianist to join them in another drink. Whiskey was sent up to the platform, and the musician drank it at a gulp, his right hand purling over the figuration of "Auf dem Wasser zu Singen." But he took no water. Then making them a little bobbing, startled bow, he began playing. Again it was something of Chopin. On his lean features there was a look of detachment; and the watchers were struck with the interesting forehead, the cheeks etched with seams of suffering, and the finely compressed lips.

"I'll bet it's some German who has boozed too much at home, and his folks have thrown him out," hinted Billy.

"German? That's no German, I swear. It's Hungarian, Bohemian or Pole. Besides, he drinks whiskey."

"Yes, drinks too much, but it has n't hurt his playing — yet: just listen to the beggar play that prelude."

The B flat minor Prelude, with its dark, rich, rushing cascade of scales, its grim iteration and ceaseless questioning, spun through the room, and again came the curious silence. Even the Oberkellner listened, his mouth ajar. The waiters paused midway in their desperate gaming with victuals, and for a moment the place was wholly given over to music. The mounting unison passage and the smashing chords at the close awakened the diners from the trance into which they had been thrown by the magnetic fluid at the tips of the pianist's fingers; the bustle began, Harry and Billy ordered more beer and drew deep breaths.

"He's a wonder, that's all I know, and I'm going to grab him. What technique, what tone, what a touch!" cried Harry, who had been assistant music critic on an afternoon paper.

A card, with a pencilled invitation, was sent to the pianist, and the place being quite dark the electric lights began hoarsely whistling in a canary colored haze. The musician came over to the table and, bowing very low, took a seat.

"You will excuse me," he said, "if I do not eat. I have trouble with my heart, and I drink whiskey. Yes, I will be happy to join you in another glass of very bad whiskey. No, I am not a Pole; I am English, and not a nobleman. I look like Paderewski, but can't play nearly as well. Here is my card." The name was commonplace, Wilkins, but was prefixed by the more unusual Feodor.

"You've some Russian in you after all?" questioned Billy.

"Perhaps. Feodor is certainly Russian. I often play Tschaïkowsky. I know that you wonder why I am in such a place. I will tell you. I like human nature, and where can you get such an opportunity to come into contact with it in the raw as this place?"

Billy winked at Harry and ordered more drinks. The pale Feodor Wilkins drank with the same precipitate gesture, as if eager with thirst. He spoke in a refined manner, and was evidently an educated man.

"I have no story, my friends. I'm not a genius in disguise, neither am I a drunkard — one may safely drink at the seaside — and if, perhaps, like Robert Louis Stevenson, I play at being an amateur emigrant, I certainly do not intend writing a book of my experiences."

The newspaper boys were disappointed. There was, then, no lovely mystery to be unravelled, no subterrene story excavated, no romance at all, nothing but a spiritual looking Englishman with an odd first name and a gift of piano playing.

Mr. Wilkins gave a little laugh, for he read the faces of his companions. As if to add another accent to their disappointment he ordered a Swiss cheese sandwich, and spoke harshly to the waiter for not bringing mustard with it. Then he turned to Harry:

" You love music?"

" Crazy for it, but see here, Mr. — Mr. Wilkins, why don't you play in public? I don't mean this kind of a public, but before a Philharmonic audience! This sort of cattle must make you sick, and for heaven's sake, man, what do they pay you?" Harry's face was big with suppressed questions. The pianist paused in his munching of bread and cheese. His fine luminous eyes twinkled: " My dear boy, I have a story — a short one — and I fancy that it will explain the mystery. I am twenty-seven years old. Yes, that's all, but I've lived and — loved."

" Ah, a petticoat!" exclaimed Harry, triumphantly; " I was sure of it."

" No, not a petticoat, but a piano was the cause of my undoing. Vaulting ambition and all that sort of thing. My parents were easy in circumstances and I was brought up to be a pianist. Deliberately planned to be a virtuoso. I was sent to Leschetizky, to Von Bülow, to Rubinstein, to Liszt. I studied scales in Paris with Planté, trills in Bologna with Martucci, octaves with Rosenthal; in Vienna I met Joseffy, and with him I studied double notes. Wait until later and I shall play for you the Chopin Study in G sharp minor! I mastered twenty-two concertos and even knew the parts for the triangle. Then at the age of twenty-five, after the best teachers in Europe had taught me their particular craft I returned to England, to London, and gave a concert. It was an elaborate affair. The best orchestra, with Hans Richter, was secured by my happy father, and after the third rehearsal he embraced me, saying that he could go to his grave a satisfied man, for his son was a piano artist. There must have been a strain of Slavic in the old man, he loved Chopin and Tschaïkowsky so. My mother was less demonstrative, but she was as truly delighted as my father. Picture to yourself the transports of these two devoted old people! And when I left them the night before the concert I really trembled.

"In my bedroom I faced the mirror and saw my secret peering out at me. I knew that if I failed it would kill my parents, who, gambler-like, were staking their very existence on my success. As the night wore white I grew more nervous, and at dawn, not being able to endure the strain a moment more, I crept out of doors and went to a public house and began drinking to settle my nerves."

"I told you it was whiskey," blurted out Billy.

"No, brandy," said Mr. Wilkins, looking into his empty glass, "now it's whiskey. Yes; thank you very much. Well, to proceed.

"I drank all day, but being young I did not feel it particularly. I went home, ran my fingers over the piano, got into a bath and dressed for the concert. At eight o'clock the carriage came, and at eight forty-five, with one more drink in me, I walked out on the platform as bold as you please, and despite the size of the audience, the glare of the lights and the air, charged with human electricity, I felt rather at ease. The orchestra went sailing into the long *tutti* of the F minor Concerto of Chopin, and Richter, I could feel, was in good spirits. My cue came; I took it, struck out and came down the piano in the introductory unisons — a divine beginning, isn't it? — and my tone seemed rich and virile. I played the first theme, and all went well until the next interlude for the orchestra; I looked about me confidently, feeling quite like a virtuoso, and soon spied my parents, when suddenly my knees began to tremble, trembled so that the damper pedal vibrated. Then my eyes blurred and I missed my cue and felt Richter's great spectacles burning into the side of my head like two fierce suns. I scrambled, got my place, lost it, rambled and was roused to my position by the short rapping of the conductor's stick on his desk. The band stopped, and Herr Richter spoke gruffly to me:

"'Begin again.'

"In a sick, dazed way I put my fingers on the keys, but they were drunk; the cursed brandy had just begun to work, and a minute later, my head reeling, I staggered through the orchestra, lurched against a contrabassist, fell down and was shoved out of sight.

"I lay in the artists' room perfectly content, and even enjoyed the pinched chalky face of my father as he stooped over me.

"'My God, the boy's drunk,' he cried, and big Richter nodded his head quite philosophically, 'Ja, er ist ganz besoffen,' and left us to go to the audience. I fell asleep. . . . The next evening I found, on awakening, a horrible head-ache and a letter from my father. I was turned out of doors, disowned, and bade to go about my business. So here I am, gentlemen, as you see, at your service, and always thirsty." . . .

The friends were about to put a hundred questions, when a thin, acid female voice broke in: "Benny, don't you think you've wasted enough of the gentlemen's time? You'd better get to work. The people are nearly all gone." Feodor Wilkins started to his feet and blushed as an old, fat woman, wearing a Mother Hubbard of gross pattern, waddled toward the table. The sad pianist with the flaming hair turned to the boys:

"My wife, Mrs. Wilkins, gentlemen!" The lady took a seat at Billy's invitation and also a small drink of peppermint and whiskey. She told them that she was tired out; business had been good, and if Benny would only quit drinking and play more popular music, why, she wouldn't complain! Then she drank to their health, and Billy thought he saw the husband make a convulsive movement in his throat. It may have been caused by hysterical mortification — the woman was undeniably vulgar — but to the practical-minded Billy it was more like an envious involuntary swallowing at the sight of another's drinking. Then the pianist mounted his wooden throne, where, amid the dust and tramplings of low conquests and in the murky air, he began to toll out the bells of the Chopin Funeral March.

"Funny how they all quit eatin' and drinkin' when he speels, isn't it?" remarked the wife with a gratified smile. "Why, if he was half a man he'd play all day as well as night and then folks out yonder would forgit their vittles altogether. I suppose he give you the same old yarn?"

Harry bristled: "What old story, madame? Mr. Feodor Wilkins told us of his studies abroad and his unsuccessful début in London. It's a beautiful story. He's a great artist, and you ought to be proud of him."

The woman burst into laughter. "Why, the

old fraud has been stringing you. Fedderr, he calls himself! His name is Benny, just plain Benny Wilkins, and he never saw London. He's from Boston way, took lessons at some big observatory up there, and he run up such a big slate with me that he married me to sponge it out. Schwamm d'rüber! you know. My first husband left a nice little tavern, and them music stoodents just flocked out after lessons was over to drink beer. Oh, dear me, Benny was a nice boy, but he always did drink too much. Then we moved to Harlem and I rented this place for the summer. I expect to make a tidy sum before I leave, if Benny only stays straight."

There was something pathetic in this last cadence, and the two boys leaned back and listened to the presto of the Chopin B flat minor Sonata, which Wilkins took at a tremendous pace.

" Sounds as if he were the wind weaving over his own grave," said Harry, mournfully. The boys had drunk too much, and the close atmosphere and music were beginning to tell on their nerves.

" He's a tramp of genius, that's what he is," growled Billy crossly.

"But we've got a story," interjected the other.

"Yes, and were taken in finely. Hanged if I didn't believe the fellow while he was yarning."

"You gentlemen won't mind me leaving you, will you? It's near closing-up time, and I've got to be the boss. Benny, he sticks close to the pianner as it gits late. I reckon he feels his licker. Ain't he a dandy with them skinny fingers o' his?"

She moved away, giving her husband a warning not to leave his perch, and went barwards to overhaul her receipts. . . .

The lights were nearly all out and the drumming of the breakers on the beach clearly could be felt. The young men paid their bill and shook hands with the pianist. He leaned over the edge of the platform and spoke to them in a low voice.

"Come again, gentlemen, come again. Don't mind what she tells you. I'm not her husband, no matter what she said just now. She owns me body and soul for this year. I swear to God it's not the drink. I need the experience in public. I must play all the time before that awful nervous terror wears off. This is the place to get in touch with common folk; if I can hold them with Chopin what won't I be able to do with an appreciative audience! Believe me, gentlemen, I pray of you; give me a year, only one year, and I'll get out of this nervousness and this nightmare, and *the* world of music will hear of me. Only give me time." Feodor Wilkins placed his hand desperately on the pit of his stomach; his wife screamed:

"Benny, come right over here and count the cash."

The boys got into the open air and scented the surf with delight, a moon enlaced with delicate cloud streamers made magic in the sky; then Harry growled:

"Say, Bill, do you believe that story?" . . .

BRYNHILD'S IMMOLATION

SHE had infinitely sad, wide eyes. The sweet
pangs of maternity and art had not been denied
this woman with the vibrant voice and temperament of fire. Singing only in the Wagner
music dramas critics awarded her the praise
that pains. She did not sing as Patti, but oh!
the sonorous heart. . . .

"Götterdämmerung" was being declaimed in
a fervent and eminently Teutonic fashion. The
house was fairly filled though it could hardly
be called a brilliant gathering; the conductor
dragged the tempi, the waits were interminable.
A young girl sat and wonderingly watched.
Her mother was the Brynhild. . . .

This daughter was a strange girl. Her only
education was the continual smatter which comes
from many cities superficially glided. She spoke
French with the accent of Vienna, and her German had in it some of the lingering lees of the
Dutch. Wherever they pitched their tent the
girl went abroad in the city, absorbing it. Thus
she knew many things denied women; and when
her mother was summoned to Bayreuth, she soon
forgot all in the mists, weavings and golden
noise of Wagner. Then followed five happy

years. The singer prospered at Bayreuth and engagements trod upon the heels of engagements. Her girl was petted, grew tall, shy, and one day they said, " She is a young woman." The heart of the child beat tranquilly in her bosom, and her thoughts took on little color of the life about her.

Once, after " Tristan und Isolde " she asked :
" Why do you never speak of my father ? "

Her mother, sitting on the bed, was coiling her glorious hair; the open dress revealed the massive throat and great white shoulders.

" Your father died years ago, child. Why do you ask now ? "

The girl looked directly at her.

" I thought to-night how lovely if he had only been Tristan instead of Herr Albert."

The other's face was draped by hair. She did not speak for a moment.

" Yes. But he never sang: your father was not a music lover." . . .

Presently they embraced affectionately and went to bed; the singer did not sleep at once. Her thoughts troubled her. . . .

Madame Stock was a great but unequal artist. She had never concerned herself with the little things of the vocal art. Nature had given her much; voice, person, musical temperament, dramatic aptitude. She erred artistically on the side of over-emphasis, and occasionally tore passion to pieces. But she had the true fire, and with time would compass repose and symmetry. Toward conquering herself she seldom gave a thought. Her unhappy marriage had left its marks; she was cynical and often reckless; but with the growth of her daughter came reflection. . . . Hilda was not to be treated as other girls. Her Scotch ancestry showed itself early. The girl did not, and could not, see the curious life about her; it was simply a myopia that her mother fostered. Thus, through all the welter and confusion of an opera-singer's life, Hilda walked serenely. She knew there were disagreeable things in the world but refused herself even the thought of them. It was not the barrier of innocence but rather a selection of certain aspects of life that she fancied, and an absolute impassibility in the presence of evil. Then her mother grew more careful.

Hilda loved Wagner. She knew every work of the Master from " Die Feen " to " Parsifal." She studied music, arduously playing accompaniments for her mother. In this way she learned the skeleton of the mighty music dramas, and grew up absorbing the torrid music as though it were Mozartean. She repeated the stories of the dramas as a child its astronomy lessons, without feeling. She saw Siegmund and Sieglinde entwined in that wondrous Song of Spring, and would have laughed in your face if you hinted that all this was anything but many-colored arabesque. It was her daily bread and butter, and like one of those pudic creatures of the Eleusinian mysteries she lived in the very tropics of passion, yet without one pulse-throb of its feverishness. It was the ritual of Wagner she worshipped; the nerves of his score had never been laid bare to her. She took her mother's tumult in good faith, and ridiculed singers of more frigid temperaments. When she writhed in Tristan's arms this vestal sat in front, a piano score on her lap, carefully listening, and later, at home, she would say:

"Dearest, you skipped two bars in the scene with Brangaene," and the singer could not contradict the stern young critic. . . .

Herr Albert sang with them longer than most tenors. They met him in Bayreuth and then in Munich. When they went to Berlin Albert was with them, and also in London. Her mother said that his style and acting suited her better than any artist with whom she had ever sung. He was a young man, much younger than Madame Stock, and a Hungarian. Tall and very dark, he looked unlike the ideal Wagner tenor. Hilda teased him and called him the hero of a melodrama. She grew fond of the young man, who was always doing her some favor. To her mother he was extremely polite; indeed he treated her as a queen.

One afternoon Hilda went back to the dressing-room. In the darkness of the corridor she ran against some one — a man. As she turned to apologize she was caught up in a pair of strong arms and kissed. It was all over in the tick of the clock, and then she ran — ran into the room, frightened, indignant, her face burning.

Her mother's back was toward her, she was preparing for the last act of "Walküre." She knew Hilda's footsteps. The girl threw herself on a couch and covered her hot face with the cushions. The woman hummed "Ho, jo to-ho!" and continued dressing. And then came her call.

Hilda sat and thought. She must tell — she would tell her. But the man, what of him? She knew who it was, knew it by intuition. She did not see his face, but she knew the man. Oh, why did he do it? Why? She blushed and with her handkerchief she rubbed her lips until they stung. Wipe away the kiss she must, or she could never look him in the face again. . . .

It seemed a long time before Brynhild re-turned. Footsteps and laughter told of her approach. The maid came in first carrying a shawl, and at the door the singer paused. Hilda half rose in fear — not knowing who was talking. Of course it was Albert. The door was partly opened, and Hilda, looking at her mother on the top steps of the little staircase, saw her lower her head to the level of the tenor's face and kiss him. . . . Fainting, the girl leaned back and covered her face with her hands. The other entered in whirlwind fashion.

"My Hilda. My God! child, have you been mooning here ever since I went on? What is the matter? You look flushed. Let us go home and have a quiet cup of tea. Albert is coming for us to go to some nice place for dinner. Come, come, rouse yourself! Marie-chen " — to the maid — " don't be stupid. Dé-pêchez-vous, dépêchez-vous ! "

And Madame Stock bustled about and half tore off her cuirass, pitched her helmet in the corner and looked very much alive and young.

"Oh, what a Wotan, Mein Gott! what a man. Do you know what he was doing when I sang 'War es so schmählich?' He had his back to the house and chewed gum. I swear it. When I grabbed his legs in anguish the beast chewed gum, his whole body trembled from the exertion; he says that it is good for a dry throat."

Hilda hardly listened. Her mother had kissed Albert, and she shook as one with the ague. . . .

She pleaded a headache, and did not go to dinner. The next day they left Hamburg, and Albert did not accompany them. Madame Stock declared that she needed a rest, and the pair went to Carlsbad. There they stayed two weeks. The nervous, excitable soprano could not long bide in one place. She was tired of singing, but she grew restless for the theatre.

"Yes, yes," she cried to Hilda, in the train

which bore them toward Berlin. "Yes, the opera is crowded every night when I sing. You know that I get flowers, enjoy triumphs enough to satisfy me. Well, I'm sick of it all. I believe that I shall end by going mad. It may become a monomania. I often say, Why all this feverishness, this art jargon? Why should I burn myself up with Isolde and weep my heart out with Sieglinde? Why go on repeating words that I do not believe in? Art! oh, I hate the word." . . .

Hilda, her eyes half closed, watched the neat German landscape unroll itself.

Her mother grumbled until she fell asleep.

Her face was worn and drawn in the twilight, and Hilda noticed the heavy markings about the mouth and under the eyes and the few gray hairs.

She caught herself analyzing, and stopped with a guilty feeling. Yes, Dearest was beginning to look old. The stress and strain of Wagner was showing. In a few years, when her voice — Hilda closed her eyes determinedly and tried to shut out a picture. But then she was not sure, not sure of herself.

She began thinking of Albert. His swarthy face forced itself upon her, and her mother's image grew faint. Why did he kiss her, why? Surely it must have been some mistake — it was dark; perhaps he mistook her. Here her heart began beating so that it tolled like a bell in her brain — mistook her, oh, God, for her mother! No! no! That could never be. Had she not caught him watching her very often? But then why should her mother have kissed him — perhaps merely a motherly interest.

Hilda sat upright and tried to discern some expression on her mother's face. But it was too dark. The train rattled on toward Berlin. . . .

The next day at the Hôtel Bellevue there was much running to and fro. Musical managers went upstairs smiling and came down raging; musical managers rushed in raging and fled roaring. Madame Stock drove a hard bargain, and, during the chaffering and gabble about dates and terms, Hilda went out for a long walk. Unter den Linden is hardly a promenade for privacy, but this girl was quite alone as she trod the familiar walk, alone as if she were the last human on the pave. She did not notice that she was being followed; when she turned homeward she faced Herr Albert, the famous Wagnerian tenor.

She felt a little shocked, but her placidity was too deep-rooted to be altogether destroyed. And so Albert found himself looking into two large eyes the persistency of whose gaze disconcerted him.

"Ach, Fräulein Hilda, I'm so glad. How are you, and when did you return?"

She had a central grip on herself, and regarded him quite steadily.

He noticed it and became abashed — he, the hero of a hundred footlights. He could not face her pure, threatening eyes.

"Herr Albert, we got back last night. Herr Albert, why did you kiss me in the theatre?"

He looked startled and reddened.

"Because I love you, Hilda. Yes, I did it because I love you," he replied, and his accents were embarrassed.

"You love me, Herr Albert," pursued the terrible Hilda. "Yet you were kissed by mamma an hour later. Do you love her too?"

The tenor trembled and said nothing. . . .

The girl insisted:

"Do you love mamma too? You must, for she kissed you and you did not move away."

Albert was plainly nervous.

"Yes, I love your mamma, too, but in a different way. Oh, dearest Hilda, you don't understand. I am the artistic associate of your mother. But I love — I love you."

Hilda felt the ground grow billowy; the day seemed supernaturally bright. She took Albert's arm and they walked slowly, without a word.

When the hotel was reached she motioned him not to come in, and she flew to her mother's room. The singer was alone. She sat at the window and in her lap was a photograph. She looked old and soul-weary.

Hilda rushed toward her, but stopped in the

middle of the room, overcome by some subtle fear that seized her throat and limb.

Madame Stock looked at her wonderingly.

"Hilda, Hilda, have you gone mad?"

Hilda went over to her and put her arms about her and whispered:

"Oh, mamma, mamma, he loves me; he has just told me so."

Her mother started:

"He! Who loves you, Hilda? What do you mean?"

Hilda's eyes drooped, and then she saw the photograph in the soprano's hand.

It was Albert's. . . .

"I love him — you have his picture — he gave it to you for me? Oh! he has spoken, Dearest, he has spoken."

The picture dropped to the floor. . . .

"Mamma, mamma, what is the matter? Are you angry at me? Do you dislike Albert? No, surely no; I saw you kiss him at the theatre. He says that he loves you, but it is a different love. It must be a Siegmund and Sieglinde love, Dearest, is it not? But he loves me. Don't be cross to him for loving me. He can't help it. And he says we must all live together, if—" . . .

The singer closed her eyes and the corners of her mouth became tense. Then she looked at her daughter almost fiercely. Hilda was terrified.

"Tell me, Hilda, swear to me, and think of what you are saying: Do you love Albert?"

"With my heart," answered the girl in all her white simplicities.

Her mother laughed and arose.

"Then you silly little goose, you shall marry him and be nice and unhappy." Hilda cried with joy: "I don't care if I am unhappy with *him*."

"Idiot!" replied the other.

That night "Götterdämmerung" was given. The conductor dragged the tempi; the waits were interminable, and a young slip of a girl wonderingly watched. Her mother was the Brynhild. The performance was redeemed by the magnificent singing of the Immolation scene. . . .

Later Brynhild faced her mirror and asked no favor of it. As she uncoiled the heavy ropes of hair her eyes grew harsh, and for a moment her image seemed blurred and bitter in the oval glass with the burnished frame that stood upon the dressing-table. But at last she would achieve the unique Brynhild! . . .

"Entbehren sollst du, sollst entbehren."

THE QUEST OF THE ELUSIVE

BALAK, *November* 5.

DEAR DARLING OLD BELLA, — How I wish you were with me. I miss you almost as much as mamma and the girls. I've had such a homesickness that even the elegant concerts, the gay city and the novelty of this out of the way foreign place do not compensate, for Why, oh *why*, does n't Herr Klug live in Berlin or Paris, or even Vienna? Think, after you leave Vienna you must travel six hours by boat and three by rail before you reach Balak, but what a city, what curious houses, and what an opera house!

Let me first tell you of my experiences with Herr Klug. I met the Ransoms; you remember those queer Michigan avenue people. They are here with their mother — snuffy Mother Ransom we used to call her — and are both studying with Herr Klug. I met them on the Ringstrasse — the principal avenue here — and they looked so dissatisfied when they saw me. Ada, the short, thin one, you know — well, she lowered her parasol — say, the weather is awful

183

hot — and, honest, I believed she was n't going to speak to me. But Lizzie is the nice one, and she fairly ate me up. They raved about Herr Klug. He is so nice, so gentle, and plays so wonderfully ! Mrs. Ransom was a trifle cool — she and ma never did get along, you remember that fight about free lager for indigent Germans in sultry weather? — well, she and ma quarrelled over the meaning of the word "indigent," and Mrs. R. said that she was indigent at ma's ignorance ; then ma burst into a fit of laughter. I heard her — it was a real mean laugh, Bella, and — but I must tell you about this place. Dear, I 'm quite out of breath !

Well, the Ransoms took me off to lunch and it was real nice at their boarding house ; they call it the Hôtel Serbe, or some such name, and I almost regretted that I went to the miserable rooms I 'm in, but I have to be economical, and as I intend practising all day and sleeping all night it does n't matter much where I am. I forgot to tell you what we had for lunch, funny dishes, sour and full of red pepper. I 'll tell you all about it in my next letter. I 'm so full of Herr Klug that I can't sit still. He is a grand man, Bella, only very old, and very small, and very nervous, and very cross. He did n't say much to me and I held my tongue, for they say he is so nervous that he is almost crazy, besides, he hates American pupils. When I went into the big lesson room it was empty, and I had a good chance to look at all the pictures on the wall. There were Bach, Beethoven and Herr Klug at every age. There must have been at least thirty portraits. He was homely in every one, and wore his hair long, and has such a high, noble forehead. You know Chicago men have such low foreheads. I love high foreheads. They are so *destingué* (is that spelt right?) and it means such a *lot* of brains. He was photographed with Liszt and with Chopin. I think it was Chopin, and — just then he came in. He walked very slowly and his shoulders were stooped. Oh, Bella, he has such a venerable look, so saintly! Well, he stood in the doorway and his eyeglasses fairly stared into me, he has such piercing gaze. I was scared out of my seven senses and stood stock still.

" *Nu was!* " he cried out; " where do you come from? " His English was maddening, Bella, just maddening, but I understood him, and with my heart in my boots I said:

" Chicago, Herr Klug." He snorted.

" Chicago. I hate Chicago, I hate Americans! There 's only one city in America — that is San Francisco. I was never there, but I like it because I never had a pupil from that city; that 's why I like it, *hein!* " He laughed, Bella, and coughed himself into a strangling fit over his joke — he thought it was a joke — and then he sharply cried out:

" You may kiss me, and play for me." I was

too frightened to reply, so I went up to him and did n't like him. He smelt of cigarettes and liquor, but I kissed him on the forehead, and he gave me a queer look and pushed me to the piano. Well, I was flabbergasted.

"Play," he said, as harsh as could be, and I dashed off the Military Polonaise of Chopin. He walked about the whole time humming out loud, and never paid any attention to me any more than if I had n't been playing. When I got to the trio I stuck, and he burst out laughing, so I stopped short.

"Aha! you girls and your teachers, how you, all swindle yourselves. You have no talent, no touch, nothing, nothing!" — his voice was like a screaming whistle — "and yet you cheat yourselves and run to Europe to be artists in a year, aha!" "Shall I go on?" I asked. I was getting mad. "No, I 've heard enough. Come to the class every Monday and Thursday morning at ten — mind you, ten sharp — and in the meantime study this piece of mine, 'The Five Blackbirds,' for the black keys, and take the first book of my 'Indispensable Studies for Stupid American Girls.'" He laughed again.

"You pay now for the music. I make no discount, for I print it myself. Your lessons you pay for one by one. Please put the money — twenty marks — on the mantelpiece when you are through playing, but don't tell me. I 'm too nervous. And now good-day; practise ten

186

hours every day. You may kiss me good-by. No? Well, next time. I hate American girls when they play; but I like to kiss them, for they are very pretty. Wait: I will introduce you to my wife." He rang a bell and barked something at a servant, and she returned followed by a nice-looking German lady, quite young. I was surprised. "My wife." We bowed and then I left.

Funny people, these foreigners. I take my lesson day after to-morrow and I must hurry home to my Blackbirds. Good-by, dear Bella, and tell the girls to write. You answer this soon and I'll write after lesson on Monday. Good-by, Bella. Don't show my ma this letter, and, Bella — say nothing to nobody about the kisses. I did n't like — now if it had been — you know — oh, dear. I hate the piano. Good-by at last, Bella, and oh, Bella, will you send me the address of Schaefer, Schloss & Cantwell's? I want to order some writing paper. Good-by.

Your devoted   IRENE.

P. S. — Any kind of Irish linen paper will do *without* any monogram.   I.

To Mrs. William Murray

BALAK, *January* 31.

MY DEAR MAMMA, — Certainly I got your last letter. I have not forgotten you at all, and the draft came all right. Bella Seymour exaggerates so. Herr Klug kisses all his pupils in the class, but just as Grandpa Murray would. He's old enough to be our grandfather; besides, as Mrs Ransom says, it is not for our beauty, but when we play well, that he rewards us. I'm sure I don't like it, and if Mrs. Klug, or his six or seven cousins who live with him, caught him they would make a lively time. I never saw such a jealous set of relatives in my life. How am I improving? Oh, splendid; just splendid. I do wish you would n't coax and worm out of Bella Seymour all I write. You know girls exaggerate so. Good-by, darling mamma. Give my love to pa and Harry. I 'll write soon. Yes, I need one new morning frock. I owe for one at a store here where the Ransoms go. Lizzie Ransom is the nicest, but I play better than she does.

Your affectionate daughter,
IRENE.

To Miss Bella Seymour

BALAK, March 2.

YOU MEAN OLD THING, — I got your letter, Bella, but I don't understand yet how you came to tell mamma the nonsense I wrote. Such a lot of things have happened since I wrote last fall. I have n't improved a bit. I have no talent, old man Kluggy says — he's such a soft old fool.

He can't play a bit, but he's always talking
about his method, his virtuosity, his wonderful
memory and his marvellous touch. He must
have played well when he was painted with
Beethoven in the same picture. Yes, he knew
Beethoven. He's as old as old what's-his-name
who ate grass and died of a colic, in the Bible.
Golly, wouldn't I like to get out of this hole,
but I promised pa I'd stick it out until spring.
I play nothing but Klug compositions, his
valses, mazurkas — mind *his* nerve, he says he
gave Chopin points on mazurkas; and Bella,
Bella, what do you think, I've found out all
about his cousins! I wrote ma that all the old
hens in his house were his cousins, and I spoke
of his wife. Bella, *he has no wife*, he has *no
cousins*. What do you think? I'll tell you how
I found it out. The Ransom girls know, but
they don't let on to their mother. The first lesson I took, Klug — I hate that man — motioned
me to wait until the other girls had gone. He
pretended to fool and fuss over some autographs
of Bach and a lot of other old idiots — I hate
Bach, too, nasty dry stuff — and I knew what he
was up to. He glared at me through his spectacles for a while and then mumbled out:

"You may kiss me before you go." Not
much, I thought, and told him so. He rang a
bell. The servant came. "Send my wife down.
Schnell, du." She hesitated and he yelled out.
"Dummkopf" and then turned to me and

smiled. The old monkey had forgotten that he had introduced me to Frau Klug two days before. In a minute I heard the swish of a silk dress and a fine-looking old lady entered. I was introduced to — what do you think? Frau Klug, please. I nearly fell over, for I remembered well the frightened-looking German girl — a pretty girl, too, only dressed *rotten*. Well, I got out the best I could — I could n't talk German or Balakian — a hideous language, full of coughing and barking sounds — so I bowed and got out. Now comes the funny part of it, Bella. Every time the old fool tries to kiss me I ask him to introduce me to his wife, and he invariably answers: "What, you have not met my wife?" and rings for the ugly servant who stands grinning until I really expect her to say "Which one?" but she never does. I 've counted seventeen so far, all sizes, ages and complexions.

The class says they are old pupils who could n't pay their bills, so Kluggy got a mortgage on them, and they have to stay with him until they work the mortgage off by sewing, washing, cooking and teaching beginners. I 've not seen them all yet, and Anne Sypher, from Cleveland, swears that there is a dungeon in the house full of girls from the eighteenth century who had n't money enough to pay for their lessons. I 'm sure ugly Babette, the servant, is an old pupil, for one day I sneaked into the dining-room and heard her playing the Bella Capricciosa, by Hummel, on an upright piano that was almost falling apart. Heavens! how she started when she saw me! The old lady he introduced me to the second time was a pupil of Steibelt's, and she played the " Storm " for us in class when the professor was sick. She must have been good-looking. Her fingers were quite lively. Honest, it is the joke of Balak, and we girls have grown so sensitive on the subject that we never walk out in a crowd, for the young men at the corners call out, " Hello, there goes the new crop for 1902." It is very embarrassing.

Bella, I want to tell you something. Swear that you will never tell my father or mother. I don't give a rap for music; I hate it, but I like the young men here in Balak, no, not the citizens. They are slow, but the soldiers, the regiment attached to the Royal Household. I 've met a Lieutenant Fustics — oh, he 's lovely, belongs to the oldest family in Serbia, is young, handsome and so fine in his uniform. He is crazy over music and America, and says he will never bear to be separated from me. Of course he 's in love and of course he 's foolish, for I 'm too young to marry — fancy, not eighteen yet, or, is it nineteen? — this place makes me forget my name — besides, pa would n't hear of such a thing. Herr Lieutenant Fustics asked my father's business, and told me all Americans

were millionaires, and I just laughed in his face.
I play for him in the salon — oh, no, not in my
room — that would be a crime in this tight-
laced old town. Now, Bella, *don't* tell mamma
this time. Why don't you write oftener? Love
to all.

Your devoted   IRENE.

P. S. — Bella, he's lovely.

To William Murray, Esq.

BALAK, *May* 12.

DEAR PA, — Yes, I need $500, and Herr
Klug says if I stay a year more I can play in
public when I go back. Five hundred dollars
will be enough *now.*

Your loving daughter,   IRENE.

To Miss Bella Seymour

BALAK, *May* 25.

DEAR, SWEET BELLA, — I'm gone; Hector,
that's his name, proposed to me — and proposed a secret marriage — he says that I can
study quietly, inspired by his love, for a year,
for his regiment will stay in Balak for another
year. Oh, Bella, I'm so happy. How I wish
you could see him. I simply don't go near the
piano. Old Klug is cross with me and I'm

192

sure the Ransoms are jealous. Good-by, Bella, don't tell mamma. Remember I trust you.

Your crazy   IRENE.

P. S. — I 'm wild to get married !

To Frau Wilhelm Murray.

BALAK, *June* 25.

HIGH RESPECTED AND HONORABLE MA-DAME, — I 've not seen your daughter, the Fräulein Irene Murray, since April, although she has been in Balak. I fear she has more talent for a military career than as a pianist. She does owe me for two lessons. Please send me the amount — 40 marks. Send it care of Frau Klug — Frau Emma Klug. With good weather,

ARMIN KLUG.

To William Murray, Esq.

August 1.

DEAR WILLIAM, — I 've found her — my heart bleeds when I think of her face, poor child — miles from Balak. Of course she followed the regiment when the wretch left, and of course he is a married man. Oh! William, the disgrace, and all for some miserable music lessons. Send the draft to Balak — to the Oriental Bank. I went as far as Belgrade. Poor, tired, daring Irene, how she cried for Chicago and for her papa! Yes, it will be all right. The girls in that old mummy's class gossiped a little, but I fixed up a story about going to Berlin and lessons there. Only the hateful Ransoms smile, and ask every day particularly for Irene. I'd like to strangle them. Have patience, William; will be back in the spring — early in the spring. My sweet, deceived child, our child William! Oh, I could kill that Fizzsticks, or whatever his name is. His regiment is off in the mountains somewhere, and I'm afraid of the publicity or I'd get our consul to introduce me to the Queen. She is a lady, and would listen to my complaint. But Irene begs me with frightened eyes not to say a word to any one. So I'll go on to Vienna and thence to Paris. For gracious sake, tell that Seymour girl — Bella Seymour — not to bother you about Irene; tell her anything you please. Tell her Irene is too busy practising to answer her silly letters. And William, not a word to Grandpa Murray — not a word, William!

Your loving wife,
MARTHA KILBY MURRAY.

P. S.— I don't know, William.

. . . .

Extract from the Daily Eagle, November 5, 1903

The most interesting feature of the concert was the début as a pianist of Miss Irene Murray, the daughter of William Murray, Esq., of the Drovers' National Bank.

THE QUEST OF THE ELUSIVE

Miss Murray, who was a slip of a girl before she went abroad two years ago to study with the celebrated Herr Armin Klug, of Balak, returns a superb, self-possessed young woman of regal appearance and queenly manners. She played a sweet bit, a fantasia by her teacher, Herr Klug, entitled "The Five Blackbirds," and displayed a wonderful command of the resources of the keyboard. For encore she dashed off a brilliant morceau by Herr Klug, entitled " Echoes de Seraglio." This was very difficult, but for the fair débutante it was child's play. She got five recalls, and after the concert held an impromptu reception in her dressing-room, her happy parents being warmly congratulated by their fellow townsmen. We predict a great career for Irene Murray. Among those present we noticed, etc., etc. . . .

AN INVOLUNTARY INSUR-GENT

Whereas it is far away from bloodshed, battle-cry and sword-thrust that the lives of most of us flow on, and the men's tears are silent to-day, and invisible, and almost spiritual. . . . — MAETERLINCK.

RACAH hated music. Even his father quoted with approval Théophile Gautier's witticism about it being the most costly of noises. Racah, as a boy, shouted under the windows of neighbors in whose rooms string-music was heard of hot summer evenings. On every occasion his nature testified to its lively abhorrence of tone, and once he was violently thrust forth from a church by an excited sexton. Racah had whistled derisively at the feebly executed voluntary of the organist. An old friend of the family declared that the boy should be trained as a music critic — he hated music so intensely. Racah's father would arch his meagre eyebrows and crisply say, "My son shall become a priest." "But even a priest must chaunt the mass; eh, what?"

The boy's sister had a piano and tried to play despite his violent mockery. One afternoon, when the sun drove the town to its siesta, he wandered into the room where stood the instrument. Moved by an automatic impulse, the lad placed one finger on a treble key. He shuddered as it tinkled under the pressure; then he struck the major third and held both keys down, trembling, while drops of water formed under his eyes. He hated the sound he made, but could not resist listening to it. Waves of disgust rolled hotly over his heart, and he almost choked from the large, bitter-tasting ball that rose in his throat. He then struck the triad of C major in a clumsy way — a quarter of an hour later his family found him in a syncope at the foot of the piano, and sent for a doctor. Racah's eyes were open, but only the whites showed. The pulse was strangely intermittent, the heart muffled, and the doctor set it down to nervous prostration brought on by strenuous attendance at church. It was Holy Week and Racah a pious boy.

He soon recovered, avoided the instrument, and kept his peace. . . . About this time he began going out immediately after supper, remaining away until midnight. This, coupled with a relaxation of religious zeal, drove his pious father into a frenzy of disappointment. But being wise in old age, he did not pester his son, especially as the pale, melancholy lad bore on his face no signs of dissipation. These disappearances lasted for over a year. Racah was chided by his mother, a large, chicken-minded woman, who liked gossip and chocolate. He never answered her, and on Sundays locked himself in his room. Once his sister listened at the door and told her father that she heard her brother counting aloud and clicking on the table with some soft, dull-edged tool, a tiny mallet, perhaps.

The father's curiosity mounted to an unhealthy pitch. He hated to break into his nightly custom of playing cards at the Inn of The Quarrelling Yellow Cats, but his duty lay as plain before him as the moles on his wrist; so he waited until Racah went out, and seizing a stout stick and clapping his hat on his head, followed his son in lagging and deceitful pursuit. The boy walked slowly, his head thrown back in reverie. Several times he halted as if the burden of his thoughts clogged his very motion. Anxiously eying him, his father sneaked after. The eccentric movements of his son filled him with a certain anguish. He was a god-fearing man; erratic behavior meant to him the obsession of the devil.

His son, his Racah, was tempted by the evil one! What could he do to save him from the fiery pit? Urged by these burdensome notions, he cried aloud, "Racah, my son, return to thy home!" But he spoke to space. No one was within hearing. The street was dark; then the sound of music fell upon his ears, and again he looked about him. Racah had disappeared. The only light came from a window hard by. With the music it oozed out between two half-closed shutters, and toward it the depressed one went. He peeped in and saw his son playing at a piano, and by his side sat a queer old man beating time. His name was Spinoza; he was a Portuguese pianist, and wore a tall, battered silk hat which he never removed, even in bed — so the town said.

Racah's father played no dominoes that night. When he returned to his house his wife thought that he was drunk. He told his story in agitated accents, and went to bed a mystified man. He understood nothing, and while his wife calmly slept he tortured himself with questions. How came Racah the priest to be metamorphosed into Racah the pianist? Then the father plucked at the counterpane like a dying fiddler. . . .

The boy showed no embarrassment when interrogated by his parents the next day. He said he did not desire to be a priest, that a pianist could make more money, and though he hated music, there were harder ways of earning one's bread. The callousness which he displayed in saying all this deeply pained his pious father. His son's secret nature was an enigma to him. In vain he endeavored to pierce the meaning of the youth's eyes, but their gaze was enigmatic and veiled. Racah had ever exhibited a certain aloofness of character, and as he grew older this trait became intensified; the riddle of his life had forced itself upon him, and he vainly wrestled with it. Music drew him as iron filings to the magnet, or as the tentacles of an octopus carry to its parrot-shaped beak its victim. It was monstrous, he abhorred it, but could no more resist it than the hasheesh eater his drug.

So in the fury of despair, and with a certain self-contempt, he strove desperately to master the technical problems of his art. He found an abettor in the person of the Portuguese pianist, to whom he laid bare his soul. He studied every night, and since he need no longer conceal his secret, he began practising at home. . . .

Racah made his début when he was twenty-one years old. The friend of the family nearly burst a blood-vessel at the concert, so enthusiastic was he over the son of his old crony. Racah's father stayed home and refused comfort. His son was a pianist and not a priest. " He has disgraced himself and God will not reply to his call for aid," and he placed his hands over his thin eyebrows and wept. Racah's mother spoke: " Take on courage; the boy plays badly — there is yet hope."

The good man, elated by the idea, went forth to play dominoes with his old crony at the inn where the two yellow cats quarrel on the dingy sign over the door. . . .

Racah sat at his piano. His usually smooth, high forehead, with its mop of heavy black curls, was corrugated with little puckering lines. His mouth was drawn at the corners, and from time to time he sighed; great groans, too, burst forth from him. But he played, played furiously, and he smote the keyboard as if he hated it. He was playing the B minor Sonata of Chopin, with its melting second movement — so moving that it could melt the heart of the right sort of a stone. Yet this lovely cantilena extorted anger from the young pianist. It was true that he played badly, but not so badly as his mother imagined. His very hatred of music reverberated in his playing and produced an odd, inverted, temperamental spark. The transposition of an emotion into a lower or higher key may change its external expression; its intensity is not thereby altered. Racah hated the piano, hated Chopin, hated music; yet potentially Racah was a great pianist. . . .

The years fugued by. Racah gradually became known as an artist of strange power. He had studied with Liszt, although he was not a favorite of the master nor in his cenacle of worshipping pupils. Racah was too grim, too much in earnest for the worldly frivolous crew that flitted over the black keys at Weimar. Occasionally aroused by the power and intensity of the young man's playing, Liszt would smile satirically and say: " Thou art well named

' Raca,' " and then all the Jews in the class would laugh at the word-play. But it gave Racah little concern whether they admired or loathed him. He was terribly set upon playing the piano and little guessed the secret of his inner struggle — the secret of the sad spirit that travailed against itself. Oddly enough his progress was rapid. He soon outpointed in brilliancy and deftness the most talented of the group of Liszt's young people, and once, after playing the Mephisto Walzer with abounding devilry, Liszt cried, " Bravo, child," and then muttered, " And how he hates it all ! "

Hypnotized as if by another's will, Racah studied so earnestly that he became a public pianist. He had success, but not with the great public. The critics called him cold, objective, a pianist made, not born. But musicians and those with cultured musical palates discerned a certain acid quality in his playing. His gloomy visage, the reflex of a disordered soul, caused Baudelaire to declare that he had added one more shiver to his extensive psychical collection. In Paris the Countess X. — charming, titled soubrette — said, " Have you heard Racah play the piano? He is a damned soul out for a holiday."

In twenty-four hours this mot spread the length of the Boulevard, and all Paris went to see the new pianist. . . .

Success did not brighten the glance of Racah.

He became gloomier as he grew older, and a prominent alienist in Paris warned him to travel or else — and he pointed to his forehead, shrugging his very Gallic shoulders. Racah immediately went to the far East. . . .

After a year's wandering up and down strange and curious countries, he came to the chief city of a barbarous province ruled by a man famous for his ferocities and charming culture. A careful education in Paris, grafted upon a nature cruel to the core, produced the most delicately depraved disposition imaginable. This Rajah was given to the paradoxical. He adored Chopin and loved to roast alive tiny birds on dainty golden grills. He would weep after reading de Musset, and a moment later watch with infinite satisfaction the spectacle of two wretched women dancing on heated copper plates. When he heard of Racah's presence in his kingdom he summoned the pianist.

Racah obeyed the Rajah's order. To his surprise he found him a man of pleasing mien and address. He was dressed in clothes of English cut, and possessed a concert piano. Racah bowed to him on entering the great Hall of the Statues.

" Do you play Chopin? "

" No," was the curt reply. The potentate glanced at the pianist, and then dropped his heavy eyelids. Racah had the air of a man bored to death.

"I entreat you" — the Rajah had winning accents — "play me something of Chopin. I adore Chopin."

"Your Highness, I abominate Chopin; I abominate music. I have taken a vow never to play again anything of that vile Polish composer. But I may play for you instead a Brahms sonata. The great one in F minor — "

"Stop a moment! You distinctly refuse to play me a Chopin valse or mazurka?"

"O Villainy!" Racah was thoroughly aroused; "I swear by the beard of your silly prophet that I will not play Chopin, nor touch your piano!"

The Rajah listened with a sweet forbearing smile. Then he clapped his hands twice — thrice. A slave entered. To him the Rajah spoke quietly, with an amused expression, and the man bowed his head. Touching the pianist on the shoulder he said:

"Come with me." Racah followed. The Rajah burst into loud laughter, and going to the piano played the D flat Valse of Chopin in a facile amateurish fashion.

Footsteps were heard; the Rajah stopped and looked up. There was bright frank expectancy in his gaze as he listened.

Then a curtain was thrust aside. Racah staggered in, supported by the attendant. He was white, helpless, fainting, and in his eyes were the shadows of infinite regret.

"Do play some Chopin," exclaimed the Rajah, gaily, as he ran his fingers over the keyboard.

The pianist groaned as the slave plucked at his arms and held them aloft. The Rajah critically viewed the hands from which the finger-tips were missing, and then, noting the remorseful anguish in the gaze of the other, he cried:

"Do you know, I really believe you love music despite yourself!"

HUNDING'S WIFE

I

CALCRAFT was very noisy in his morning humors, and the banging of windows caused his wife to raise a curious voice.

From the breakfast-room she called, "What is the matter with you this morning, Cal? Did n't Wagner agree with you last night? Or was it the —?"

"Yes, it was *that*," replied a surly voice.

"Have you hung your wrists out of the window and given them a good airing?"

"I have." Calcraft laughed rudely.

"Then for goodness' sake hurry in to breakfast, if you are cooled off; the eggs are." Mrs. Calcraft sighed. It was their usual conversation; thus the day began. . . . Her husband entered the room. Of a thick-set, almost burly figure, Calcraft was an enormously muscular man. His broad shoulders, powerful brow, black, deep-set eyes, inky black hair and beard — the beard worn in Hunding fashion — made up a personality slightly forbidding. The suppleness of his gait, the ready laughter and bright expression of the eye, soon corrected this aversion; the critic was liked, and admired, — after the criti-

cal fashion. Good temper and wit in the evening ever are. The recurring matrimonial duel
over the morning teacups awoke him for the
day's labors; he actually profited from the ver-
bal exercising of Tekla's temper.

"After what you promised!" she inquired in
her most reproachful manner. Calcraft smiled.
"And your story in the *Watchman*. Now, Cal,
are n't you a bit ashamed? We have heard
much worse Siegmunds."

"Not much," he grunted, swallowing a huge
cup of tea at a draught.

"Yet you roasted the poor boy as you would
never dare roast a singer with any sort of reputation. Hinweg's Siegmund was —"

"Like himself, too thin," said her husband;
"fancy a thin Siegmund! Besides, the fellow
does n't know how to sing, and he can't act."

"But his voice; it has all the freshness of
youth." . . . She left the table, and lounging to
the window regarded the streets and sky with a
contemptuous expression. Tekla was very tall,
rather heavy, though well built, with hair and
skin of royal blond. She looked as Scandinavian as her name.

"My dear Tek, you are always discovering
genius. You remember that young pianist with
a touch like old gold? Or was it smothered
onions? I've forgotten which." He grinned as
he spilled part of an egg on his beard.

She faced him. "If the critics don't encourage youthful talent, who will? But they never do." Her voice took on flat tones: "I wonder, Cal, that you are not easier as you grow older, for you certainly do not improve with age, yourself. Do you know what time you got in this morning?"

"No, and I don't want to know." The man's demeanor was harsh; there were deep circles under his large eyes; his cheeks were slightly puffed, and, as he opened his newspaper, he looked like one who had not slept.

Tekla sighed again and stirred uneasily about the room. "For heaven's sake, girl, sit down and read — or, something!"

"I don't wonder your nerves are bad this morning," she sweetly responded; "the only wonder is that you can keep up such a wearing pace and do your work so well."

"This isn't such a roast," said Calcraft irrelevantly. He had heard these same remarks every morning for more than ten years. "Last night," he proceeded, "the new tenor — "

"Oh! Cal, please don't read your criticism aloud. I saw it hours ago," she implored, — her slightly protuberant, blue eyes were fixed steadily upon him.

"Why, what time is it?"

"Long past twelve."

"Phew! And I promised to be at the office at midday! Where's my coat, my overshoes! Magda! Magda! Hang that girl, she's always

gadding with the elevator boy when I need her."
Calcraft bustled about the room, rushed to his
bedchamber, to the hall, and reappeared dressed
for his trip down-town.

"Cal, I forgot to say that Hinweg called this
morning and left his card. Foreigners are so
polite in these matters. He left cards for both
of us."

"He did, did he?" answered Calcraft grimly.
"Well, that won't make him sing Wagner any
better in the *Watchman*. And as a matter of
politeness — if you will quote the polite ways of
foreigners — he should have left cards here before he sang. What name is on his pasteboard?
I've heard that his real one is something like
Whizzina. He's a Croat, I believe."

She indifferently took some cards from a
bronze salver and read aloud: "Adalbert Viznina, Tenor, Royal Opera, Prague."

"So-ho! a Bohemian. Well, it's all the
same. Croatia is Czech. Your Mr. Viznina
can't sing a little bit. That vile, throaty German tone-production of his — but why in thunder does he call himself Hinweg? Viznina is a
far prettier name. Perhaps Viznina is Hinweg
in German!"

Tekla shrugged her strong shoulders and
gazed outdoors. "What a wretched day, and
I have so much to do. Now, Cal, do come home
early. We dine at seven. No opera to-night,
you know. And come back soon. We never

spend a night home alone together. What if this young man should call again?"

"Don't stop him," her husband answered in good-humored accents as he bade her good-by. He was prepared to meet the world now, and in a jolly mood. "Tell your Hinweg or Whizzerina, or whatever his name is, to sing Tristan better to-morrow night than he did Siegmund, or there will be more trouble." He skipped off. She called after him:

"Cal, remember your promise!"

"Not a drop," and the double slamming of the street doors set Tekla humming Hunding's motif in "Die Walküre."

II

Her morning-room was hung with Japanese umbrellas and, despite the warning of friends, peacock-feathers hid from view the walls; this comfortable little boudoir, with its rugs, cozy Turkish corner, and dull sweet odors was originally a hall-bedroom; Tekla's ingenuity and desperate desire for the unconventional had converted the apartment into the prettiest of the Calcraft flat. Here, and here alone, was the imperious critic forbidden pipe or cigar. Cigarettes he abhorred, therefore Tekla allowed her favorites to use them. She became sick if she merely lighted one; so her pet attitude was to loll on a crimson divan and hold a freshly rolled Russian cigarette in her big fingers covered with opals. Her male friends said that she reminded them of a Frankish slave in a harem; she needed nothing more but Turkish-trousers, hoop ear-rings, and the sad, resigned smile of the captive maiden. . . .

It was half-past five in the dark, stormy afternoon when the electric buzzer warned Tekla of visitors. A man was ushered into the drawing-room and Magda, in correct cap and apron, fetched his card to her mistress.

"Show him in here, Magda, and Magda" — there were languid intonations in the voice of this vigorous woman — "light that lamp with the green globe."

In the fast disappearing daylight Tekla peeped at herself in a rhomboid crystal mirror, saw her house frock, voluminously becoming, and her golden hair set well over her brow: she believed in the eternal charm of fluffiness. After the lamp was ready the visitor came in. He was a very tall, rather emaciated looking, blond young man, whose springy step and clear eyes belied any hint of ill-health. As he entered, the gaze of the two met in the veiled light of the green-globed lamp, and the fire flickered high on the gas-log hearth. He hesitated with engaging modesty; then Tekla, holding out a hand, moved in a large curved way, to meet him.

"Delighted, I am sure, my dear Herr Viznina, to know you! How good of you to call on such a day, to see a bored woman." He bowed, smiled, showing strong white teeth under his boyish moustache, and sat down on the low seat near her divan.

"Madame," he answered in Slavic-accented English, "I am happy to make your acquaintance and hope to meet your husband, M. Calcraft." She turned her head impatiently. "I only hope that his notice will not discourage you for Tristan to-morrow night. But Mr. Calcraft is really a kind man, even if he seems severe in print. I tell him that he always hangs his fiddle outside the door, as the Irish say, which means, my dear Herr Viznina, that he is kinder abroad than at home." Seeing the slightly bewildered look of her companion she added, "And so you didn't mind his being cross this morning, did you?" The tenor hesitated.

"But he was not cross at all, Madame; I thought him very kind; for my throat was rough — you know what I mean! sick, sore; yes, it was a real sore throat that I had last night." It was her turn to look puzzled.

"Not cross? Mr. Calcraft not severe? Dear me, what do you call it, then?"

"He said I was a great artist," rejoined the other.

Tekla burst into laughter and apologized. "You have read the wrong paper, Herr Viznina, and I am glad you have. And now you must promise to stay and dine with us to-night. No, you sha'n't refuse! We are quite alone and you must know that, as old married folks, we are always delighted to have some one with us. I told Mr. Calcraft only this morning that we should go out to dinner if he came home alone. Don't ask for which paper he writes until you meet him. Nothing in the world could make me tell you." She was all frankness and animation, and her guest told himself that she was of a great charm. They fell into professional talk. She spoke of her husband's talents; how he had played the viola in quartet parties; of his successful lecture, "The Inutility of Wagner," and his preferences in music.

"But if he does not care for Wagner he must be a Brahmsianer." The last word came out with true Viennese unction.

"He now despises Brahms, and thinks that he had nothing to say. Wagner is, for him, a decadent, like Liszt and the rest."

"But the classics, Madame, what does M. Calcraft write of the classics?" demanded the singer.

"That they are all used-up romantics; that every musical dog has his day, and the latest composer is always the best; he voices his generation. We liked Brahms yesterday; to-day we are all for Richard Strauss and the symphonic poem."

"*We?*" A quizzical inflection was in the young man's voice. She stared at him.

"I get into the habit of using the editorial 'we.' I do it for fun; I by no means always agree with my husband. Besides, I often write criticism for Mr. Calcraft when he is away — or lecturing." She paused.

"Then," he exclaimed, and he gazed at her tenderly, "if you like my Tristan you may, perhaps, write a nice little notice. Oh, how lovely that would be!"

The artist in him stirred the strings of her maternal lyre. "Yes, it would be lovely, but Mr. Calcraft is not lecturing to-morrow night, and I hope that — "

The two street doors banged out a half bar of the Hunding rhythm. Calcraft was heard in the hall. A minute later he stood in the door of his wife's retreat; there was a frown upon his brow when he saw her companion, but it vanished as the two men shook hands. Viznina asked him if he spoke German; Magda beckoned to Mrs. Calcraft from the middle of the drawing-room. When Tekla returned, after giving final instructions for dinner, she found critic and tenor in heated argument over Jean de Reszké's interpretation of the elder Siegfried. . . .

The dining-room was a small salon, oak-panelled, and with low ceilings. A few prints of religious subjects, after the early Italian masters, hung on the walls. The buffet was pure renaissance. Comfortable was the room, while the oval table and soft leather chairs were provocative of appetite and conversation.

"Very un-American," remarked the singer, as he ate his crab bisque.

"How many American houses have you been in?" irritably asked Calcraft. Viznina admitted that he was enjoying his début.

"I thought so." Calcraft was now as bland as a May morning, and his eyes sparkled. His wife watched Magda serve the fish and fowl, and her husband insisted upon champagne as the sole wine. The tenor looked surprised, and then amused.

"Americans love champagne, do they not? I never touch it."

"Would you rather have claret or beer?" hastily inquired the host.

"Neither; I must sing Tristan to-morrow."

"You singers are saints on the stage." The critic laughed. "I am old-fashioned enough to believe that good wine or beer will never hurt the throat. Now there was Karl Formes, and Niemann the great tenor — "

Tekla interrupted. "My dear Cal, pray don't get on one of your interminable liquid talks. Herr Viznina does not care to drink, whether he is singing or not. I told him, too, that we always liked a guest at dinner, for we are such old married people."

Calcraft watched the pair facing one another. He was in a disagreeable humor because of his

wife's allusion to visitors; he liked to bear the
major burden of conversation, even when they
were alone. If Tekla began he had to sit still
and drink — there was no other alternative. She
asked Viznina where he was born, where he had
studied, and why he had changed his name. The
answers were those of a man in love with his art.
Hinweg, he explained, was his mother's name,
and assumed because of the anti-Slav prejudice
existing in Vienna.

Calcraft broke in. "You say you are Bohemian, Herr Viznina? You are really as Swedish
looking as Mrs. Calcraft."

"What a Sieglinde she would make, with her
beautiful blond complexion and grand figure,"
returned the tenor with enthusiasm.

Tekla sighed for the third time that day. She
burned to become a Wagner singer. Had she
not been a successful elocutionist in Minnesota?
How this talented young artist appreciated her
gift, intuitively understood her ambition! Calcraft noted that they looked enough alike to
be brother and sister; tall, fair and blue-eyed
as they were. He laughed at the conceit.

"You are both of the Wölfing tribe," he
roared and ordered beer of Magda. "I always
drink dark beer after champagne, it settles the
effervesence," he argued.

"You can always drink beer, before and after
anything, Cal," said his wife in her sarcastic,
vibrant voice.

The guest was hopelessly bored, but, being a man of will, he concentrated his attention upon himself and grew more resigned. He did not pretend to understand this rough-spoken critic, with his hatred of Wagner and his contradictory Teutonic tastes. Tekla with eyes full of beaming implications spoke:

"I should tell you, Cal, that Herr Viznina does not know, or else has forgotten, which paper you write for, and I let him guess. He thinks you praised his Siegmund."

"Saturday morning after the Tristan performance he will know for sure," answered the critic sardonically, drinking a stein of Würzburger.

"You rude man! of course he will know, and he will love you afterwards." If Calcraft had been near enough she would have tapped him playfully on the arm.

"Ah! Madame, what would we poor artists do if it were not for the ladies, the kind, sweet American ladies?"

"That's just it," cried Calcraft.

"What an idea, Warrington Calcraft!" Tekla was thoroughly indignant. "Never since I've known you have I attempted to influence you."

"You could n't," said he.

"No, not even for poor Florence Deliba, who entered into a suicidal marriage after she read your brutal notice of her début."

"And a good thing it was for the operatic stage," chuckled the man.

"If I write the notices of a few minor concerts I always try to follow your notions." She was out of breath and Viznina admired her without reserve.

Calcraft was becoming slow of utterance. "You women are wonders when it comes to criticism." The air darkened. Viznina looked unhappy and Mrs. Calcraft rose: "Come, let us drink our coffee in my den, Herr Viznina, I hate shop talk." She swept out of the room and the tenor, after a dismissal from the drowsy critic, joined her.

"My headstrong husband does n't care for coffee," she confessed, apologetically. "Sit down where you were before. The soft light is so becoming to you. Do you know that you have an ideal face for Tristan, and this green recalls the forest scene. Now just fancy that I am Isolde and tell me what your thoughts and feelings are in the second act."

Sitting beside her on the couch and watching her long fingers milky-green with opals, Viznina spoke only of himself, with all the meticulous delicacy of a Wagnerian tenor, and was thoroughly happy playing the part of a tame Tristan.

III

Tristan and Isolde were in the middle of their passionate symphony of flesh and spirit, when Tekla was ushered to the regular Calcraft seats in the opera house. Her husband, who had been in the city all day, returned to the house late for dinner, through which meal he dozed. He then fell asleep on a couch. After dressing and waiting wearily until nearly nine o'clock she had a carriage called and went to the opera alone; not forgetting, however, to bid Magda leave a case of imported beer where Mr. Calcraft could find it when he awoke. . . .

Rather flustered, she watched the stage with anxious eyes. Brangaene — an ugly, large person in a terra-cotta cheese-cloth peplum — had already warned the desperate pair beneath the trees that dawn and danger were at hand. But the lovers sang of death and love, and love and death; and their sweet, despairing imagery floated on the oily waves of orchestral passion. The eloquence became burning; Tekla had forgotten her tribulations, Calcraft and time and space, when King Marke entered accompanied by the blustering busy-body Melot.

"Oh, these tiresome husbands!" she thought, and not listening to the noble music of the deceived man, she presently slipped into the lobby. The place was deserted, and as she paced up and down, she recollected with pleasure the boyish-looking Tristan. How handsome he was! and how his voice, husky in "Die Walküre," now rang out thrillingly! There! — she heard it again, muffled indeed by the thick doors, but pure, free, full of youthful fire. What a Tristan!

And he had looked at her the night before with
the same ardor! A pity it was, that she, Tekla
Calcraft, born Tekla Björnsen, had not studied
for the opera; had not sung Sieglinde to
his Siegmund; was not singing at this moment
with such a Tristan in the place of that fat
Malska, old enough to be his mother! and instead of being the wife of an indifferent man
who — . . .

The act was over, the applause noisy. People
began to press out through the swinging doors,
and Tekla, not caring to be caught alone, walked
around to the stage entrance. She met the
Director, who made much of her and took her
through the archway presided over by a hoarse-
voiced keeper.

In his dressing-room Tristan welcomed her
with outstretched hands.

"You are so good," and then quickly pointed
to his throat.

"And you were superb," she responded
unaffectedly.

"Your husband, is he here?" he asked, forgetting his throat.

"He is not here yet; he is detained down-
town."

"But he will write the critique?" inquired
Viznina with startled eyes. Tekla did not at
first answer him.

"I don't know," she replied thickly. He
seized her hands.

" Oh, you will like my third act! I am there at my best," he declared with all the muted vanity of a modest man. She was slightly disappointed.

" I like everything you do," she slowly admitted. Viznina kissed her wrists. She regarded him with maternal eyes.

As Tekla mounted the stairs her mind was made up. Fatigued as she was by the exciting events of the past twenty-four hours, she reached the press-room in a buoyant mood. It was smoky with the cigars and cigarettes of a half dozen men who invented ideas, pleasant and otherwise, about the opera, for the morning papers. Mrs. Calcraft was greeted with warmth; like her husband she was a favorite, though an old man grumbled out something about women abusing their privilege. Jetsam, one of her devoted body-guard, gave her a seat, pen and paper, and told her to go ahead; there were plenty of messenger boys in waiting. It was not the first time Tekla had been in the press-room, the room of the dreaded critical chain-gang, as Cal had named it. All asked after Calcraft.

" He has gone to the Symphony Concert," replied Tekla unblushingly, and young Jetsam winked his thin eyes at the rest. Feeling encouraged at this he persisted:

" I thought Gardner was ' doing ' the concert for Cal? "

"Oh! you know Cal!" she put a pen in her mouth, "he hates Wagner; perhaps he thinks Mr. Gardner needs company once in a while."

"Perhaps he does," gravely soliloquized Jetsam.

"How many performances of Tristan does this make, Mr. Jetsam?"

"I'm sure I don't know — I am never much on statistics."

When she was told the correct number the scratching of pens went on and the smoke grew denser. Messenger after messenger was dismissed with precious critical freightage, and soon Tekla had finished, envious eyes watching her all the while. Every man there wished that his wife were as clever and helpful as Mrs. Calcraft.

Driving home she forgot all about the shabby cab having memories only for the garden scene, its musical enchantments. The spell of them lay thick upon her as she was undressed by Magda. When the lights were out, she asked Magda if Mr. Calcraft still slept.

"No, ma'am; after drinking the beer he went out."

"Oh! he went out after all, did he?" responded Tekla in a sleepy voice and immediately passed into happy dreams. . . .

It was sullen afternoon when she stood in her room regarding with instant joy a large bunch of roses. Calcraft came in without slamming the doors as usual. She turned a shining face to him. He looked factitiously fresh, with a Turkish bath freshness, his linen was spotless, and in his hand he held a newspaper.

"That was a fine, dark potion you brewed for me last night, Sieglinde!" he mournfully began. "No wonder your Tristan sang so well in the *Watchman* this morning!" The youthful candors of her Swedish blue eyes with their tinted lashes evoked his sulky admiration.

"I knew, Cal, that you would do the young man justice for his magnificent performance," she replied, her cheeks beginning to echo the hues of the roses she held; her fingers had just closed over an angular bit of paper buried in the heart of the flowers. . . .

For answer, Calcraft ironically hummed the Pity motif from "Die Walküre" and went out of the house, the doors closing gently after him to the familiar rhythm of that sadly duped warrior, Hunding.

THE CORRIDOR OF TIME

Ah! to see behind me no longer on the Lake of
Eternity the implacable Wake of Time.
— Ephraïm Mikaël.

When Cintras was twenty he planned an
appeal to eternity. He knew "Émaux et
Camées" as pious folk their Bible; he felt
that naught endured but art. So he became a
pagan, and sought for firmness and delicacy in
the texture, while aiming to fill his verse
with the fire of Swinburne, the subtlety of
Rossetti and the great, clear day-flame of
Gautier. A well-nigh impossible ideal; yet
he cherished it for twice ten years, and at
forty had forsworn poetry for prose. . . .

Then he read the masters of that "other
harmony of prose" until he dreamed of long,
sweeping phrases, drumming with melody,
cadences like the humming of slow, uplifting
walls of water tumbling on sullen strands. He
knew Sir Thomas Browne, and repeated with
unction: "Now since these dead bones have
already outlasted the living ones of Methusaleh,
and in a yard under ground, and thin walls of
clay, outworn all the strong and spacious

buildings above it; and quietly rested under the drums and tramplings of three conquests; what prince can promise such diuturnity unto his relicks." . . . He wondered if Milton, De Quincey, Walter Pater or even Jeremy Taylor had made such sustained music. He marvelled at the lofty structures of old seventeenth century prose-men, and compared them with the chippy staccato of the modern perky style, its smug smartness, its eternal chattering gallop. He absorbed the quiet prose of Addison and Steele and swore it tasted like dry sherry. Swift, he found brilliantly hard, often mannered; and he loved Dr. Goldsmith, so bland, loquacious, welcoming. In Fielding's sentences he heard the clatter of oaths; and when bored by the pulpy magnificence of Pater's harmonies went back to Bunyan with his stern, straightforward way. For Macaulay and his multitudinous prose, Cintras conceived a special abhorrence, but could quote for you with unfailing diction Sir William Temple's "Use of Poetry and Music," and its sweet coda: "When all is done, human life is at the greatest and the best, but like a froward child that must be played with and humored to keep it quiet till it falls asleep, and then the care is over."

Cintras had become enamoured with the English language, and emptied it into his eyes from Chaucer to Stevenson. He most affected Charles Lamb and Laurence Sterne; he also loved the

Bible for its canorous prose, and on hot afternoons as the boys lolled about his room, he thundered forth bits of Job and the Psalms. Cintras was greatly beloved by the gang, though it was generally conceded that he had as yet done nothing. This is the way Berkeley put it, down at Chérierre's, where they often met to say obvious things in American-French. . . .

"You see boys, if Cintras had the stuff in him he would have turned out something by this time. He's a bad poet — what, have n't you ever read any of his verse? — and now he's gone daft on artistic prose. Artistic rubbish! Who the devil cares for chiselled prose nowadays? In the days when link-boys and sedan chairs helped home a jag they had the time to speak good English. But now! Good Lord! With typewriters cutting your phrases into angular fragments, with the very soil at your heels saturated with slang, what hope in an age of hurry has a fellow to think of the cadence? I honestly believe Stevenson was having fun when he wrote that essay of his on the technical elements of style. It's a puzzle picture and no more to be deciphered than a Bach fugue."

"When Bill Berkeley gets the flow on, he's worse than Cintras with his variable vowels. Say, Bill, I think you're jealous of old Pop Cintras." It was Sammy Hodson, a newspaper man, who spoke, and as he wrote on space he was usually the cashier of the crowd. . . .

THE CORRIDOR OF TIME

Chérierre's is on University Place, and the spot where the artistic set — Berkeley, Hodson, Pauch, the sculptor, and Cintras — happened to be hanging about just then. The musician of the circle was a tall thin young man named Merville. It was said that he had written a symphony; and one night they all got drunk when the last movement was finished, though not a soul had heard a note. Every one believed Merville would do big things some day.

Cintras entered. He was hopelessly uninteresting looking and wore a beard. Berkeley swore that if he shaved he would be sent to prison; but Cintras pleaded economy, a delicate throat, also the fact that his nose was stubby. But set him to talking about the beauties of English prose, and his eyes blazed with a green fire. The conversation turned on good things to drink; wine at twenty-five cents a litre was ordered, and the chatter began. . . .

"It seems to me, Berkeley," Cintras spoke, "that you modern fellows are too much devoted to the color scheme. I remember when I was a boy, Gautier set us crazy in Paris with his color sense. His pages glowed with all the pigments of the palette; he vied with the jeweller in introducing precious stones of the most ravishing brilliancy within the walls of his paragraph; I sickened of all this splendor, this Ruskin word-painting, and went in for cool grays, took up Baudelaire and finally reached Verlaine,

whose music is the echo of music heard in misty
mediæval parks while the peacock dragging by
with its twilight tail, utters shrill commentary on
such moonshine. After that I reached Chopin
and found him too dangerous, too treacherous,
too condensed, the art too filed out; and so I
finally landed in the arms of Wagner, and I 've
been there ever since."

"Look here, Cintras, you 're prose-mad and
you 've landed nowhere." Berkeley lighted one
of Hodson's cigarettes. "When a new, big fellow comes along you follow him until you find
out how he does the trick and then you get
bored. Don't you remember the day you
rushed into my studio and yelled, ' Newman is
the only man who wrote prose in the nineteenth
century,' and then persisted in spouting long
sentences from the ' Apologia'? First it was
Arnold, then it was Edmund Burke." "It will
always be Burke," interrupted Cintras. "Then
it was Maurice de Guérin, and I suppose it
will be Flaubert forever and ever." They all
laughed.

"Yes, Billy, it will always be Gustave Flaubert, and I worship him more and more every
day. It took him forty years to write four books
and three stories, and, as Henry James says, he
deliberately planned masterpieces."

Hodson broke in: "You literary men make
me tired. Why, if I turned out copy at the
rate of Slobsbert — what 's his name? — I 'd

starve. What's all the fuss about, anyhow? Write natural English and any one will understand you " — " Ah, natural English, that's what one man writes in a generation," sighed Cintras. " And when you want something great," continued the young man, " why, read a good ' thriller' about the great Cemetery Syndicate, and how it robbed the dead for gold fillings in teeth. The author just slings it out — and such words ! "

" Yes, with a whitewash brush." Berkeley scowled.

" Why," pursued Hodson, unmoved, " why don't you get married, Cintras, and work for your living? Then you 'll have to write syndicate stuff and that will knock the nonsense out of you. Or, fall in love and be miserable like me." Hodson paused to drink.

> " O triste, triste était mon âme,
>   À cause, à cause d'une femme."

" That 's Verlaine; Hoddy, my boy, when you grow up, quit newspapering and become cultured, you may appreciate its meaning and beauty."

" When I am cultured I 'll be a night city editor; that 's my ideal," said the youth, stoutly.

" Let 's go over to Merville's room and make him play Chopin," suggested Pauch, the sculptor, who seldom spoke, but could eat more than four men. . . . They drank their coffee and went across into Twelfth street, and at the top of the house they found the musician's room. It was large, but poorly fitted out. An old square-piano, a stove, a bed, three chairs, a big lounge and a washstand completed the catalogue. Merville made them comfortable and sat down to the piano. Its tone, as his fingers crept over the keys, was of faded richness and there were re-verberations of lost splendors in the bass. Merville started with a Chopin nocturne, but Hodson hurt the cat as it brushed against him, and the noise displeased the pianist. He stopped.

" I don't feel like Chopin, it's too early in the day. Chopin should be heard only in the early evening or after midnight. I'll give you some Brahms instead. Brahms suits the after-noon, this gray, dull day." All were too lazy to reply and the pianist began, with hesitating touch, an Intermezzo in A minor. It sounded like music heard in a dream, a dream anterior to this existence. It seemed as if life, tired of the external blaze of the sun, sought for the secret of hidden spaces; searched for the message in the sinuous murmuring shell. It was an art of an art, the penumbra of an art. Its faint outlines melted into one's soul and refused to be turned away. The recollection of other music seemed gross after this curiously introspective, this almost whorl-like, music. It was the return to the invertebrate, the shadow of a shadow, and the hearts of Merville's guests were downcast and purified. . . .

When he had finished, Cintras asked: " If that is Brahms, why then he has solved the secret of the age's end. He has written the song of humanity absorbed in the slime of a dying planet."

" Very morbid, very perverse in rhythms, I should say," broke in Berkeley; they all shivered. Merville arose, his face glum and drawn, and brought whiskey and glasses.

Cintras was the first to speak:

" Hodson, you are a very young fellow and I wish to give you good advice. Yours to me was better than you supposed. Now don't you ever bother with art, music or artistic prose. Just marry a nice girl who goes to comic operas. You stick to her and avoid Balzac. He is too strong meat for you — " " Yes, but he 's great; I read him ! " " And no more understand him than you do Chopin. Because he is great he is readable, but his secret is the secret of the sphinx; it may only be unravelled by a few strong souls. So go your road and be happy in your plush way, read your historical hog-wash, and believe me when I swear that the most miserable men are those who have caught a glimpse of the eternal beauty of art, who pursue her ideal face, who have the vision but not the voice. I once wrote a little prose poem about this desire of beauty; I will see if I can remember it for you."

"Go ahead, old man; I'll stand anything to-day," sang out Hodson.

"Here it is:" and Cintras recited his legend of

THE RECURRING STAIRCASE

I first saw her on the Recurring Staircase. I had turned sharply the angle of the hall and placed my foot upon the bottom step and then I saw her. She was motionless; her back I saw, and O! the grace of her neck and the glory of her arrested attitude. I feared to move, but some portent, silent, inflexibly eloquent, haled me to the staircase. That was years ago. I called to her, strange calls, beautiful sounding names; I besought her to bend her head, to make some sign to my signals of urgency; but her glance was aloft, where, illumined by the scarlet music of a setting sun, I saw in a rich, heavy mullioned embrazure, multi-colored glass shot through with drunken despairing daylight. Again I prayed my Lady of the Recurring Staircase to give me hope by a single dropped glance. At last I conjured her in Love's fatal name, and she moved languorously up the steep slope of stairs. As if the spell had been thwarted, I followed the melodious adagio of her footsteps. That was many years ago. She never mounted to the heavy mullioned embrazure with the multi-colored glass shot through with drunken, despairing daylight. I never touched the hand of the

232

Lady of the Recurring Staircase; for the stairs were endless and I stood ever upon the bottom step; and the others below slipped into eternity; and all this was many years ago. I never have seen the glorious glance of My Lady on the Recurring Staircase.

They all applauded, Hodson violently. "I say, old chap, what would you have gained by overtaking the lady?" Cintras sniffed; Berkeley laughingly remarked that the staircase reminded him of the sort you see at a harvest with a horse on the treadmill.

"Don't, fellows!" begged Merville. "Cintras is giving one ideas to-day for a symphonic poem. Go on, Cintras, with more, but in a different vein. Something in the classical style."

"I can't do that," responded Cintras, trying not to look flattered, "but I will show you my soul when overtaken by doubt." "Cintras, your soul, like Huysmans's, is a cork one." They were aghast, for Hodson the uncultured one had spoken.

"And where, Hoddy, my brave lad, did you ever in the world hear of Huysmans?" he was asked. "I read that; I thought it fitted Cintras. His soul is like a cork ball that is always rebounding from one idea to another." "Bravo! you will be the literary, not the night city editor, before you die, Hoddy." . . . Then Cintras read another prose-poem which he had named

THE MIRROR OF UNFAITH

I looked into my mirror the next morning. With scared cry I again looked into my mirror. With brutish, trembling fingers I tried to cleanse the mist from my eyes, and once more I looked into my mirror, scraped its surface tenderly, but it availed not. There was no reflection of my features in its polished depths; naught but vacancy, steely and profound. There is no God, I had proclaimed; no God in high heaven, no God with the world, no spirit ever moved upon the vasty waters, no spirit ever travailed in the womb of time and conceived the cosmos. There is no God and man is not made in his image; eternity is an eyeless socket—a socket that never beheld the burning splendors of the Deity. There is no God, O my God! And my cries are futile, for have I not gazed into my mirror, gazed with clear ironic frantic gaze and missed my own image! There is no God; yet has my denial been heard in blackest Eblis, and has it not reverberated unto the very edges of Time? There is no God, and from that moment my face was blotted out. I may never see it in the moving waters, in mirrors, in the burnished hearts of things, or in the liquid eyes of woman. I denied God. I mocked His omnipotence. I dared him to mortal combat, and my mirror tells me there is no Me, no image of the man called by my name. I denied God and God denies me!

" If I were in such a mental condition," Hodson eagerly commented, " I 'd call a doctor or join the Salvation Army." "Why have n't you written more short stories?" inquired Merville. "Because I 've never had the time," Cintras sadly answered. "Once I tried to condense what novelists usually spread over hundreds of pages, and say it in a couple of paragraphs. Every word must illuminate the past, in every sentence may be found the sequel."

"Cintras, I vow your case is hopeless. You are a regular cherry-stone carver. Here you 've shown us the skeletons of two stories and yet given none of them flesh enough to live upon." "Berkeley you belong to a past full of novelistic monsters. You are the three volume man with the happy ending tacked on willy-nilly. It is the tact of omission —" "Hang your art-for-art theories. I 'll make more money than Cintras ever did when I publish my "Art of Anonymous Letter Writing!" cut in Hodson. Cintras calmly continued, "Here is my title and see if you can follow me."

INELUCTABLE

The light waned as with tense fingers he turned the round, bevelled-edge screw of the lamp. Darkness, immitigable, profound, and soft, must soon succeed yellow radiance. To face this gloom, to live in it and breathe of it, set his heart harshly beating. Yet he slowly turned with tense fingers the bevelled-edge screw of the lamp. He would presently be forced to

a criticism of the day, that day, which must brilliantly
flame when night closed upon him. As in the vivid
agony endured between two bell-strokes of a clock,
he strove to answer the oppressing shape threatening
him. And his fingers lingeringly revolved the lamp-
screw with its brass and bevelled-edge. If only some
gust of resolution would arise like the sudden scud of
the squall that whitens far-away level summer seas,
and drive forth pampered procrastinations! Then
might his fingers become flexile, his mind untied.
Poor, drab seconds that fooled with eternity and
supped on vain courage as they went trooping by.
Could not one keen point of consciousness abide?
Why must all go humming into oblivion like untuned
values? He grasped at a single strand of recollection;
he saw her parted lips, the passionate reproach of
her eyes and felt her strenuous tacit acquiescence;
he sensed the richness of her love. So he stood,
unstable, vacillating and a treacherous groper amidst
cruel shards of an ineluctable memory, powerless
to stay the fair phantom and fearful of looking
night squarely in the front. And he remained
a dweller in the shadows, as he faintly fingered the
bevelled-edge screw of the lamp. . . .

" If Maeterlinck would feed on Henry James
and write a dream fugue on your affected title,
this might be the result," muttered Berkeley.
" Hush!" whispered Merville; " can't you see
that it is his own life he is unconsciously relating
in this sequence of short stories; the tale of his
own pampered procrastinations? If he had only

made up his mind perhaps he could have kept her by his side and been happy but " — " But instead," said Berkeley sourly " he wrote queer impossible things about bevelled-edge lamp screws and she could n't stand it. I don't blame her. I say, nature before art every time." . . . Then Hodson shouted, dispelling dangerous reveries :

"Cintras, why don't you finish that book of yours? Ten years ago you told me that you had finished it nearly one-half." "Yes, and in ten years more he will finish the other," remarked Berkeley.

"If you knew how I worked you would not ask why I work slowly." "Flaubert again!" interjected Berkeley.

"The title cost me much pain, and the first two lines infinite travail. I really write with great facility. I once wrote a novel in three weeks for a sensation monger of a publisher; but because of this ease I suspect every sentence, every word, aye, every letter that drops from my pen."

"Hire a typewriter and you 'll suspect nobody," suggested Hodson. . . .

The party began to break up ; Cintras pressed hands and went first. There was some desultory conversation, during which Berkeley endeavored to persuade Hodson to buy him his dinner. Then they left Merville and Pauch alone. The musician looked at the sculptor.

" And these makers of words think they have the secret of art; as if form, as if music, is not infinitely greater and nearer the core of life." Pauch grunted.

"There's a man, that Brahms, you played, Merville; his is great art which will girdle the centuries. The man built solidly for the future. He reminds me of Rodin's Calais group: harsh but eternal; secret and sweetly harsh. Brahms is the Bonze of his art; his music has often the immobility of the Orient — I think the ' Vibrationists ' would describe it as ' kinetic stability.' . . . Cintras is done. He never did anything; he never will. He theorizes too much. If you talk too often of the beautiful things you are going to execute they will go sailing into the air for some other fellow to catch. Mark my words! No man may play tag with his soul and win the game. He is a study in temperament, or, rather the need of one, is Cintras. He must have received a black eye some time. Was he ever in love?"

" Yes, but she went off with another fellow."

" That explains all." Pauch stolidly asked for beer, and getting none strolled home. . . .

Cintras died. Among his effects was found a bulky mass of manuscript; almost trembling with joy and expectation Berkeley carried the treasure to Merville's room. On the title-page was read: " The Corridor of Time: A Novel. By George Cintras."

Frantic with curiosity the friends found on the next page the following lines:

"And the insistent clamor of her name at my heart is as the sonorous roll of the sea on a savage shore."

The other pages were virginal of ink. . . .

AVATAR

Somewhere ; in desolate wind-swept space,
　In Twilight-land — in No-man's land —
Two hurrying shapes met face to face
　And bade each other stand.

" And who are you ? " cried one agape
　Shuddering in the gloaming light ;
" I know not," said the second shape,
　" I only died last night ! "

— ALDRICH.

MYCHOWSKI was considered by grave critical
authorities, the best living interpreter of Chopin.
He was a Pole — any one could tell that by the
way he spelt his name — and a perfect foil to
Paderewski, being short, thick-set and with hair
as black as a kitchen beetle. His fat amiable
face, flat and corpulent fingers, his swarthy skin
and upturned nose, were called comical by the
women who thronged his recitals ; but Mychowski at the keyboard was a different man
from the Mychowski who sat all night at a
table eating macaroni and drinking Apollinaris
water. Then the funny profile vanished and
the fat fingers literally dripped melody. His
readings of the Polish master's music were distinguished by grace, dexterity, finesse, pathos

and subtilty. The only pupils of Chopin alive
— there were only six now — hobbled to Mychowski's concerts and declared that at last
their dead idol was reincarnated, at last the
miracle had taken place: a genuine interpreter
of Chopin had appeared — then severe coughing, superinduced by emotion, and the rest of
the sentence would finish in tears. . . .

The Chopin pupils also wrote to the papers
letters always beginning, "Honored Sir, —
Your numerous and intelligent readers would
perhaps like to know in what manner Chopin's
performance of the F minor Ballade resembled
Mychowski's. It was in the year 1842 that — "
A sextuple flood of recollections was then let
loose, and Mychowski the gainer thereby. Still
he obstinately refused to be lionized, cut his
hair perilously near the prizefighter's line, and
never went into society, except for money.
He was a model business man; the impresarios
worshipped him. Such business ability, such
frugality, such absence of eccentricity, such
temperance, were voted extraordinary.

"Why, the man never gambles," said a manager, "drinks only at his meals" — "which are
many," interrupted some one — "and always
sends his money home to his wife and family in
Poland. Yet he plays like a god. It is un-
heard of." . . .

The Polish servant Mychowski brought with
him from home sickened in Paris and died.

Although the pianist was playing the Erard, he went often to the Pleyel piano warerooms and there told a friend that he was without a valet.

"We have some one here who will suit you. His father was Chopin's body-servant, who, as you must have read, was an Irish-Frenchman named Daniel Dubois. We call the son Daniel Chopin; he looks so much like some of the pictures of your great countryman. Best of all, he does n't know one note of music from another."

"Just the man," cried Mychowski; "my last valet always insisted on waking me in the morning with a Bach Invention. It was awful." Mychowski shuddered.

"Wait, then; I 'll send upstairs for him," said the amiable representative of the Maison Pleyel, and soon there appeared, dressed after the fashion fifty years ago, a man of about thirty, whose face and expression caused Mychowski to bound out of his seat and exclaim in his native tongue:

"Slawa Bohu! but he looks like Frédéric."

The man started a little, then became impassive. "My father was Daniel Dubois, in whose arms the great master died. May he keep company with the angels! When my mother bore me she wore a medallion containing a portrait of the great master, and my father, who was his pupil, played the nocturnes for her."

AVATAR

The speaker's voice was slightly muffled in timbre, its accent was languid, yet it was indubitably the voice of a cultivated man. Mychowski regarded him curiously. A slim frame of middle height; fragile but wonderfully flexible limbs; delicately formed hands; very small feet; an oval, softly-outlined head; a pale, transparent complexion; long silken hair of a light chestnut color parted on one side; tender brown eyes, intelligent rather than dreamy; a finely-curved aquiline nose, a sweet, subtle smile; graceful and varied gestures — such was the outward presence of Daniel Dubois.

" He looks just like the description given by Niecks," murmured the pianist. " Even the eyes are *piwne*, as we say in Poland, couleur de bière.

"Yet you do not play the piano?" he continued. The man smiled and shook his head. Terms were arranged, and the valet sent to Mychowski's rooms.

" And the mother, who was she?" Mychowski asked later.

"Pst!" enjoined his friend discreetly. Mychowski smiled, sighed, shook his head, settled himself before a new piano and plunged into the preludes, playing the entire twenty-five without pause, while business was suspended in the ancient and honorable Maison Pleyel, so captivating, so miraculous, was the poetic performance of this commonplace and kind-hearted virtuoso. . . .

Mychowski discovered in Daniel an agreeable servant. He was noiseless, ubiquitous. He could make an omelette or sew on a button with woman's skill. His small, well-kept hands knew no fatigue, and his master often watched them, almost transparent, fragile and aristocratic, as they shaved his rotund oily face. Daniel was admirable in his management of the musical library, seeming to know where the music of every composer had to be placed. Mychowski wondered how he contrived to find time to learn so much and yet keep his hands from the keyboard. After the first month Mychowski began to envy his servant the possession of such a poetic personality.

"Now if I had such a face and figure how much better an effect I should produce. I see the women laugh when I sit down to play, and if it was n't for my fat fingers where would I be?" Mychowski sighed. He had conquered the musical world, but not his reflection in the mirror. He had made some charming conquests, but his better guides had whispered to him that it was his music, not his face, that had won the women. He was vain, sensitive and without the courage of his nose, unlike Cyrano de Bergerac. Nothing was lacking; talent, wealth, health, a capital digestion and success! Had they not poured in upon him? From his twentieth year he enjoyed the sunshine of popular favor and after ten years was enamoured of

it as ever. He almost felt bitter when he saw
Daniel's high-bred and delicate figure. He questioned him a hundred times, but could find out
nothing. Where had he been raised? Who was
his mother, and why did he select a servant's life?
Daniel replied with repose and managed to
parry or evade all inquiries. He confessed,
however, to one weakness — insatiable love for
music — and begged his master to be allowed
the privilege of sitting in the room during the
practising hours. When a concert was given
Daniel went to the hall and arranged all that was
necessary for the pianist's comfort. Mychowski
caught him at a recital one night with a score of
the F minor Ballade of Chopin, and warm and
irritable as he was, for he had just played the
work, he could not refrain from asking his
servant how it had pleased him. Daniel shook
his head gently. Mychowski stared at him
curiously, with chagrin. Then a lot of women
rushed in to congratulate the artist, but stopped
to stare aghast at Daniel.

"Ah, M. Mychowski!" — it was the beautiful
Countess d'Angers — "We know now why you
play Chopin so wonderfully, for have you not
his ghost here to tell you everything? Naughty
magician, why have you not come to me on my
evenings? You surely received cards!" Mychowski looked so annoyed at the jest that
Daniel slipped out of the room and did not
appear until the carriage was ready. . . .

At the café where Mychowski invariably went for his macaroni Daniel usually had a place at the table. The pianist was easy in his manners, and not finding his man presumptuous he made him a companion. They had both eaten in silence, Mychowski gluttonously. Looking at Daniel and drinking a glass of chianti, he said in his most jocular manner:

"Eh bien, mon brave! now tell me why you didn't like my F minor Ballade." Daniel lifted his eyes slowly to the other's face and smiled faint protestation. Mychowski would take no refusal. He swore in Polish and called out in lusty tones, "Come now, Daniel Chopin, what didn't you like, the tempo, the conception, the coda, or my touch?"

"Your playing, cher maître, was yourself. No one can do what you can," answered Daniel evasively.

"Hoity-toity! What have we here, a critic in disguise?" said Mychowski good humoredly, yet at heart greatly troubled. "Do you know what the pupils of Chopin say of my interpretation?" Daniel again shook his head.

"They know nothing about Chopin or his music," he calmly replied. A thunderbolt had fallen at Mychowski's feet and he was affrighted. Know nothing of Chopin or his music? Here was a pretty presumption. "Pray, Daniel," he managed to gasp out, "pray how does your lordship happen to know so much about Chopin and his music?" Mychowski was becoming angry. In a stifled voice Daniel replied:

"Dear master, only what my father told me. But do let me go home and get your bed ready. I feel faint and I ask pardon for my impertinence. I am indeed no critic, nor shall I ever presume again." "You may go," said his master in gruff accents, and regretted his rudeness as soon as Daniel was out of sight. If any one of the managers who so ardently praised Mychowski's temperate habits had seen him guzzling wine, beer and brandy that night, they might have been shocked. He seldom went to excess, but was out of sorts and nettled at criticism from such a quarter. Yet — had he played as well as usual? Was not overpraise undermining his artistic constitution? He thought hard and vainly endeavored to recapture the mood in which he had interpreted the Ballade, and then he fell to laughing at his spleen. A great artist to be annoyed by the first adverse feather that happened to tickle him in an awkward way. What folly! What vanity! Mychowski laughed and ordered a big glass of brandy to steady his nerves.

All fat men, he thought, are nervous and sensitive. I must really go to Marienbad and drink the waters and I think I'll leave Daniel Chopin behind in Paris. Chopin — Chopin, I wonder how much Chopin is in him? Pooh! what nonsense. Chopin only loved Sand and before that Constantia Gladowska. He never stooped to commonplace intrigue. But the resemblance, the extraordinary resemblance! After all, nature plays queer pranks. A thunderstorm may alarm a Mozart into existence, and why not a second Chopin? Ah, if I had that fellow's face and figure or he had my fingers what could n't we do? If he were not too old to study — no, I won't give him lessons, I 'll be damned if I will! He might walk away with me, piano and all. Chopin face, Chopin fingers.

Mychowski was rapidly becoming helpless and at two o'clock the patron of the café sent a message to Daniel, who was hard by, that he had better fetch his master away. The pianist was lifted into a carriage, though he lived just around the corner, and with the aid of the concierge, a cynical man of years, was helped into his apartment and put to bed. It was a trying night for Daniel, whose nature revolted at any suggestion of the grosser vices. . . .

From dull, muddy unconsciousness the soul of Mychowski struggled up into thin light. He fought with bands of villainous appearing men holding tuning forks; he was rolled down terrific gulfs a-top of pianos; while accompanying him in his vertiginous flight were other pianos, square, upright and grand; pianos of sinister and menacing expression; pianos with cruel grinning teeth; pianos of obsolete and anonymous shapes; pianos that leered at him, sneered

at him with screaming dissonances. The din
was infernal, the clangor terrific; and as the
pianist, hemmed in and riding this whirlwind
of splintered sounding-boards, jangling wires
and crunching lyres, closed his eyes expecting
the last awful plunge into the ghastly abyss, a
sudden, piercing tone penetrated the thick of
the storm; as if by sorcery, the turmoil faded
away, and, looking about him, Mychowski's disordered senses took note of an exquisite valley
in which rapidly flowed a tiny silvery stream.
Carpeted with green and fragrant with flowers,
the landscape was magical, and most melancholy
was the music made by the running waters.
Never had the artist heard such music, and
in the luminous haze of his mind it seemed
familiar. Three tones, three Gs in the treble
and in octaves, sounded clear to him; and again
and once more they were heard in doubled
rhythm. A rippling prelude rained upon the
meadows and Mychowski lay perfectly en-
tranced. He knew what was coming and
knew not the music. Then a melody fell from
the trees as they whispered over the banks of
the brook and it was in the key of F minor. A
nocturne; yet the day was young. Its mournful reiterations darkened the sky; but about all,
enchantment lay. In G flat, so the sensitive
ear of the pianist warned him, was his life being
borne; but only for a time. Back came the
first persistent theme, bringing with it over-

powering richness of hue and scent, and then it melted away in prismatic vapors. . . .

"What is all this melodic madness?" asked Mychowski. He knew the music made by the little river and trees, yet he groped as if in the toils of a nightmare to name it. That solemn narrative in six-eight time in B flat, where had he heard it? The glowing, glittering arabesques, the trilling as if from the throats of a thousand larks, the cunning imitations as if leaf mocked leaf in the sunshine! Again the first theme in F minor, but amplified and enlarged with a spray of basses and under a clouded sky. Without knowing why, the unhappy man felt the impending catastrophe and hastened to escape it. But in vain. His feet were as lead, and suddenly the heavens opened, fiercely lightened, the savage thunder leaping upon him in chromatic dissonances; then a great stillness in C major, and with solemn, silent steps he descended in modulated chords until he reached an awful crevasse. With a howl the tempest again unloosed, and in screeching accents the end came, came in F minor. For many octaves Mychowski fell as a stone from a star, and as he crashed into the very cellarage of hell he heard four snapping chords and found himself on the floor of his bedroom. . . .

"The F minor Ballade, of course," he cried; "and a nice ass I made of myself last night. Oh, what a head! But I wonder how I came to dream of the Ballade? Oh, yes, talking about it with Daniel, of course. What a vivid dream! I heard every note, and thought the trees and the brook were enjoying a duo, and — Bon Dieu! what's that?"

Mychowski, his face swollen and hair in disorder, slowly lifted himself and sat on the edge of the bed as he listened.

" Who the devil is playing at this hour? But what's this? Am I dreaming again? There goes that damnable Ballade." Mychowski rushed out of his room, down the short hall and pushed open the door of the music-room. The music stopped. Daniel was dusting some music at the end of the piano as he came in.

" Ah! dear master, I hope you are not sick," said the faithful fellow, dropping his feather-duster and running to Mychowski, who stood still and only stared.

" Who was playing the piano? " he demanded. " The piano? " quoth Daniel. " Yes, the piano. Was any one here? "

"No one has called this morning," answered Daniel, " except M. Dufour, the patron of the café, who came to inquire after your health." " It's none of his business," snapped Mychowski, whose nerves were on edge, " I heard piano playing and I wasn't dreaming. Come, no nonsense, Daniel, who was it? "

Just then his eyes fell on the desk; he strode to it and snatched the music. " There," he hoarsely said, "there is damning proof that you have lied to me; there is the Ballade in F minor by Chopin, and who, in the name of Beelzebub, was playing it? Not you?"

Daniel turned white, then pink, and trembled like a cat. Mychowski, his own face white, with cold shivers playing zither-wise up and down his back, looked at the servant and, in a feeble voice, asked him, "Who are you, man?" Daniel recovered himself and said in soothing tones, "Cher maître, you were up too late last night and you are nervous, agitated. I ask your pardon, but I never did tell you that I drum a little on the piano, and thinking you fast asleep I ventured on the liberty, and — "

"Drum a little! You call that drumming?" said Mychowski slowly. The two men looked into each other's eyes and Daniel's drooped. "Don't do it again; that's all. You woke me up," said Mychowski roughly, and he went out of the room without hearing Daniel reply:

"No, Monsieur Mychowski, I will not do it again." . . .

From that time on Mychowski was obsessed. He weighed the evidence and questioned again and again the validity of his dream, in the margin between sleep and waking. During the daytime he was inclined to think that it had been an odd trance, music and all; but when he had drunk brandy he grew superstitious and swore to himself that he really had heard

Daniel play; and he became so nervous that he never took his man about with him. He drank too much, and kept such late hours that Daniel gently scolded him; finally he played badly in public and then the critical press fairly pounced upon him. Too long had he been King Pianist, and his place was coveted by the pounding throng below. He drank more, and presently there was talk of a decadence in the marvellous art of M. Mychowski, the celebrated interpreter of Chopin.

All this time Mychowski watched Daniel, watched him in the day, watched him in the night. He would prowl about his apartment after midnight, listening for the tone of a piano, and, after telling Daniel that he would be gone for the day, he would sneak back anxious and expectant. But he never heard any music, and this, instead of calming his nerves, made him sicker. "Why," he would ask himself, " if the fellow can play as he does, why in the name of Chopin does he remain my servant? Is it because his servant blood rules, or — His servant blood? Why, he may have Polish blood in his veins, and such Polish!" Mychowski grew white at the idea. He could not sleep at night for he felt lonely, and drank so much that his manager declined to do business with him. Daniel prayed, expostulated and even threatened to leave; but Mychowski kept on the broad, downward path that leads to the mirage called Thirst.

One afternoon Mychowski sat at his accustomed table in the café. He was sick and sullen after a hard night of drinking, and as he saw himself in the mirror he bitterly thought, " He has the face, he has the figure, and, by God, he plays like Chopin." A voice interrupted him.

" Bon jour, Monsieur Mychowski; but how can you duplicate yourself, for just a minute ago I passed your apartment and heard such delicious piano playing? "

" The devil! " cried Mychowski, jumping up, and meeting the gaze of one of the six original Chopin pupils. " No, not the devil," said the other; " but Chopin. Surely you could not have been playing the F minor Ballade so marvellously and so early in the day? Now, Chopin always asserted that the F minor Ballade was for the dusk —"

" No," interrupted Mychowski, " it was not I; it was only Daniel, my valet, and my pupil. The lazy scamp! If I catch him at the piano instead of at his work I'll break every bone in his body." Mychowski's eyes were evil.

" But I assure you, cher monsieur, this was no servant, no pupil; this sounded as if the master had come back." " You once said that of me," returned the pianist moodily, and as he got up, his face ugly with passion, he reiterated:

" I tell you it was Daniel Chopin. But I'll answer for his silence after I've finished with him."

Mychowski hurried home. . . .

THE WEGSTAFFES GIVE A MUSICALE

I HAD promised Mrs. Wegstaffe and so there was no escape; not that my word was as good as my bond — in the matter of invitations it was not — but I liked Edith Wegstaffe, who was pretty, even if she did murder Bach. Hence the secret of my acceptance of Mrs. Wegstaffe's rather frigid inquiry as to whether I was engaged for the fourteenth. I am a bachelor, and next to cats, hate music heartily. Almost any other form of art appeals to my æstheticism, which must feed upon form, color, substance, but not upon impalpabilities. Silly sound waves, that are said to possess color, form, rhythm — in fact, all attributes of the plastic arts. "Pooh! What nonsense," I cried on the evening of the fourteenth, as I cursed a wretched collar that would not be coerced. . . . When I reached the Wegstaffe mansion I found my progress retarded by half a hundred guests, who fought, but politely, mind you, for precedence. At last, rumpled and red, I reached the men's dressing room, and the first person I encountered was Tompkins, Percy Tompkins, a man I hated for his cocksure manner of speech and

know-it-all style on the subject of music. Often
had he crushed my callow musical knowledge
by an apt phrase, and thinking well of myself
— at least Miss Edith says I do — I disliked
Tompkins heartily. " Hello ! " with a perceptible
raising of his eyebrows, " what are you doing
here?" "The same as yourself," I tartly answered, for he was not l'ami de la maison any
more than I, and I did n't purpose being sat
upon, that night at least. " My good fellow,
I 'm here to listen and — to be bored," he replied in his wittiest way.

" Indeed ! well I 'm in the same boat about
the music, but I hope I sha'n't be bored."

" But good heavens, man, it 's an amateur
affair — musicale, as the Wegstaffes call it in
true barbarous American jargon — and I fear
Edith Wegstaffe will play Chopin ! "

This angered me; I had long suspected
Tompkins of entertaining a sneaking admiration
for Edith, and resolved to tell her of this slur at
the first opportunity. I did n't have a chance
to answer him; a dozen men rushed into the
room, threw their hats and coats on the bed and
rushed out again.

" They 're in a hurry for a drink before the
music begins," said Tompkins. . . .

Going slowly down the long staircase we
found a little room on the second floor crowded
with men puffing cigarettes and drinking brandy
and soda. Old Wegstaffe was a generous host,

and knew what men liked best at a musicale. On the top floor four or five half-grown boys were playing billiards, and the ground floor fairly surged with women of all ages, degrees and ugliness. To me there was only one pretty girl in the house, Edith Wegstaffe; but of course I was prejudiced.

It was nine o'clock before Mrs. Wegstaffe gave the signal to begin. The three long drawing-rooms were jammed with smart looking people, a fair sprinkling of Bohemians, and a few professionals, whose hair, hands and glasses betrayed them. The latter stood in groups, eying each other suspiciously, while regarding the rest of the world with that indulgent air they assume at musicales. Everything to my unpractised eye seemed in hopeless disorder; a frightful buzz filled the air, and a blond girl at the big piano was trying to disentangle a lot of music. Near her stood a long-haired young man who perspired incessantly. "Ah!" I gloated. "Nervous! serves him right; he should have stayed at home!"

Just then Mrs. Wegstaffe saw me. "You're just the man I'm looking for," said she hurriedly. "Now be a good fellow; do go and tell all those people in the other room to stop talking. It's nine o'clock, and we're a half hour behind time." Before I could expostulate she had gone, leaving me in the same condition as the long-haired young man I had just derided.

"How tell them to stop talking?" I madly asked myself. Should I go to each group and politely say: "Please stop, for the music is about to begin," or should I stand in a doorway and shout:

"Say, quit gabbling, will you? the parties in the other room are going to spiel." My embarrassment was so hideous that the latter course would probably have been adopted, but Miss Edith touched me on the arm and I followed her to the hall.

"Oh, Mr. Trybill!" she gasped; "I'm so nervous that I shall surely faint when it comes my turn. Won't you please turn the music for me? I shall really feel better if some one is near me."

I looked at the sweet girl. There was not a particle of coquetry in her request. Dark shadows were under her eyes, two pink spots burnt in her pretty cheeks and her hands shook like a cigarette-smoker's.

"But think, think of your technique, your mamma, your guests," I blurted out desperately. She shook her head sadly and I shuddered. Are all amateur musicales such torturing things? . . .

The house was packed. A strong odor of flowers, perfumes and cooking mingled in the air; one stout woman fought her way to a window and put her head out gasping. It was Madame Bujoli, the famous vocal teacher,

three of whose crack pupils were on the programme. Not far from her sat Frau Makart, the
great instructor in the art of German Lieder interpretation, a hard-featured woman who sneered
at Italians, Italian methods and Italian music.
Two of her pupils were to appear, and I saw
trouble ahead in the superheated atmosphere.

Crash! went the piano. " They're off!"
hoarsely chuckled a sporting man next to me,
with a wilted collar, and Moszkowski's " Nations" welled up from the vicinity of the piano,
two young women exploiting their fingers in
its delivery. The talking in the back drawing-
rooms went on furiously, and I saw the hostess
coming toward me. I escape her by edging
into the back hall, despite the smothered com-
plaints of my displaced neighbors.

I got into the doorway, or rather into the
angle of a door leading into the back room.
The piano had stopped; while wondering what
to do next my attention was suddenly attracted
by a conversation to which I had to listen; it
was impossible to move away. " So she is going to sing, is she? Well, we will see if this
great and only true Italian method will put
brains into a fool's head or voice into her
chest." This was said in a guttural voice, the
accent being quite Teutonic. A soprano voice
was heard, and I listened as critically as I could.
The voice sang the Jewel Song from " Faust,"
and it seemed to me that its owner knew some-

thing about singing. I understood the words. She sang in English, and what more do you want in singing?

But the buzz at my left went on fiercely. "So the Bujoli calls *that* voice-production, does she? Humph! In Germany we would n't call the cows home with such singing." It was surely Frau Makart who spoke. There was a huge clapping of hands, fans waved, and I heard whispers, "Yes, rather pretty; but dresses in bad taste; good eyes; walks stiffly. Who is she? What was it she sang?"

More chatter. I wriggled away to my first position near the piano, but not without much personal discomfort. I was allowed to pass because, for some reason or other, I was supposed to be running the function. Upon reaching the piano Edith beckoned to me rapidly, and I slid across the polished floor, where she was talking to that hated Tompkins, and asked what I could do for her.

"Hold my music until I play; that 's a good fellow." I hate to be considered a "good fellow," but what could I do? Edith, who seemed to have recovered her aplomb, continued her conversation with Percy Tompkins.

"You know, Mr. Tompkins, Chopin is for me the only composer. You know, his nocturnes fill me with a sense of nothingness — the divine *néant, nirvana,* you call it. Now, Grünfeld — "

Tompkins interrupted rudely: "Grünfeld

can't play Chopin. Give me the 'Chopinzee.'
He plays Chopin. As Schumann says: 'The
Chopin polonaises are cannon buried in flowers.'
Now, Grünfeld is a —"

"No poet!" said I, indignantly, for I never
could admire the chubby Viennese pianist.
Tompkins turned and looked at me, but never
noticed my correction.

"Oh, Miss Wegstaffe," he continued viva-
ciously — how I hated that vivacity — "did you
hear that new story about a wit and the young
man who asked him to define George Meredith's
position in literature? 'Meredith,' said the
other, pompously, 'Meredith is a prose Browning,' and the young man thanked the great man
for this side light thrown on English letters,
when the poet added with a twinkle in his eye,
'Browning himself was a prose Browning.'
Now, is n't that delicious, Miss Wegstaffe; is n't
that —"

A volley of *hists-hists* and *hushes* came over the
room as I vainly tried to see the point of Tompkins' story. Every one laughed at his jokes, but
to me they seemed superficial and flippant.

The piano by this time was being manipu-
lated by a practical hand. Herr Wunderheim,
a Bulgarian pianist, was playing what the programme called a sonata in X dur, by Tschaïkowsky, op. 47, A, B, C, D, E, F, G. I
listened: I did n't understand it all, but I was
sitting next to Edith and would have endured

the remainder of the alphabet rather than let Tompkins gain one point.

The piano thundered and roared; lightning flew over the keys, and we were of course electrified. Herr Wunderheim jammed the notes in an astounding manner, and when he reached the letter G the sporting man said to me in a pious whisper, "Thank God! we didn't go to H —— altogether, but near it, my boy, near it!" I shrugged my shoulders and longed for my club.

Mighty was the applause. Herr Wunderheim looked delighted. Mrs. Wegstaffe, sailing up to the distinguished Bulgarian pianist, said loudly:

"Dear Herr Wunderheim, charmed, I assure you! We are all charmed; dear Tschaïkowsky, charming man, charming composer. Dear Walter Damrosch assured me that he was quite the gentleman; charming music altogether!"

The pianist grew red in the face. Then, straightening himself quite suddenly, he said in tones that sounded like a dog barking:

"Dot vas n't Schykufski I blayed, lieber madame; dot vas a koprice by me, myself."

Even the second drawing-room people stopped talking for a minute. . . .

The musicale merrily proceeded. We heard the amateur tenor with the cravat voice. We heard the society pianist, who had a graceful bow and an amiable technic; then two of Frau Makart's pupils sang. I could n't get near the

THE WEGSTAFFES GIVE A MUSICALE

Italian contingent, but they chattered loudly. One of the girls sang Dvořák's " Gute Nacht," and her German made me shiver. The other tried a Brahms song and everybody talked. I turned to ask Edith the girl's name but she had gone — so had Tompkins.

This angered me but I could n't get up then. Opposite me was a Yankee college professor — an expert on golfing poetry — who had become famous by an essay in which he proved that Poe should not have written Poe; next to me sat a fat lady who said to her daughter as she fanned herself vigorously, " Horrid music, that Brahms. He wrote 'The Rustic Cavalier,' did n't he? And some nasty critics said it was written by De —— "

" No, mamma. He wrote — " more buzzing and I fled upstairs.

The men's room was crowded to suffocation. Everybody was drinking hard, and old Wegstaffe was telling a story to a group of young men among whom I recognized the fat author of that affected book " How to play Chopin though Happy." He was pretty far gone.

" Shee here, bhoys; thish bloody music — thish classhic music — makesh me shick — I mean tired. I played Bluebottle for plashe to-day — 50 to 1 shot — whoop ! "

Another bottle was opened.

In a corner they were telling the story of Herr Schwillmun, the famous pianist who was

found crazy with wine in a Fourth Avenue undertaker's shop trying to play the Dvořák Concerto
on the lid of a highly polished coffin. The
Finnish virtuoso thought he was in a piano
wareroom. Another lie, I knew, for Schwillmun
was most poetic in appearance and surely not
an intemperate man!

Wherever I went I heard nothing but malicious remarks, slurring accusations and tittle-
tattle. Finally I joined a crowd in the upper
hall attracted by the appearance of a white-
haired man of intelligent aspect, who, with
kindly smile and abundant gesture was making
much merriment about him. I got close enough
to hear what he was saying.

"Music in New York! There is none. You
fellows ought to work for your grub, as I do,
on a daily, and write up the bosh concerts
that advertise. Humbug, boys; rank humbug!
Modern music is gone to the devil. Brahms
was a fraud who patched up a compound of
Beethoven and Schumann, put in a lot of mysti-
fying harmonic progressions, and thought he
was new. Verdi, the later Verdi was helped out
by Boito: Just compare 'Otello' and 'Falstaff'
with 'Mefistofele'! Dvořák, old 'Borax' as
they call him, went in for 'nigger' music and
says there's no future for American music unless
it is founded on plantation tunes. Hence the
'coon' song and its long reign. Tschaïkowsky!
Well, that tartar with his tom-tom orchestra

makes me tired; he should have been locked up in the 'Ha-Ha House.' Rubinstein never could do ten bars of decent counterpoint. Saint-Saëns, with his symphonic poems, his Omphalic Roués, is a Gallic echo of Bach and Liszt — a Bach of the Boulevards. The English have no composers; the Americans never will have, and, begad, sir, we're all going to the dogs. Music — rot!"

I was shocked. Here was a great critic abusing the gods of modern music and not a dissenting voice was raised. I determined to do my duty. I would ask this cynical old man why he belittled his profession. "Sir!" said I, raising my voice, but got no further, for a household servant, whose breath reeked, caught me by the arm and in a whisper explained:

"Oh, Mr. Trybill, Miss Edith is a-lookin' for you everywheres and sent me to tell you as how you're wanted in the music-room. It's her turn next."

My heart sank below my boots but I waded downstairs, spoiling many a tête-à-tête by my haste, for which I was duly and audibly execrated. Why do people at musicales flirt on the stairs?

Upon reaching the front drawing-room I found Edith taking her seat at the demon piano. Tompkins was nowhere visible, and I felt relieved. The guests looked worn out, and knots of men were hanging suspiciously about the closed doors of the supper room.

The musical part of the entertainment was about over, Edith's solo being the very last. Suddenly all became still; every one had to listen to the daughter of the hostess.

She looked positively radiant. Her eyes sparkled, and of her early nervousness not a trace remained.

" Do turn over the leaves nicely, that's a good fellow, Mr. Trybill " — again that odious phrase — " I feel so happy I'm sure I'll play well." Naturally, I was flattered at the inference. I was near her — the darling of my wildest dreams. Of course she would play well, and of course I would turn over the music nobly.

She began. The piece was Liszt's Polonaise in E. My brave girl, how proud I felt of her as she began. How she rushed on! I could scarcely turn the leaves fast enough for my little girl, my wife that was to be. How sweet her face seemed. I was ravished. I must tell her all to-night, and she will put her plump little hand in mine and say, "Yes"; the sweet little —

Bang! Smash, crash-bang! "Stupid fellow, I hate you!" I awoke as from a dream. Edith was standing up and in tears. Alas! Fatal dreamer that I am, I had turned over two pages at once, and trouble ensued, for Edith never memorized. . . .

THE WEGSTAFFES GIVE A MUSICALE

As I stood in horrid silence Mrs. Wegstaffe swooped down on Edith and took her away, saying in a harsh voice, "The young man knows nothing of the divine art!" Then the supper signal was sounded, and a cyclone's fury was not comparable to the rush and crush.

Old Wegstaffe, in a very shaky condition, led a gallant band of unsteady men in a gallop to the supper room, crying, "Bluebottle's the horsh for me." I lost heart. All my brilliant visions fled. As I stood alone in the hall Mrs. Wegstaffe triumphantly passed me on the arm of Herr Wunderheim. She looked at me a moment, then, seeming to pity my loneliness, leaned toward me, saying in acidulously sweet accents:

"Ah, no partner yet, Mr. Trybill? Your first partner is engaged, and to Mr. Tompkins. Do go in and congratulate him, that's a good fellow."

She swam away in the bedlam of shrieks and clattering of dishes and knives. I walked firmly upstairs, found my coat and hat, and left the house forever. It was my first and last experience at that occidental version of the Hara-Kiri, called a musicale.

THE IRON VIRGIN

*For there is order in the streets, but in the soul —
confusion. — MAXIM GORKY.*

THE carriage stood awaiting them in the Place
Boïeldieu. Chardon told the coachman to
drive rapidly; then closed the door upon
Madame Patel and himself. Cautiously trav-
ersing the crowded boulevards they reached
the Madeleine; a sharp turn to the left, down
the Rue Royale, they were soon crossing the
vast windy spaces of the Place de la Concorde
and there he spoke to his companion.

"It was a glorious victory! The Opéra
Comique looked like a battlefield after the conflict." Chardon's voice trembled as if with
timidity. Madame Patel turned from the half-
opened window.

"Yes, a glorious triumph. And *he* is not
here to enjoy it, to exult over his detractors."
Her tone was bitter as winter.

"My poor friend," the other answered as he
laid his hand gently on her arm. She shuddered. "Are you cold? Shall I close the
window?" "Thanks, no; it is too warm. How
long this ride seems! Yet he always de-

lighted in it after conducting." Chardon was silently polite. They were riding now at high speed along the Avenue Montaigne which the carriage had entered after leaving the Champs Élysées. From the Quai de Billy to the Quai de Passy their horses galloped over naked well-lighted avenues. The cool of the river penetrated them and the woman drew herself back into the corner absorbed in depressing memories. Along Mirabeau and Molitor, after passing the Avenue de Versailles; and when the street called Boileau appeared the carriage, its lanterns shooting tiny shafts of light on the road, headed for the *Hameau*, named after the old poet of Auteuil. There it stopped. Madame Patel and Chardon, a moment later, were walking slowly down the broad avenue of trees through which drawled the bourdon of the breeze this night in early May.

It was one o'clock when they entered the pretty little house, formerly the summer retreat of the dead composer Patel. A winner of the *Prix de Rome* he had produced many operas and oratorios until his death, just a year previous to the *première* of "The Iron Virgin." Of its immense success widow and librettist were in no doubt. Had they not witnessed it an hour earlier! Such furore did not often occur at the Comique. All recollection of Patel's mediocre work was wiped away in the swelter and glow of this passionate music, more modern than

Wagner, more brutal than Richard Strauss.
" Who would have believed that the old dried-up
mummy had such a volcano in his brain? " —
this the bereaved woman had overheard as she
descended the marble stairway of the theatre,
and Chardon hurried her to the carriage fearing
that the emotions of the evening — the sou-
venirs of the dead, the shouting of the audience
and the blaring of the band as it had saluted her
trembling, bowing figure in the box — finally
would prove too strong for her. He, too, had
come in for some of the applause, a sort of
inverted glory which like a frosty nimbus
envelopes the head of the librettist. Now he
recalled all this and rejoiced that his charge
was safely within doors.

Madame Patel retained only one servant in
her dignified, miniature household, for she was
not rich; but the lamps were burning brightly,
and on the table stood cold food, wine and fruit.
The music-room was familiar to her late husband's associate. Patel's portrait hung over the
fireplace. It represented in hard, shallow tones
the face of a white-haired, white-bearded man
whose thin lips, narrow nose and high forehead
proclaimed him an ascetic of art. The deep-
set eyes alone told of talent — their gaze inscrutable and calculating; a disappointed life
could be read in every seam of the brow.

Near the piano, where Chardon turned as he
waited Madame Patel's return from her dressing-

room, there swung a picture whose violence was not dissipated by the gloom of the half-hidden corner. He approached it with a lamp. Staring eyes saluted him, eyes saturated with the immitigable horror of life; eyes set in grotesque faces and smothered in a sinister Northern landscape. It was one of Edvard Munch's ferocious and ironic travesties of existence. And on the white margin of the lithograph the artist had pencilled: "I stopped and leaned against the balustrade almost dead with fatigue. Over the blue-black fjord hung clouds red as blood — as tongues of flame. My friends passed on, and alone, trembling with anguish, I listened to the great infinite cry of Nature."

She tapped him on the shoulder. "Come," she said gravely, "leave that awful picture and eat. You must be dead — you poor man!" Chardon blushed happily until he saw her cold eyes. "I was trying to catch the color of that painter's mind — that Norwegian, Munch. Disordered, farouche as is his style its spiritual note enchains me. The title of the picture means nothing, yet everything — 'Les Curieux,' is it not?" "Yes, you know it well enough by this time. What M. Patel could see in it I can't say." As she sat down to the table — not at the head: that was significantly empty — he admired her figure, maidenly still despite her majestic bearing; admired the terse contour of her head and noticed, not without a sigh, her small selfish ear. Madame Patel was nearing forty and her November hair had begun to whiten, but in her long gray eyes was invincible youth, poised, self-centred youth. She was deliberate in her movements and her complexion a clear brown. Chardon followed her example, eating and drinking, for they were exhausted by the ordeal of hearing under the most painful conditions, a posthumous opera.

"The great, infinite cry of Nature," — he returned to the picture. "How difficult that is to get into one's art." "Yes, *mon ami ;* but our dead one succeeded, did he not?" She was plainly obsessed by the theme. "His enemies — ah! the fools, fools. What a joy to see their astonished faces! Did you notice the critics, did you notice Millé in particular? He was in despair; for years that man pursued with his rancorous pen every opera by M. Patel." She paused. "But now he is conquered at last. Ah! Chardon, ah! Robert, Patel loved you, trusted you — and you helped him so much with your experience, your superior dramatic knowledge, your poetic gifts. You have been a noble friend indeed." She pressed his hand while he sat beside her in a stupor. "The great, infinite cry of Nature," he muttered. "And think of his kindness to me, a poor singer, so many years younger than himself! No father could have treated a daughter with such delicacy!" . . .

Chardon looked up. " Yes," he assented, " he was very, very old — too old for such a beautiful young wife." She started. " Not too old, M. Chardon," she said, slightly raising her contralto voice : " What if he was thirty years my senior ! He married me to spare me the peril and fatigue of a singer's life ; few women can stand them — I least of all. He loved me with a pure, narrow affection. I was his daughter, his staff. You, he often called ' Son.' " She grazed the hem of tears. Chardon was touched ; he seized her large, shapely hand, firm and cold as iron, and spoke rapidly.

" Listen, Madame Patel, listen Olivie — you were like a daughter to him, I know it, he told me. I was his adopted son. I tried to repay him for his interest in a young, unknown poet and composer — well, I compose a bit, you know — and I feel that I pleased him in my libretto of 'The Iron Virgin.' You remember the summer I spent at Nuremberg digging up the old legend, and the numberless times I visited the torture chamber where stands the real Iron Virgin, her interior studded with horrid spikes that cruelly stabbed the wretches consigned to her diabolical embraces? You recall all this ? " he went on, his vivacity increasing. " Now on the night of the successful termination of our artistic enterprize, the night when all Paris is ringing with the name of Patel, with 'The Iron Virgin ' " — he did not dare to add his own name — " let me tell you what you know already : I love you, Olivie. I have always loved you and I offer you my love, knowing that our dear one — " She dragged her hand from his too exultant grasp and sat down breathless on a low couch. Her eye never left his and he wavered at the thought of following her.

" So this is the true reason for your friendship ! " she protested in sorrowful accents. " For this you cultivated the good graces of an unsuspecting old man." " Olivie ! " he exclaimed. " For this," she sternly pursued, " you sought my company after his death. Oh, Chardon ! Robert ! How could you be so soon unfaithful to the memory of a man who loved you? He loved you, Robert, he made you ! Without him what would you be?" " What am I ? " She did not reply for she was gazing at the portrait over the fireplace. " A neglected genius," she mused. " He was forced to conduct operas to support his life — and mine. Yet he composed a masterpiece. He composed 'The Iron Virgin.' " " Could he have done it without me?" Madame Patel turned upon him : " You ask such a question, *you ?* " Chardon paced between table and piano. He stopped to look at the Munch picture and bit his lips : " The great, infinite cry of Nature ! Much Patel knew of music, of nature and her infinite cries." His excitement increased with every step.

" Olivie Patel, we must come to an understanding. You wonder at that picture, wonder what dread thing is happening. Perhaps the eyes are looking into this room, peering into our souls, into my soul which is black with sin and music." Like some timid men aroused he had begun to shout. The woman half rose in alarm but he waved her back. His forehead, full of power, an obstinate forehead, wrinkled with pain; his hands — the true index of the soul — were clasped, the fingers interlocked, wiry fingers agile with pen and piano. "Hear me out, Olivie," he commanded. "I 've been too good a friend to dismiss because I 've offended your sense of propriety" — she made an indignant gesture — "well, your idea of fidelity. But there is the other side of the slate: I 've been a faithful slave, I 've worked long years for my reward; and disciple of Nietzsche as I am, I have never attempted to assert my claims." "Your claims!" she uttered scornfully. "Yes, my claims, the claims of a man who sees his love sacrificed to miserable deception. Sit still! You must hear all now. I loved poetry but I loved you better. It was for that I endured everything. I spoke of my black soul — it is black, I 've poisoned it with music, slowly poisoned it until now it must be deadened. Like the opium eater I began with small doses of innocent music: I absorbed Haydn, Mozart. When Mozart became too mild I turned to Beethoven; from Beethoven to the mad stuff of

Schubert, Schumann, Chopin — sick souls all of them. They sustained me until even they failed to intoxicate. My nerves needed music that would bite — I found it in Liszt, Wagner and Tschaïkowsky; and like absinthe-drinkers I was wretched without my daily draughts." "You drink absinthe also, do you not?" she asked in her coldest manner. He did not notice her. "My soul gradually took on the color of the evil I sucked from all this music. Why? I can't say; perhaps because a poet has nothing in common with music — it usually kills the poetry in him. That is why I wonder what music Edvard Munch hears when he paints such pictures. It must be dire! Then Richard Strauss swept the torrid earth and my thirsty soul slaked itself in his tumultuous seas. At last I felt sure I had met my match. Your husband was like a child in my hands." She listened eagerly. "I did with him what I wished — but to please you I wrote 'The Iron Virgin.'" . . .

"The book," she calmly corrected. "As I wrote 'The Iron Virgin' I thought of you: You were my iron virgin, you, the wife of Patel. Will you hear the truth at last, the truth about a soul damned by music? Patel knew it. He promised me on his death-bed — " Olivie pushed by him and stood in the doorway. He only stared at her. "You are an Oread," he mumbled, "you still pine for your lost Narcissus till nothing is left of you but a voice — a voice which echoes him, echoes Ambroise Patel."

She watched him until his color began to return. "Robert," she said almost kindly, "Robert, the excitement of to-night has upset your nerves. Drink some brandy, and sit down." He eyed her piteously, then covered his face with nervous hands, his hair falling over them. She felt surer of him. "You called me an echo a moment ago, Robert," she resumed, her voice deepening. "I can never forget Patel. And it was because of this and because of my last promise to him that your offer shocked me; I ask your pardon for my rudeness. You have been so like a brother for the past years that marriage seems sacrilegious. Come, let us be friends — we have been trusty comrades. 'The Iron Virgin' is a success" — "Yes," he whispered, "the iron virgin is always a success." "— and why should our friendship merely be an echo of the past? Come, let us be more united than ever, Patel, you and I." Her smooth voice became vibrant as she pointed triumphantly at the portrait. He followed her with dull eyes from which all fire had fled.

"The echo," he said, drinking a tumbler of brandy. "The echo! I have it now: they *see* the echo in that picture back of me. Munch is the first man who painted tone; put on canvas that ape of music, of our souls, the ape which mocks us, leaps out after our voice, is always ready to follow us and show its leering shape

when we pass under dark, vaulted bridges or stand in the secret shadow of churches. The echo! What is the echo, Olivie, you discoursed of so sweetly? It is the sound of our souls escaping from some fissure of the brain. It has color, is a living thing, the thin wraith that pursues man ever to his grave. Patel was an echo. When his soul leans naked against the chill bar of heaven and bears false witness, then his echo will tell the truth about his music — this damnable reverberating *Doppelgänger* which sneaks into corners and lies in wait for our guilty gliding footsteps." She began to retreat again; she feared him, feared the hypnotism of his sad voice. "Robert, I firmly believe that picture has bewitched you — you, a believer in the brave philosophy of Nietzsche!" He moved toward her. "Madame Patel, it is you who are the cruel follower of Nietzsche. So was the original iron virgin; so is the new 'Iron Virgin' which I had the honor to surround with — "
"You mean instrumentation," she faltered. "Ah! you acknowledge so much?"

"Patel told me."

"He did not tell you enough."

Chardon laughed, shook her hand, put on his top-coat and descended the steps that led into the garden.

"Where are you going?" she asked affrightedly, regret stirring within her. "To Nuremberg to see the real iron virgin," he answered without sarcasm. They looked hard into each other's eyes — his were glowing like restless red coals — and then he plunged down the path leaving her strained and shaken to the very centre of her virginal soul. Had he spoken the truth! Ambroise Patel, upon whose grave would be strown flowers that belonged to the living! It was vile, the idea. "Robert!" she cried.

A smoky, yellow morning mist hung over Auteuil. A long, slow rain fell softly. Chardon pulled the chord at the gate of the *Hameau* roughly summoning the *concierge*. He soon found himself under the viaduct on the Boulevard Exelmans, where he walked until he reached Point-du-Jour. There a few workingmen about to take the circular railway to Batignolles regarded him cynically. He seemed like a man in the depths of a crazy debauch. He blundered on toward the Seine. "The echo! god of thunders, the echo!" he moaned as he heard his steps resound in the hollow arches. Near the water's edge he found a café and sat before a damp tin table. He pounded it with his walking stick. "The iron virgin," he roared; and laughed at the joke until the tears rolled over his tremulous chin. Lifting his inflamed eyes to the dirty little waiter he again brought his cane heavily upon the table. "Garçon," he clamored "the iron virgin!" The waiter brought absinthe; Chardon drank five. Doggedly he began his long journey.

DUSK OF THE GODS

A MASQUE OF MUSIC

STANNUM invited the pianist to his apartment
several times, but concert engagements inter-
vened, and when Herr Bech actually appeared
his host did not attempt to conceal his pleasure.
He admired the playing of the distinguished
virtuoso, and said so privately and in print.
Bech was a rare specimen of that rapidly disappearing order — the artist who knows all composers equally well. Not poetic, nor yet a
pedantic classicist, he played Bach and Brahms
with intellectual clearness and romantic fervor.
All these things Stannum noted, and the heart
of him grew elate as Bech sat down to the big
concert piano that stood in the middle of his
studio. It was a room of few lights and lofty,
soft shadows; and the air was as free from
sound as a diving bell. Stannum leaned back
on his wicker couch smoking a cigar, while the
pianist made broad preludes in many keys. . . .

The music, from misty weavings, tentative
gropings in remote tonalities, soon resolved
itself into the fluid affirmations of Bach's Chro-

matic Fantasia. Stannum noticed the burnished, argent surface of an old-fashioned Egyptian mirror of solid tin hanging in front of him, and saw in leaden shadows his features, dim and distorted. Being a man of astrological lore he mused, and presently mumbled, "Tin is the sign of Jupiter in alchemy and stands for the god of Juno and Thunders," and immediately begged Bech's pardon for having interrupted him. The pianist made no sign, having reached the fugue following the prelude. Stannum again speculated, his head supported by his hands. He stared into the tinny surface, and it seemed to take on new echoes of light and shade, following the chromatic changes of the music. . . . Presently rose many-colored smoke, as if exhaled from the enchantments of some oriental mage, and Stannum's eyes strove to penetrate the vaporous thickness. He plunged his gaze into its tinted steamy volutes, and struggled with it until it parted and fell away from him like the sound of falling waters. He could not see the source of the great roaring — the roaring of some cosmical cataract. He pushed boldly through the dense thunder-world into the shadow land, still knew that he lived. A few feet away was his chamber wherein Bech played Bach. Faintly the air cleared, yet never stopped the terrifying hum that attracted his attention. And now Stannum stood on the Cliff of the World, saw and heard the travailing and groaning of light and sound in the epochal and reverberating Void. A pedal bass, a diapasonic tone, that came from the bowels of the firmament struck fear to his heart; the tone was of such magnitude as might be overheard by the gods. No mortal ear could have held it without cracking and dying. This gigantic flood, this overwhelming and cataclysmic roar, filled every pore of Stannum's body. It blew him as a blade of grass is blown in a boreal blast; yet he sensed the pitch. Unorganized nature, the unrestrained cry of the rocks and their buried secrets; crushed aspirations, and the hidden worlds of plant, mineral, animal, and human, became vocal. It was the voice of the monstrous abortions of nature, the groan of the incomplete, experimental types, born for a day and shattered forever. All God's mud made moan for recognition; and Stannum was sorrowful. . . .

Light, its vibrations screeching into thin and acid flame-music, transposed his soul. He saw the battle of the molecules, the partitioning asunder of the elements; saw sound falling far behind its lighter-winged, fleeter-footed brother; saw the inequality of this race, " swifter than the weaver's shuttle," and felt that he was present at the very beginnings of Time and Space. Like unto some majestic comet that in passing had blazed out " Be not light; be sound ! " the fire-god mounted to the blue basin of Heaven and left time behind, but not space;

for in space sound abides not and cycles may be cancelled in a tone. Thus sound was born, and of it rhythm, the planets portioning it; and from rhythm came music, primordial, mad, yet music, and Stannum heard it as a single tone that never ceased, a tone that jarred the sun with mighty concussions, ruled the moon, and made rise etheric waves upon the rim of the interstellar milky way. Then quired the morning stars, and at their concordance Stannum was affrighted. . . .

His ear was become a monstrous labyrinth, a cortical lute of three thousand strings, and upon it impacted the early music at the dawn of things. In the planetary slime he heard the screaming struggles of fishy beasts; in the tanglewood of hot, aspiring forests were muffled roarings of gigantic mastodons, of tapirs that humped at the sky, beetles big as camels, and crocodiles with wings. Wicked creatures snarled crepitantly, and their crackling noises were echoed by lizard and dragon, ululating snouted birds and hissing leagues of snaky lengths. Stannum fled from these disturbing dreams seeking safety in the mountains. The tone pursued him, but he felt that it had a less bestial quality. Casting his eyes upon the vague plateau below he witnessed two-legged creatures pursuing game with stone hatchets; while in the tropical-colored tree-tops nudging apes eyed the contest with malicious regard. The cry of the pursuers had a suggestive sound; occasionally as one fell the shriek that reached Stannum plucked at his heart, for it was a cry of human distress. He went down the mountain, but lost his way, his only clue in the obscurity of the woods being the tone. . . .

And now he heard a strange noise, a noise of harsh stones bruised together and punctuated with shouts and sobbings. There was rhythmic rise and fall in the savage music, and soon he came upon a sudden secret glade of burial. Male and female slowly postured before a fire, scraping flints as they solemnly circled their dead one. Stannum, fascinated at this revelation of primeval music, watched until the tone penetrated his being and haled him to it, as is haled the ship to the whirlpool. It was night. The strong fair sky of the south was sown with dartings of silver and starry dust. He walked under the great wind-bowl with its few balancing clouds and listened to the whirrings of the infinite. A dreamer ever, he knew that he was near the core of existence; and while light was more vibratile than sound, sound touched Earth, embraced it and was content with its eld and homely face. Light, a mischievous Loge: Sound, the All-Mother Erda. He walked on. His way seemed clearer. . . .

Reaching a mighty and fabulous plain, half buried in sand he came upon a great Sphinx, looming in the starlight. He watched her face and knew that the tone enveloped him no longer. Why it had ceased set him to wondering not unmixed with fear. The dawn filtered over the head of the Sphinx, and there were stirrings in the sky. From afar a fluttering of thin tones sounded; as the sun shone rosy on the vast stone the tone came back like a clear-colored wind from the sea. And in the music-filled air he fell down and worshipped the Sphinx; for music is a window that looks upon eternity. . . .

Then followed a strange musical rout of the nations. Stannum saw defile before him Silence, "eldest of all things"; Brahma's consort Saraswati fingered her Vina; and following, Siva and his hideous mate Devi, who is sometimes called Durga; and the brazen heavens turned to a typhoon that showered appalling evils upon mankind. All the gods of Egypt and Assyria, dog-faced, moon-breasted and menacing, passed, playing upon dreams, making choric music black and fuliginous. The sacred Ibis stalked to the silvery steps of the Houris; the Graces held hands. Phœbus Apollo appeared; his face was as a silver shield, so shining was it. He improvised upon a many-stringed lyre made of tortoise shell, and his music was shimmering and symphonious. Hermes and his Syrinx wooed the shy Euterpe; the maidens went in woven paces: a medley of masques flamed by; and the great god Pan

breathed into his pipes.   Stannum saw Bacchus
pursued by the ravening Mænads; saw Lamia
and her ophidian flute; and sorrowfully sped
Orpheus searching for his Eurydice.   Neptune
blew his wreathéd horn, the Tritons gambolled in
the waves, Cybele clanged her cymbals; and with
his music Amphion summoned rocks to Thebes.
Jephtha's daughter danced to her death before
the Ark of the Covenant, praising the Lord God
of Israel.   Behind her leered unabashed the
rhythmic Herodias; while were heard the
praiseful songs of Deborah and Barak, as
Cæcilia smote her keys.   Miriam with her
timbrel sang songs of triumph.   Abyssinian girls
swayed alluringly before the Persian Satrap in
his purple litter; the air was filled with the
crisp tinklings of tiny bells at wrist and anklet
as the Kabaros drummed; and hard by, in the
brake, brown nymphs, their little breasts pointing
to the zenith, moved in languorous rhythms,
droning hoarse sacrificial chaunts.   The colos-
sus Memnon hymned; priests of Baal screamed
as they lacerated themselves with knives;
Druid priestesses crooned sybillic incantations.
And over this pageant of woman and music the
proud sun of old Egypt scattered splendid
burning rays. . . .

From distant strands and hillsides came the
noise of strange and unholy instruments with
sweet-sounding and clashing names.   Nofres
from the Nile, Ravanastrons of Ceylon, Javanese

gongs, Pavilions from China, Tambourahs, Sack-
buts, Shawms, Psalteries, Dulcimers, Salpinxes,
Keras, Timbrels, Sistras, Crotalas, double flutes,
twenty-two stringed harps, Kerrenas, the Indian
flute called Yo and the quaint Yamato-Koto.
Then followed the Biwa, the Gekkin and its
cousin the Genkwan; the Ku, named after the
hideous god; the Shunga and its cluttering
strings; the Samasien, the Kokyu, the Yamato
Fuye — which breathed moon-eyed melodies —
the Hichi-Riki and the Shaku-Hachi. The Sho
was mouthed by slant-haired yellow boys; while
the sharp roll of drums covered with goat-skins
never ceased. From this bedlam there occasionally emerged a splinter of tune, like a plank
thrown up by the sea. Stannum could discern
no melody, though he grasped its beginnings;
double flutes gave him the modes, Dorian,
Phrygian, Æolian, Lydian and Ionian; after
Sappho and her Mixolydian mode, he longed
for a modern accord. . . .

The choir went whirling by with Citharas, Re-
becs, Citoles, Domras, Goules, Serpents, Crwths,
Pentachords, Rebabs, Pantalons, Conches, Fla-
geolets made of Pelican bones, Tam-Tams, Caril-
lons, Xylophones, Crescents of beating bells,
Mandoras, Whistling Vases of Clay, Zampognas,
Zithers, Bugles, Octochords, Naccaras or Turkish castanets and Quinternas. He heard blare
the two hundred thousand curved trumpets which
Solomon had made for his temple, and the forty

thousand which accompanied the Psalms of
David. Jubal played his Magrepha; Pythag-
oras came with his Monochord; Plato listened
to the music of the spheres; the priests of
Joshua blew seven times upon their Shofars or
Rams-Horns. And the walls of Jericho fell.

To this came a challenging blast from the
terrible horn of Roland — he of Roncesvalles.
The air had the resonance of hell, as the Guate-
malan Indians worshipped their black Christ
upon the plaza; and naked Istar, Daughter of
Sin, stood shivering before the Seventh Gate.
Then a great silence fell upon Stannum. He
saw a green star drop over Judea, and thought
music itself slain. The pilgrims with their Jews-
harps dispersed into sorrowful groups; blackness usurped the sonorous sun: there was no
music upon all the earth and this tonal eclipse
lasted long. Stannum heard in his magic mirror the submerged music of Dufay, Ockeghem,
Josquin Deprès and Orlando di Lasso, Goudi-
mel and Luther; the cathedral tones of
Palestrina; the frozen sweetness of Arezzo,
Frescobaldi, Monteverde, Carissimi, Tartini,
Correlli, Scarlatti, Jomelli, Pergolese, Lulli,
Rameau, Couperin, Buxtehude, Sweelinck,
Bryd, Gibbons, Purcell, Bach: with their Lutes,
Monochords, Virginals, Harpsichords, Clavi-
cytherums, Clavichords, Cembalos, Spinets,
Theorbos, Organs and Piano-fortes and accom-
panying them was an army, vast and formidable,

of all the immemorial virtuosi, singers, castrati, the night moths and midgets of music. Like wraiths they waved desperate ineffectual hands and made sad mimickings of their dead and dusty triumphs. . . . Stannum again heard the Bach Chromatic Fantasia which seemed old yet very new. In its weaving sonant patterns were the detonations of the primeval world he had left; and something strangely disquieting and feminine. But the man in Bach predominates, subtle, magnetic and nervous as he is.

A mincing, courtly old woman bows low. It is Haydn, and there is sprightly malice in his music. The glorious periwigged giant of Halle conducts a chorus of millions; Handel's hail-stones rattle upon the pate of the Sphinx. "A man!" cries Stannum, as the heavens storm out their cadenced hallelujahs. The divine youth approaches. His mien is excellent and his voice of rare sweetness. His band discourses ravishing music. The tone is there, feminized and graceful; troupes of stage players in paint and furbelows give startling pictures of rakes and fantastics. An orchestra mimes as Mozart disappears. . . .

Behold, the great one approaches and the earth trembles at his tread — Beethoven, the sublime, the conqueror, the demi-god! All that has gone before, all that is to be, is globed in his symphonies, is divined by the seer: a man, the first since Handel. And the eagles triumphantly jostle the scarred face of the Sphinx. . . . Then appear Von Weber and Meyerbeer, player folk; Schubert, a pan-pipe through which the wind discourses exquisite melodies; Gluck, whose lyre is stringed Greek fashion, but bedecked with Paris gauds and ribbons; Mendelssohn, a charming girlish echo, Hebraic of profile; Schumann and Chopin, romantic wrestlers with muted dreams, strugglers against ineffable madness and stricken sore at the end; Berlioz, a primitive Roc, half monster, half human, a Minotaur who dragged to his Crete all the music of the masters; and then comes the Turk of the keyboard, Franz Liszt, with cymbalom, čzardas and crazy Kalamaïkas. But now Stannum notices a shriller accent, the accent of a sun that has lost its sex and is stricken with soft moon-sickness. A Hybrid appears, followed by a vast cohort of players. The orchestra begins playing, and straightway the Sphinx smiles. . . .

Stannum saw what man had never seen before — the tone-color of each instrument. Some malign enchanter had seduced and diverted from its natural uses the noble instrumental army. He saw strings of rainbow hues, red trumpets, blue flutes, green oboes, garnet clarinets, golden yellow horns, dark-brown bassoons, scarlet trombones, carmilion ophecleides while the drums punctured space with ebon holes. That the triangle had always been silver he never questioned; but this new chromatic blaze, this new tinting of tones — what did it portend? Was it a symbol of the further degradation and effeminization of music? Was art a woman's sigh? A new, selfish goddess was about to be placed upon high and worshipped — soon the rustling of silk would betray her sex. Released from the wise bonds imposed upon her by Mother Church, music is a novel parasite of the emotions, a modern Circe whose feet " take hold on hell," whose wand transforms men into listening swine. Gigantic as antediluvian ferns, as evil-smelling and as dangerous, music in the hands of this magician is dowered with ambiguous attitudes, with anonymous gestures, is color become sound, sensuality in the mask of Beauty. This Klingsor tears down, evirates, effeminates and disintegrates. He is the great denier of all things natural, and his revengeful, theatric music is in the guise of a woman. The art nears its end; its spiritual suicide is at hand. Stannum lifted his gaze. Surely he recognized that little dominating figure directing the orchestra. Was it the tragic-comedian Richard Wagner? Were those his ardent, mocking eyes fading in the mist? A fat cowled monk marches stealthily after Wagner. He shades his eyes from the fierce rays of the noonday sun; more grateful to him are moon-rays and the reflected light of lonely pools. He is the Arch-Hypocrite of Tone who speaks in divers tongues. It is Johannes Brahms, and he wears the mask of a

musical masker. . . . Then swirled near a band
of gypsies and moors, with guitars, tambourines,
mandolins and castanets, led by Bizet; Africa
seemed familiar land. Gounod and his simpering
" Faust " went on tiptoe; a horde of Calmucks
and Cossacks stampeded them, Tschaïkowsky and
Rimski-Korsakoff at their head.   These yelled
and played upon resounding Svirelis, Bala-
laïkas, and Kobzas dancing the Ziganka all the
while; and as a still more horrible uproar fell
upon Stannum's ears, he was aware of a change
in the face of the Sphinx: streaked with gray, it
seemed to be crumbling.   As the clatter increased Stannum diverted his regard from the
great stone and beheld an orgiastic mob of men
and women howling and playing upon instruments of fulgurating colors and vile shapes.
Their skins were of white, their hair yellow, and
their eyes of victorious blue.   " Nietzsche's
Great Blond Barbarians, the Apes of Wagner ! "
exclaimed Stannum, and he felt the earth falling
away from him.   The naked music, pulsatile and
drowsy, turned hysterical as Zarathustra-Strauss
waved on his Übermensch with an iron hammer
and in frenzied, philosophic motions.   Music
was become vertiginous; a mad vortex, wherein
whirled mad atoms, madly embracing.   Dancing, the dissonant corybantes of the Dionysian
evangel flitted by, scarce touching earth in their
efforts to outvie the Bacchantes.   With peals of
thunderous and ironical laughter the Sphinx

sank into the murmuring sand, yawning, " Music is Woman." . . .

And then the tone grew higher and ultra-violet; the air darkened with vapors; the shrillness was so exceeding that it modulated into Hertzian waves and merged into light; this vibratile, argent light pierced Stannum's eyes. He found himself staring into the Egyptian mirror while about him beat the torrential harmonies of Richard Strauss. . . . Herr Bech had just finished his playing, and, as he struck the last chord of " Death and Transfiguration," acidly remarked:

" Tin must be a great hypnotizer, lieber Stannum! "

" In alchemy, my dear Bech, tin is the sign of Jove, and Jove, you know, hath power to evoke apocalyptic visions! "

" Both you and your Jove are fakirs! " The pianist then went away in a rage because Stannum had slept while he played.

SIEGFRIED'S DEATH

But, as you will! we'll sit contentedly,
And eat our pot of honey on the grave.
— GEORGE MEREDITH.

I

IT was finally arranged that the two women should not be present together at the funeral. The strain might prove too great; and as Marsoc wiped his forehead he congratulated himself that for the present at least a horrid scandal might be averted. He had pleaded in a most forceful manner with Selene, his sister, and it seemed to him that his arguments had taken root. Ever since Brazier's death there had been much talking, much visiting — and now he felt it soon would end. Oh, for the relief of a quiet house; for the relief that must follow when the newspaper men would stop haunting the neighborhood. The past two days had well-nigh worn him out, and yet he hated leaving Selene to face her troubles alone. Marsoc believed in blood and all its entailed obligations. . . .

The pitiless comment of the press he had hidden from his sister, but the visit of the other woman was simply unavoidable. There were certain rights not to be ignored, and the perfidy of the dead man placed beyond Marsoc's power all hopes of reprisal. Brazier had acted badly, but then, too, he had been forced by a fatal temperament into a false position — a position from which only sudden death could rout him; and death had not turned a deaf ear to his appeal. It came with implacable swiftness and with one easy blow created two mourning women, a world of surmise and much genuine indignation.

Selene sent for her brother. He went to her chamber in rather a doubting mood. If there was to be any more backing and filling, any new programme, then he must be counted out. He had accepted his share of the trouble that had thrust itself into their life, and could endure no more. On this point he solemnly assured himself as he knocked at Selene's door. To his quick gaze she did not appear to be downcast as on the night before.

"I sent for you, my dear Val," she said in rather acid tones, "because I wanted to reassure you about to-morrow morning. I have considered the matter a hundred times and have made up my mind that I shall not allow Bellona Brydges to sit alone at the head of his coffin —"

"But you said —" interrupted her brother.

"I know I said lots of things, but please remember that Sig Brazier was my husband, quite as much, if not more than Belle's, that he committed — that he died under our roof, and simply because the divorce laws of this country are

idiotic is no reason why I should abdicate my
rights as a wife — at least his last wife. If Belle
attempts her grand airs or begins to lord it over
me I 'll make a scene — "

Marsoc groaned. He knew that his sister was
capable of making, not one, but half a dozen
scenes with a well defined tragic crescendo at
the close of each. The situation was fast becoming unbearable. With a gesture of despair
he turned to leave the room but Selene detained him.

"You poor fellow, how you do worry! But
it is all your fault. You introduced Sig here —"

"How the deuce did I know that he had a
wife up in the hills somewhere?" cried Marsoc.

"Very true; but you knew of his habits,"
his sister rejoined gently. "You knew what a
boastful, vain, hard-drinking, immoral man he
was, and at least you might have warned me."

"What good would that have done?" asked
her brother, in heated accents. . . . He was
tall, very blond and his eyes were hopelessly
blue. Brother and sister they were — that a dog
might have discovered — but there was more reserve, chilliness of manner, coldness in the
woman. She could never give herself to any
one or anything with the same vigor as Val.
She lacked enthusiasms and had a doubtful
temper. Even now, as they faced each other,
she forced him to drop his eyes; then the door-
bell rang.

"If it's Belle, send her up at once. Run, Val, and see." Selene almost pushed her brother down the short flight that led to the landing on the second floor. The house was old-fashioned, the drawing-room upstairs. Val went down grumbling and wondering what sort of a girl was his sister. He almost ran into a woman dressed in deep mourning.

"Why, Belle — why, Mrs. Brazier, is that you?" he exclaimed, and then felt like biting his tongue.

Bellona Brydges was as big as Brünnhilde and dark as Carmen. Her tread was majestic and her black eyes, aquiline nose and firm, large-lipped mouth, gave an expression of power to her countenance. Her bearing was one of command, her voice as rich as an English horn, and her manner forthright.

"Never mind the Brazier part of it, Val," she replied, in an off-hand, unembarrassed tone. "I want to see Selene and have this dreadful business over before the funeral. Where is she?"

Val motioned upstairs and the clear voice of his sister was heard:

"Is that you, Belle? Come up right away. . . ."

II

Both women were dry-eyed as they embraced. Belle showed signs of fatigue, so Selene made her comfortable on the divan.

"Shall I ring for tea, Belle?" The other
nodded. Then she burst forth: "And to think,
Selene, to think that we should be the unlucky
victims. To think that my dearest friend should
be the wife of my husband." She began to laugh.
Selene would not smile. The tea was brought
by a man-servant, who did not lift his eyes, but
the corners of his mouth twitched when he
turned his back. Belle sipping the hot, comforting drink looked about her curiously. The
apartment reflected unity of taste. It was
rather low, and long, the ceiling panelled and
covered with dull gilt arabesques. The walls
were hung with soft material upon which were
embroidered fugitive figures heavily powdered
with gold dust. One wide window with a low sill
covered the end of this room, and over the fireplace was swung a single painting, "The Rape of
the Rhinegold," by a German master. The grand
piano loaded with music occupied the lower
part of the room and there were plenty of books
in the cases. Belle reflected that Sig's taste was
artistic and sighed at the recollection of her —
of their — big, bare, uncanny house on the hill.
Selene began:

"Belle, dear, I 'm glad to see you, sorry to see
you. The odious newspapers were the cause of
your discovering the crime — don't stop me —
the crime of that wretch downstairs —" Belle
started. "I sha'n't mince words with you.
Sig was a scamp, a gifted rascal; his singing

and artistic love-making the cause of many a woman's downfall."

"Oh, then there are some more?" asked Belle, in a most interested voice.

"Yes, there are many more; but my dear girl, we mustn't become morbid and discuss the matter. I'm afraid what we are doing now is in rather bad taste, but I'm too fond of you, too fond of the girl I went to school with to quarrel because a bad man deceived us. I've been laying down the law to Val, Belle; we must *not* be present at the funeral. We've got to bury our headstrong husband and we both can see the last of him from the closed windows, but neither of us must be present. Now, don't shake your head! In this matter I'm determined; besides what would the newspapers say? One miserable sheet actually compared us to Brünnhilde and Gutrune because — oh, you know why!"

"When Sig left the opera-house," continued Belle, in a calm voice, "he always took a special train home and I suppose the railroad men gave the story to the reporters."

"Not always; excuse me, Belle," contradicted Selene, in her coldest manner; "the last time Sig sang 'Götterdämmerung' he returned here." Belle stood up and waved her teaspoon.

"Now, don't be ridiculous, Selene; this was not as much his home as ours in the mountains, and —"

"There is no necessity of becoming excited, Belle; he told me of his affair with you." Selene's blue eyes were opened very wide. The other woman began to blaze.

"Affair? Why, foolish child, I am his first wife —" "Common-law wife," interjected Selene. "His first, his legal wife, and I mean to test it in the courts. His property —" "You mean his debts, Belle," interrupted Selene, contemptuously. "Sig owes even for his Siegfried helmet. He gambled his money away. He played poker-dice when he was n't singing Wagner, and flirted when he was n't drunk."

Belle sat down and laughed again, and this time Selene joined in.

"Tell me, dear, how and when he persuaded you," inquired Belle. Selene grew snappish. "Oh, you read the papers. We were married last month with Val as witness; then some fool got hold of the story; it was printed. Sig came home after the opera and told me that he was ruined because he had expected a fortune from Mrs. Madison — you know the old bleached blonde who sits in the first tier box at the opera — and, of course, I smelt another affair. I scolded him and sent for Val. Well, Val was a perfect fool on the subject of Sig, and when he heard of the gambling debts he said a lawyer might straighten the affair out. That night Sig began drinking absinthe and brandy, and in the morning James, the butler, found him dead.

If the papers had n't got hold of your story, the thing could have been nicely settled. As it is we are simply ridiculous, and the worst of all is that the management and the stockholders insist on a public funeral and speeches; Sig was such a favorite. Think! he was the first great American Wagner singer; and so here are we, a pair of fools in love with the same man "— "Excuse me, Selene, I never loved him. He forced me to marry him." "And my own brother, Belle, with his nonsensical Wagner worship, drove me to marry a man I had only met twice." Selene sighed.

"We were fools," they said in chorus, as Val entered, his eyes red from weeping. "You silly, silly boy, Sig never cared a rap for any one on earth but himself. Look at us and follow our example in grieving," and the widows laughed almost hysterically. . . .

III

As early as seven o'clock there was a small crowd in front of the Marsoc residence, from which was to be buried the famous tenor, Siegfried Brazier. His death, his many romances, his marriages, his debts and his stalwart personality canalized public curiosity, and after the doors had been thrown open a constantly growing stream of men, women, children, and again women, women, women, flowed into the house through the hall, into the big reception-room, past the modest coffin with its twin bouquets of violets, out of the side door and into the street again. The fact that at midday there were to be imposing public obsequies, did not check the desire of the morbid-minded to view the corpse in a more intimate fashion. No members of the family were downstairs; but over the broad balustrade hung two veiled women, their eyes burning with curiosity. As the tide of humanity swept by Belle felt her arm pinched:

"There, there! the old woman in a crape veil. That's mother Madison. She'll have to alter her will now. Perhaps she's done it already. She was in love with Sig. Yes, that old thing." Selene gave a husky titter. "And she's sneaking in to see the poor boy and thinks no one will recognize her. I'd like to call out her name." Belle clapped her hand over Selene's mouth.

"Look, now," said the latter, releasing herself; "look at those chorus girls. What cheek! All with violets, because it was *his* favorite flower. What a man; what a man!" . . .

Belle's companion leaned heavily on her, and Val came up and persuaded his sister to go to the front room. His eyes were hollow and his voice broke as he whispered to Belle that they might be seen. Besides, it was nearly time — he went downstairs. . . .

From the latticed window the two women watched. First, the police cleared the way; the ragamuffins were driven into the street. Then the fat undertaker appeared with Val and stood on the curb as the coffin, an oak affair with silver handles and plate, was carried to the hearse. Val and the undertaker got into a solitary carriage, and amidst much gabbling and wondering gossip were driven off. It was a plain, very plain, funeral, every one said, and without a note of music. As the crowd dribbled away, Selene recognized two of the prima donnas and the first contralto of the opera, and she nudged Belle in a sardonic manner.

"More of them, Belle, more of them. We ought to feel flattered," then both women burst into hysterical sobbing and embraced desperately. They read in each other's eyes a mutual desire.

"Shall we risk it?" whispered Belle. Selene was already putting on her heavy mourning veil. Belle at once began to dress, and James was despatched for a carriage. The street was clear when the widows went forth, and in half an hour they reached the opera-house. Here they were delayed. A mounted policeman tried to turn their hansom away.

Selene beckoned to him and explained:

"I am Mrs. Brazier," and the officer bowed. They were driven to a side entrance, and the assistant-manager took the pair to his box.

There they sat and trembled behind their long crape veils. . . .

Some one on the stage was speaking of music, the "Heavenly Maid," and the women dissolved in tears at the glowing eulogies upon their husband. The huge auditorium was draped entirely in black. In it was thronged a sombre-coated mass of men and the women known in the fashionable and artistic world. The stage was filled with musicians, and in its centre, banked by violets,. violets only, was the catafalque. The numerous candles and flowers made the air dull and perfumed; the large chandeliers burned dimly, and when the Pilgrims' Chorus began, Belle felt that she was ready to swoon.

The stage-setting was the last scene of "Götterdämmerung", and the chorus was in costume. A celebrated orator had finished; the chorus welled up solemnly, and Selene said again and again:

"Oh, Sig! Sig! what a funeral, what a funeral for such a man!" "It 's just the kind he would have liked," remonstrated Belle, in a barely audible voice, and Selene shivered. When the music ceased a soprano sang the Immolation music and there was weeping heard in the body of the house. The ushers with difficulty kept the aisles clear, and the lobbies were packed with perspiring persons. Wherever Selene peeped she saw faces, and they all wore an expression

of grief. Nearly all the women carried handker-
chiefs to their eyes, and many of the men
seemed shamefaced at the tears they could not
keep back. In one of the front stalls a solitary
figure knelt, face buried in hands.

"There's Val, Belle. There, near the stage,
to the left. I do believe he's praying. And
for what? For a man who had no brains, no
heart; a reckless, handsome man, who was
simply a voice, a sweet, lying voice."

"For shame, Selene, for shame! He was
your — he was our husband." Belle's lips
were white and trembling as she murmured,
"May God rest his poor soul. He was a sweet
boy, poor Sig, may God rest his soul. Oh, how
I wish he were alive!" Selene looked disdainful, and her eyes grew black.

"I don't," she said, so loudly that a man in
the next box leaned over, and then as "Siegfried's Trauermarsch" sounded, the coffin was
carried in pompous procession from the building.
There was a brief conflict between the ushers
and a lot of women over the flowers on the
stage, and every one, babbling and relieved,
went out into the daylight. . . . The widows
waited until the police had emptied the house,
then sent for their carriage. They lunched at
home and later, after many exchanges of affection, Belle drove away to catch the evening
train. Selene watched her from the window.

"I do believe she loved him after all! I wish

she'd set her cap now for Val. Pooh! what a soft fool she is. Sig was *my* legal husband, and I alone can bear his name, for she has no certificate. What an interesting name, Mrs. Siegfried Brazier, widow of the famous Wagnerian tenor. Is that you, Val?" Val came in, dusty and exhausted.

"Did you go to the cemetery?" "Yes." "Was any one there?" "Only one old woman." "Mrs. Madison!" cried Selene, in rasping, triumphant tones.

"No," wearily answered the man, lying. . . .

INTERMEZZO

In his hand Frank Etharedge held a cable-gram. The emotion of the moment was one of triumph mixed with curiosity; his sensitive face a keyboard over which his feelings swept the oc-tave. He was alone in his office, and from the windows on the top floor of this giant building he saw the harbor, saw the river maculated with craft; saw the bay, the big Statue — best of all saw steamships. This caught his fancies into one chord and the keynote sounded: Yes, life was a good thing sometimes. A few months more, in the spring, he would be sailing on just such an iron carrier of joy, sailing to Paris, to Edna. He looked at the pink message again. It announced in disconnected words that Mrs. Etharedge had been bidden to the Paris Grand Opéra. The cable was ten days old, and on each of these days the lawyer had gone to his private consulting room immediately after luncheon, and, facing seaward, read the precious revelation: " Engaged by Gailhard for Opéra. Will write. Edna." That was all — but it was the top of the hill for both after three years of separation and work. He was not an expansive

man and said little to his associates of this good
fortune, though there were times when he felt
as if he would like to throw open the windows
and shout the glorious news across the chimneys
of the world.

Etharedge was a slim, nervous man with dark
eyes and pointed beard. He believed in his
wife. Europe, artistic Europe, had for him the
fascination which sends fanatics across hot sands
to Mecca shrines. He had never seen Paris but
knew its people, palaces, galleries. His whole
life was a preparation for deliberate assault upon
the City by the Seine. He spoke American-
French, ate at French-American table d'hôtes,
and had been married four years to a girl of
Gallic descent whose singing held such promise
of future brilliancy that finally their household
was disrupted by music and its fluent decep-
tions. The advice of friends, the unfortunate
praise of a few professional critics, and Edna
Etharedge accompanied by her cousin, a widow,
sailed for Paris. Each summer he made up his
mind to join her; once the death of his mother
had stopped him, and a second time money
matters held him in a vise of steel, but the third
season — he did not care to dwell upon that
last summer: his conscience was ill at ease.
And Edna worked like the galley slave into
which operatic routine transforms the most
buoyant spirit. For the first two years her
letters were as regular as the mail service —

and hopeful. She was getting on famously. Her cousin corroborated the accounts of plain living and high singing. There were no vacations in the simple pension on the Boulevard de Clichy. She had the best master in Paris, the best répétiteur; and the instructor who came to coach her in stage business declared that madame held the future in the hollow of her pretty palm. But the third year letters began to miss. Edna wrote irregularly in pessimistic phrases. Art was so long and life so gray that she felt, thus she assured her husband, as if she must give up everything and return to him. Did he miss her? Why was he cool — above all, patient? Didn't he long for wings to fly across the Atlantic? Then a silence of three weeks. Etharedge grew frantic. He neglected business, spent much money in telegraph tolls, and was at last relieved by a letter from Emmeline relating Edna's severe illness, her close sailing to the perilous gate, and her slow recovery. He was told not to come over as they were on the point of starting for Switzerland where the invalid had been ordered. Frank felt happy for the first time since his wife had gone away. After that, letters began again — old currents ran smooth and the climax came with the wonderful news.

He would go to Paris — go in a few months, go without writing. Then, gaining the beautiful city, he would read the announcements of

Edna's singing. With what selfish, subtle joy
would he buy a box and listen to the voice of
his beautiful wife, watch the lithe figure, hear
the applause after her aria! He had sworn
this was to reward his long months of loneliness,
of syncopated hopes, of tiresome labor; his
profession had become unleavened drudgery.
Perhaps Edna would make him her business
man, her constant companion. Ah! what enchantment to stand in the *coulisses* and hold her
wraps while she floated near the footlights on
the pinions of song. He would give up his distasteful practice and devote the remainder of
his life to the service of a great artist, hear all
the music he longed for, see the Paris of his
dreams.

The door opened. Plunged in reverie he felt
that this was but an extension of his vision.
"Edna!" he cried and flung wide his arms.
"Frank, you dear old boy, how thin you've
grown! Heavens! You're not sick? Wait,
wait until I raise the window." She pushed up
the sash noisily and Frank felt the brisk air on
his temples. He smiled though his heart nipped
sadly. It was Edna, Edna his wife in the flesh;
and the excitement of holding her in his willing
arms drove from his brain the vapors of idle
hope. She was looking down at him a strong,
handsome girl with eyes too bright and hair too
golden. "Edna," he cried, "your hair, what
have you done to your lovely black hair?"

"There's a salute from a loving husband. No surprise, though I've dropped from the clouds. But my hair is quizzed. Now, what do you mean, Frank Etharedge?" Both were agitated, both endeavored to dissemble. Then his eyes fell on the cablegram. He started.

"In the name of God, Edna, is anything the matter? This cable! Why are you here? Are you in trouble?" The dark shadows under her eyes lightened at the commonplace questions. She had time to tune her whirring thoughts.

"Frank, don't ask too much at once. I'm here because I am. We have just landed. I left Emmeline on the pier with the custom officers and came to you immediately. Say you're glad to see me — my old Frank!"

"But, but — " he stammered.

"Yes, I know what you are thinking. I was engaged for the Paris Opéra — " "Was?" he blankly ejaculated — "and I couldn't stand it. Locatéli — " "Who?" "Locatéli. You remember him, Frank, my old teacher? He got me into the Opéra and he got me out of it." "Do you mean that low-lived scamp who gave you lessons here, the man I kicked out of doors?" She flushed. Etharedge stared at her. He was near despair. His dream of an artistic life on the Continent was as a bubble burst in the midday sunlight. He loved his wife, but the shock of her unheralded arrival, the hasty

311

ill-news, proved too much for this patient man's
nerves. So he transposed his wrath to Locatéli.

"Well, I'm damned!" he blurted, kicking
aside the chair and walking the floor like a
caged cat. "And to think that scoundrel of
an Italian —" "Frenchman, Frank," she interposed — "that foreigner, who ought to have
been shot for insulting you, that Locatéli, followed you to Paris and mixed up in your af--
fairs! And you say he had you pushed out of
the Opéra? The intriguing villain! How did
you come to see him?"

"He gave me lessons in Paris." "Locatéli
gave you — Lord!" The man was speechless.
He put his hand to his forehead several times,
and then gazed at his wife's hair. She fell to
sobbing. "Frank," she wailed, "Frank! I've
come back to you because I couldn't stand it
any longer — it was killing me. Can't you see
it? Can't you believe me? No woman, no
American girl can go through that life and come
out of it — happy. It made me sick, Frank, but
I did not like to tell you. And now, after I've
thrown up a career simply because I can't be
your wife and a great artist at the same time,
your suspicions are driving me mad." Her
tone was poignant. He looked out on the harbor as another steamer passed the Statue bound
for Europe.

"Ask Emmeline!" She, too, followed the

vessel with hopeless expression and clasped his shoulder. " Oh! Sweetheart, are n't you glad to have me back again? It 's Edna, your wife! I 've been through lots for the sake of music. Now I want my husband — I 'm not happy away from him." He suddenly embraced her. Forgotten the disappointment, forgotten the fast vanishing hope of a luxurious life, of seeing his dream — Paris; forgotten all in the fierce joy of having Edna with him forever. Again he experienced a thrill that must be happiness: as if his being were dissolving into a magnetic slumber. He searched her eyes. She bore it without blenching.

" Are you my same little Edna? " " Oh, my husband! " There was a knock at the door; an office boy entered and gave Etharedge a letter which bore a foreign stamp. She put out her hand greedily. " It will keep until after dinner, Edna. We 'll go to some café, drink a bottle of champagne and celebrate. You must tell me your story — perhaps we may be able to go to Paris, after all." " To Paris! " Edna shivered and importuned for the letter until he showed it. " Why, it 's mine! " she exclaimed. " It 's the letter I wrote you before we sailed." " You said nothing about it when you came in? " He put it in his pocket and looked for his hat. She was the color of clay. " It is my letter. Let me have it," she begged. " Why, dear, what 's the matter? I 'll give it to you after I have read it. Why this excitement? Besides, the address is not in your handwriting." He trembled. "Emmeline wrote it for me; I was too busy — or sick — or —" "Hang the letter, my dear girl. I hear the elevator. Let's run and catch it. This is the happiest hour of my life. An 'intermezzo' you musicians call it, don't you?" "Yes," she desperately whispered following him into the hall, "an intermezzo of happiness — for you!"

Suddenly with a grin the man turned and handed her the letter: "Here! I'd better not juggle with the future. You can tell me all about it — tomorrow."

And now for the first time Edna hated him.

A SPINNER OF SILENCE

She was only a woman famish'd for loving.
  Mad with devotion and such slight things.
And he was a very great musician
  And used to finger his fiddle strings.

Her heart's sweet gamut is cracking and breaking
  For a look, for a touch — for such slight things
But he 's such a very great musician
  Grimacing and fing'ring his fiddle strings.
                              — THÉOPHILE MARZIALS.

I

IN his study Belus sat before a piano, his
slender troubled fingers seeking to follow the
quick drift of his mind. He played Liszt's
" Waldesrauschen," but murmured, " She is
the first to doubt me." He laughed, and shifted
by an almost unconscious cut to the F minor
Nocturne of Chopin. With the upward curve
of his thoughts the music grew more joyous;
then came bits of a Schubert impromptu, boil-
ing scales and flashes of clear sky. The window
he faced looked out upon the park. Beyond
the copper gleam from the great, erect syna-
gogue was the placid toy lake with its rim of
moving children; the trees swept smoothly in a
huge semi-circle, and at their verge was the

315

driveway. The glow of the afternoon, the purity of the air, and the glancing metal on the rolling carriages made a gay picture for the artist. But he was not long at ease, though his eyes rested gratefully upon the green foliage. The interrogative note in the music betrayed inquietude, even mental turbulence.

A certain firmness of features, long, narrow eyes set under a square forehead, heavily accented cheek-bones, almost Calmuck in width, a straight feminine nose, beckoning black hair — these, and a distinction of bearing made Belus the eighth wonder of his day. That is what the hypnotized ones averred. Master of a complex art, his nature complex, the synthesis was irresistible. His expression was complicated; he had not a frank gaze, nor did he meet his friends without a nameless reticence. This veiled manner made him difficult to decipher. Upon the stage Belus was like a desert cat, a gliding movement almost incorporeal, a glance of feline intensity, and then — the puissant attack upon the keyboard. As in sullen dreams one struggles to throw off the spell of hypnotic suggestion, so there were many who mutely fought his power, questioning with rebellious soul his right to conquer. But conquer he did — so all the conservatory pupils said. A steady stream of victorious tone came from under his supple fingers, and his instrument of shallow thunders and tinkling wires sang as if an archangel had smote it, celestially sang. Belus was the Raphäel of the piano, and master of the emotional world. His planetary music gathered about him women, the ailing, the sorrowful, the mad, and there were days when these Mænads could have slain him in their excess of nervous fury, as was slain Bacchus of old. Thus wrote some enthusiastic critics of the impressionist school.

Zora came in. She was brune and broad, her eyes of changeful color, and her temper wifely. Belus flashed his fingers in the air, and she bowed her head. His own language was Hungarian, that tongue of tender and royal assonances, but Zora had never heard it. She was quite deaf; and so, barred from the splendors of this magician's inner court, she ever watched his face with a curiosity that honeycombed her very life.

The man's love of paradox had piqued him to select this deaf woman; he confessed to his intimate friends that the ideal companion for a musician was one who could never hear him practise his piano. She rapidly made a request in her little voice, the faded voice of the deaf: "Can't I go to the concert with you? Oh, do not put me off. I am crazy to see you play, to see the public." He drew back at once. "If you go you will make me nervous — and the recital is sold out," he signalled. She regarded him steadily. "Your art usually ends in the

box-office." They drank their coffee sadly.
Leaving her with a pad upon which he had
scribbled "Patience, Fatima, wife of Blue-
beard!" Belus went to his concert, she to her
hushed dreams. . . .

II

Zora drowsed on the balcony. The park
was a great, shapeless, soft flowing river of trees
over which the tall stars hung, while the creeping plumes of rhythmic steam, and the earthly
echoes of light from the flat-faced hotels on the
west side set her wondering if any one really
stayed at home when Belus played Chopin. No
one but herself, she bitterly thought. Her
mood turned jealous. His magnetism, her
husband's magnetism, that vast reservoir upon
which floated the souls of many, like tiny lamps
set adrift upon the bosom of the Ganges by
pious Mahommedan widows, must it ever be
free to all but herself? Must she, who worshipped at his secret shrine, share her adoration,
her idol, with the first sentimental school girl?
It was revolting. She would bear with it no
longer. The ride through the park cooled her
blood and eased her headache. Just to be
nearer to him; that might set her throbbing
nerves at rest. As if she had been cut off from
the big central current of life, so this woman
suffered during the absence of her husband. In

trance-like condition she stepped out of the carriage, and slowly walked down Seventh avenue. When Fifty-sixth Street was reached, she turned eastward and went up the few steps that led into the artists' room.

A man half staggered by her at the dimly lighted door, but steadied himself when he saw her.

"I am Madame Belus," she said in her pretty English streaked with soft Magyar cadences. He stared at her, and she thought him crazy. "All right, ma'am," he said after a pause. His speech was thick, yet he was not drunk; it was more the behavior of a drug eater.

"Don't go back there, lady!" he begged, "don't go back to the professor. He is doing wonderful things with the piano, but somehow I couldn't stand it, it made me dizzy. I had no business there anyhow. . . . You know his orders. Every door locked in the building when he plays. If the public knew it, what a row!" The man gasped in the spring air. Zora was terrified. What secret was being withheld from her? Who could be with him? Perhaps he was deceiving her, Belus, her husband! She tried to pass the man, who stared at her vacantly.

"Don't go in, ma'am, don't go in. Every door is locked, all except the two little doors looking out on the stage. My God, don't go there! I saw a mango tree — I know the

mango, for I've been in India — I saw the tree
bloom out over the keys, and its fruit fell on the
stage. I saw it. And I swear to the ladder,
the rope ladder, which he threw up with his
left hand while he kept on playing with the
other. If you had only seen what came tumbling down that rope as he played the cradle-
song! Baby faces, withered faces, girls and
mothers, the sweetest and the most fearful you
ever saw. They all came rolling down and the
people in front sat still, the old ones crying
softly. And there were wings and devilish
things. I couldn't stand the air, it was alive;
and your man's face, white and drawn, with the
eyes all gone like those jugglers I knew when I
was a boy in India — out there in India."

She trembled like the strings of a violin.
Then after a sharp struggle with her beating
heart, and bravely pushing the man aside, she
went on rapid feet up the circular stairway, her
head buzzing with the clamor of her nerves.
India! Belus had once confessed that his youth
had been spent in Eastern lands. What did it
mean? As she mounted to the little doors she
listened in vain for the sound of music. She
heard nothing, not even the occasional singing
of the electric lights. Not a break in the air
told her of the vast assembly on the other side
of the wall. Belus, where was he? Possibly in
his room above. But why had she met none of
the usual officials? What devilry was loosed in

the large spaces of this hall? Again her heart roared threateningly and she was forced to sit on a chair to catch her breath. A humming like the wind plucking at the wires of a thousand Æolian harps set her soul shivering in fresh dismay. The two little arched doors were in front of her, but they seemed leagues away. To go to one and boldly open it she must; yet her tissues were dissolving, her eyes dim. That door! — if she could see him, see Belus, then all would be well. Across the stair she wavered, a wraith blown across the gulf of time. She grasped at the cold knob of the door — gripped but could not turn it, for it was locked. Zora fell to her knees, her heart weeping like the eyes of sorrow. Oh! for one firm, clangorous chord struck by Belus; it would be as wine to the wounded. Zora crawled to the other door, perhaps — ! It was not locked, and slowly she opened it and peered out upon the stage, the auditorium.

The humming of the harps ceased and the chaplet of iron that bound her brow relaxed. The house was full of faces, pink human faces, the faces of women, and as these faces rose tier after tier, terrifying terraces of heads, Zora recalled the first council of the Angel of Light; Lucifer's council sung of by Milton and mezzo-tinted by John Martin. The faces were drained of expression, but in the rows near by she saw staring eyes. Belus — what was he doing?

He sat at the piano and over its keyboard his long, ghost-like fingers moved with febrile velocity. But no music reached her ears. Instead she saw suspended above him the soul of Belus. It was like a coat of many colors. It glistened with the subtle hues of a flying fish; and it swam in the air with passionate flashes of fire. This soul that wriggled and leapt, this burning coal that blistered the hearts of his audience, was it truly the soul of her husband? As the multitude rose in cadenced waves of emotion, the soul seemed to shrink, to become more remote. Then leaf by leaf it dropped its petals until only an incandescent core was left. And this, too, paled and died into numb nothingness. Where was the soul of Belus? What was the soul of Belus? A bit of carbon lighted by the world's applause? A trick-nest of boxes each smaller than the other, with black emptiness at the end? A musical mirage of the world?

Belus was bowing. Then she saw the faces ravished with delight, the swaying of crazy people. They had heard — but she alone knew the secret. . . .

III

Belus shook Zora's shoulders when he returned from the concert. "Why, your hair is wet; you must have been asleep on the balcony in the rain," he irritably fingered in the deaf

code.   Still possessed by the melodious terror of
her dream, the rare audible dream of one born
to silence, she arose from her chair and waved
him a gentle good-night.   He stared moodily
after her and rang for the servant. . . .

The hearts of some women are as a vast
cathedral.   Its gorgeous high altars, its sounding gloom, its lofty arches are there; and perhaps a tiny taper burns before an obscure
votive shrine.   Many pass through life with
this taper unlighted, despite the pomps and
pleasures of the conjugal comedy.   But others
carry in the little chapel of their hearts a solitary glimmering lamp of love which only flames
out with death.   Zora knows this glimmering
light is not love, but renunciation.   Is not she
the wife of a great artist?

THE

DISENCHANTED SYMPHONY

The Earth hath bubbles —
— MACBETH.

POBLOFF began to whistle the second theme of
his symphony. He was a short, round-bellied
man with a high head upon which stood quill-like
hair; when he smiled, his little lunar eyes closed
completely, and his vast mouth opened — a
trap filled with white blocks of polished bone;
when he laughed, it sounded like a snorting
tuba. . . . Nature had hesitated whether to endow him with the profile of Punch or Napoleon.
He was dark, not in the least dangerous, and a
native of Russia, though long a resident of Balak.
Pobloff's wife dusted the music on the top of
his old piano. " In God's name, Luga, let my
manuscript in peace," he adjured her. She
snapped at him, but he continued whistling.
" More original music? " She was ironically
inquisitive as she danced about the white porcelain stove, tumbled over scores that littered
the apartment as grass grown wild in a deserted
alley; pushed violin cases that rattled; upset an
empty bird-cage and finally threw wide back the
metal-slatted shutters, admitting an inundation of

sunshine. . . . It was early May, but in Balak, with its southeastern Europe climate, the weather was warm as a July day in Paris. " Hurrah ! " Pobloff suddenly bellowed, " I have it, I have it ! " Luga glanced at him sourly. " I suppose you 'll set the world on fire this time for sure, my man ; and then little Richard Strauss will be asking for advice ! What are you going to call the new symphonic poem, Pobloff ? Oh, name it after me ! " She shrieked down the passage way at a slouching maid, and ran out, leaving Pobloff jolly and unruffled.

" Ouf ! " he ejaculated, as her sarcasm finally penetrated his consciousness, " I 'll call it ' The Fourth Dimension ' — that 's what I will. Luga ! Where 's that idle cat ? Luga, some tea, tea, I 'm thirsty." And he again whistled the second theme of his new symphony.

I

Pobloff loved mathematics more than music — and he adored music. He was fond of comparing the two, and often quoted Leibnitz : " Music is an occult exercise of the mind unconsciously performing arithmetical calculations." For him, so he assured his friends, music was a species of sensual mathematics. Before he left St. Petersburg to settle in Balak as its Kapellmeister he had studied at the University under the famous Lobatchewsky, and absorbed from him not a few of the radical theories containing the problematic fourth dimension. He read with avid interest of J. K. F. Zöllner's experiments which drove that unfortunate Leipzig physicist into incurable melancholia. Ah, what madmen these! Perpetual motion, squaring the circle, the fourth spatial dimension — all new variants of the old alchemical mystery, the vain pursuit of the philosophers' stone, the transmutation of the baser metals, the cabalistic Abracadabra, the quest of the absolute! Yet sincere and certainly quite sane men of scientific training had considered seriously this mathematic hypothesis. Cayley, Pobloff had read, and Abbot's " Flatland "; while the ingenious speculations of W. K. Clifford and the American, Simon Newcomb, fascinated him immeasurably. He cared little — being idealist and musician — for the grosser demonstrations of hyper-normal phenomena, though for a time he had wavered before the mysterious cross-roads of demoniac possession, subliminal divinations, and the strange rappings that emanate from souls smothered in hypnotic slumber. The testimony of such a man as Professor Crookes who had witnessed feats of human levitation greatly stirred him; but in the end he drifted back to his early passions — music and mathematics.

Zöllner had proved to his own satisfaction the existence of a fourth dimension, when he turned an India-rubber ball inside out without tearing it; but Pobloff, a man of tone, was more absorbed in the demonstration that Time could be shown in two dimensions. He often quoted Hugh Craig, who compared Time to a river always flowing, yet a permanent river: If one emerged from this stream at a certain moment and entered it an hour later, would it not signify that Time had two dimensions? And music — where did music stand in the eternal scheme of things? Was not harmony with its vertical structure and melody's horizontal flow, proof that music itself was but another dimension in Time? In the vast and complicated scores of Richard Strauss, the listener has set in motion two orders of auditions: he hears the music both horizontally and vertically. This combination of the upright and the transverse amused Pobloff immensely. He declared, with his inscrutable giggle, that all other arts were childish in their demands upon the intellect when compared to music. " You can see pictures, poems, sculpture, and architecture — but music you must hear, see, feel, smell, taste, to apprehend it rightfully: and all at the same time!" Pobloff shook his heavy head and tried to look solemn. "Think of it! With every sense and several more besides, going in different directions, brilliantly sputtering like wet fireworks, roaring like mighty cataracts! Ah, it was a noble, crazy art, and the only art, except poetry, that moved. All the rest are beautiful gestures arrested. . . .

Pobloff ate five meals a day, and sometimes

expanding his chest to its utmost and extending his arms to the zenith, yawned prodigiously. Born a true pessimist, he often was bored to the extreme by existence. In addition to the fortnightly symphony concerts and their necessary rehearsals, he did nothing but compose and dream of new spaces to conquer. He was a Czar over his orchestra, and though a fat, good-humored man, had a singularly nasty temper.

Convinced that in music lay the solution of this particular mathematical problem, he had been working for over a year on a symphonic poem which he jocularly christened " The Abysm." Untouched by his wife's daily tauntings — she was an excellent musician and harpist in his band — he could not help admitting to his interior self, that she was right in her aspersions on his originality: Richard Strauss had shown him the way. Pobloff decided to leave map and compass behind, and march out with his music into some new country or other — he did not much care where. Could but the fourth dimension be traced to tone, to his tones, then would his name resound throughout the ages; for what was the feat of Columbus compared with this exploration of a vaster spiritual America! Pobloff trembled. He was so transported by the idea, that his capacious frame and large head became enveloped in a sort of magnetic halo. He diffused enthusiasm as a swan sheds water; and his men did not grumble at the numerous extra rehearsals, for they realized that their chief might make an important discovery.

The composer was a stern believer in absolute music. For him the charms of scenery, lights, odor, costume, singers, and the subtle voice of the prompter seemed factitious, mere excrescences on the fair surface of art. But he was a born colorist, and sought to arouse the imagination by stupendous orchestral effects, frescoes of tone wherein might be discerned terrifying perspectives, sinister avenues of drooping trees melting into iron dusks. If Pobloff was a mathematician, he was also a painter-poet. He did not credit the theory of the alienists, that the confusion of tone and color — *audition colorée* — betrayed the existence of a slight mental lesion; and he laughed consumedly at the notion of confounding musicians with madmen.

"Then my butcher and baker are just as mad," he asserted; and swore that a man could both pray and think of eating at the same time. Why should the highly organized brain of a musician be considered abnormal because it could see tone, hear color, and out of a mixture of sound and silence, fashion images of awe and sweetness for a wondering, unbelieving world? If Man is a being afloat in an ocean of vibrations, as Maurice de Fleury wrote, then any or all vibrations are possible. Why not a synthesis? Why not a transposition of the *neurons* — according to Ramon Y Cajal being little erectile bodies in the cells of the cortex, stirred to reflex motor impulse when a message is sent them from the sensory nerves? The crossing of filaments occurs oftener than imagined, and Pobloff, knowing these things, had boundless faith in his enterprise. So when he cried aloud, " I have it ! " he really believed that at last he saw the way clear; and his symphonic poem was to be the key which would unlock the great mystery of existence.

II

Rehearsal had been called at eight o'clock, a late hour for Balak, which rises early only to get ready the sooner for the luxury of a long afternoon siesta. The conductor of the Royal Filharmonie Orchestra had sent out brief enough notice to his men; but they were in the opera house before he arrived. Pobloff believed in discipline ; when he reached the stage, he cast a few quick glances about him: fifty-two men in all sat in their accustomed places; his concertmaster, Sven, was nodding at the leader. Then Pobloff surveyed the auditorium, its depths dimly lighted by the few clusters of lights on the platform; white linen coverings made more ghastly the background. He thought he saw some one moving near the main door. " Who's that? " He rapped sharply for an answer but none came. Sven said that the women who cleaned the opera house had not yet arrived.

THE DISENCHANTED SYMPHONY

" Lock the doors and keep them out," was the response, and one of the double-bass players ran down the steps to attend to the order. The men smiled; and some whispered that they were evidently in for a hard morning — all signs were ominous. Again the conductor's stick commanded silence.

In a few words he told them he would rehearse his new symphonic poem, " The Abysm: " " I call it by that title as an experiment. In fact the music is experimental — in the development-section I endeavor to represent the depths of starry space; one of those black abysms that are the despair of astronomer and telescope. Ahem! " Pobloff looked so conscious as he wiped his perspiring mop of a forehead that the tenor trombone coughed in his instrument. The strange cackle caused the composer to start: " How 's that, what 's that? " The man apologized. " Yes, yes, of course you did n't do it on purpose. But how did you do it? Try it again." The trombone blatted and the orchestra roared with laughter. " Gentlemen, gentlemen, this will never do. I needed just such a crazy tone effect and always imagined the trombone too low for it." " Try the oboe, Herr Kapellmeister," suggested Sven, and this was received with noisy signs of joy. " Yes, the crazy oboe, that 's the fellow for the crazy effects! " — they all shouted. Luga, at her harp, arpeggiated in sardonic excitement.

"What's the matter with you men this morning?" sternly inquired Pobloff. "Did you miss your breakfasts?" Stillness ensued and the rehearsal proceeded. It was very trying. Seven times the first violins, divided, essayed one passage, and after its chromaticism had been conquered it would not go at all when played with the wood-wind. It was nearly eleven o'clock. The heat increased and also the thirst of the men. As the doors were locked there was no relief. Grumbling started. Pobloff, very pale, his eyes staring out of his head, yelled, swore, stamped his feet, waved his arms and twice barely escaped tumbling over. The work continued and a glaze seemed to obscure his eyes; he was well-nigh speechless but beat time with an intensity that carried his men along like chips in a high surf. The free-fantasia of the poem was reached, and, roaring, the music neared its climacteric point. "Now," whispered Pobloff, stooping, "when the pianissimo begins I shall watch for the Abysm." As the wind sweepingly rushes to a howling apex so came the propulsive crash of the climax. The tone rapidly subsided and receded; for the composer had so cunningly scored it that groups of instruments were withdrawn without losing the thread of the musical tale. The tone, spun to a needle fineness, rushed up the fingerboard of the fiddles accompanied by the harp in a billowing glissando and — then on ragged rims of wide thunder a gust of air seemed to melt lights, men, instruments into a darkness that froze the eyeballs. With a scorching whiff of sulphur and violets, a thin, spiral scream, the music tapered into the sepulchral clang of a tam-tam. And Pobloff, his broad face awash with fear saw by a solitary wavering gas-jet that he was alone and upon his knees. Not a musician was to be seen. Not a sound save dull noises from the street without. He stared about him like a man suffering from some hideous ataxia, and the horror of the affair plucking at his soul, he beat his breast, groaning in an agony of envy.

"Oh, it is the Fourth Dimension they have found — my black abysm! Oh, why did I not fall into it with the ignorant dogs!" He was crying this over and over when the doors were smashed and Pobloff taken, half delirious, to his home. . . .

III

The houses of Balak are seldom over two storeys high; an occasional earthquake is the reason for this architectural economy. Pobloff's sleeping apartment opened out upon a broad balcony just above the principal entrance. As he lay upon his couch his thoughts revolved like a coruscating wheel of fire. What! How! Where! And Luga, was she lost to him in that no-man's land of a fourth dimension? He closed his weary wet eyes. Then pricked by a sudden thought he sat up in jealous rage. No-man's land? Yes, but the entire orchestra of fifty-two men were with her — and he hated the horn-player, for had he not intercepted poison-ous glances between Luga and that impertinent jackanapes? In his torture Pobloff groaned aloud and wondered how he had reached his home: he could remember nothing after the ebon music had devoured his band. How did it come about? Why was he not drawn within the fatal whirlpool of sound? Or was he out-side the fringe of the vortex? As these questions thronged the chambers of his brain the consciousness of what he had discovered, accomplished, flashed over him in a supe-rior hot wave of exultation. " I am greater than Pythagoras, Kepler, Newton ! " he raved, only stopping for breath. Too well had he calculated his trap for the detection of a third dimension in Time, a fourth one in Space, only to catch the wrong game; for he had counted upon studying, if but for a few rapt moments, the vision of a land west of the sun, east of the moon — a novel territory, perhaps a vast play-ground for souls emancipated from the gyves of existence. But this ! — he shuddered at the catastrophe: a very Pompeian calamity depriv-ing him at a stroke of his wife, his orchestra — all, all had been engulfed. Forgetting his newly won crown, forgetting the tremendous import of his discovery to mankind, Pobloff began howling, "Luga, Luga, *Akh!* Wife of my bosom, my tender little violet of a harpist!"

His voice floated into the street, and it seemed to him to be echoed by a shrill chorus. Soprano voices reached him and he heard his name mentioned in a foreboding way.

"Where is the pig? Pobloff! Pobloff! Why don't you show your ugly face? Be a man! Where are our husbands?" He recognized a voice — it was the wife of the horn-player who thus insulted him. She was a tall, ugly woman and, as gossip averred, she beat her man if he did not return home sober with all his wages. Pobloff rushed out upon the balcony; it was not many feet above the level of the street. In the rays of a sinking sun he was received with jeers, groans, and imprecations. Balakian women have warm blood in their veins and are not given to measuring their words over-nicely. He stared about him in sheer wonderment. A mob of women gazed up at him and its one expression was unconcealed wrath. Children and men hung about the circle of vengeful amazons laughing, shouting and urging violence. Pobloff, in his dressing-gown, was a fair target. "Where are our husbands? Brute, beast, in what prison have you locked them up? Where is your good woman, Luga? Have you hidden her, you old tyrant?" "No!" shrieked the horn-player's wife, "he's jealous of her." "And she's run away with your man," snapped the wife of the crazy oboist. The two women struggled to get at each other, their fingers curved for hairplucking, but others interfered — it would not be right to promote a street fight, when the cause of the trouble was almost in their clutches. A disappointed yell arose. Pobloff had sneaked away, overjoyed at the chance, and, as his front door succumbed to angry feminine pressure, he was safely hidden in the opera house which he reached by running along back alleys in the twilight. There he learned from one of the stage hands that the real secret was his and his alone.

Alarmed by the absence of their husbands, the musicians' wives hung around the building pestering the officials. Pobloff has been found, they were informed, in a solitary fit, on the floor of the auditorium. The stage was in the greatest confusion — chairs and music stands being piled about as if a tornado had visited the place. Not a musician was there, and with the missing was Luga, the harp-player. A thousand wild rumors prevailed. The men, tired of tyrannical treatment, brutal rehearsals and continual abuse, had risen in a body and thrashed their leader; then fearing arrest, fled to the suburbs carrying off Luga with them as dangerous witness. But the summer-garden, where they usually foregathered, had not seen them since the Sunday previous — Luga not for weeks. This had been

ascertained by interested scouts. The fact that
Luga was with the rebels gave rise to disconcert-
ing gossip. Possibly her husband had discovered a certain flirtation — heads shook knowingly.
At five o'clock the news spread that Pobloff had
by means of a trap in the stage, dropped the entire orchestra into the cellar, where they lay
entombed in a half-dying condition. No one
could trace this tale to its source, thought it was
believed to have emanated from the oboe-play-
er's wife. Half a hundred women rushed to the
opera house and fell upon their hands and knees,
scratching at the iron cellar gratings, and calling
loudly through the little windows whose thick
panes of glass were grimed with age. Finding
nothing, hearing nothing, the dissatisfied crew
only needed an angry explosion of bitterness
from the lips of the horn-player's spouse to hatch
hatred in their bosoms and to set them upon
Pobloff at his home.

Now knowing that he was safe for the moment
behind the thick walls of the opera house, he
consoled himself with some bread and wine which
his servant fetched him. And then he fell to
thinking hard.

No, not a soul suspected the real reason for
the disappearance of the band — that secret was
his forever. By the light of a lamp in the property room he danced with joy at his escape from
danger; and the tension being relaxed, he burst
out sobbing: "Luga! Luga! Oh, where are

you, my little harpist! I have not forgotten you,
my violet. Let me go to you!" Pobloff rolled
over the carpetless floor in an ecstasy of grief,
the lamp barely casting enough light to cover
his burly figure, his cheeks trilling with tears.

IV

A thin rift of sunshine fell across Pobloff's
nose and awoke him. He sat up. It took fully
five minutes for self-orientation, and the fixed
idea bored vainly at his forehead. He groaned
as he realized the hopelessness of the situation.
Sometime the truth would have to be told. The
king — what would His Majesty not say! Pobloff's life was in danger; he had no doubt on that
head. At the best, if he escaped the infuriated
women he would be cast into prison, or else
wander an exile, all his hopes of glory gone.
The prospect was chilling. If he had only kept
the score — the score, where was it? In a moment he was on his feet, rummaging the stage
for the missing music. It had vanished. Pobloff
jumped from the platform to the spot where he
had fallen; his sharp eye saw something white
beneath the overturned music-stand. It did not
take long to reveal the missing *partitur*. All
was there, not a leaf missing, though some rumpled and soiled. When Pobloff had tumbled
into the aisle, miraculously escaping a dislo-
cated neck, the music and the rack had kept

him company. Curiously he fingered the manuscript. Yes, there was the fatal spot! He gazed at the strange combination of instruments on the page in his own nervous handwriting. How came the cataclysm? Vainly the composer scanned the various clefs, vainly he strove to endow with significance the sparse bunches of notes scattered over the white ruled paper. He saw the violins in the highest, most screeching position; saw them disappear like a battalion of tiny balloons in a cloud. No, it was not by the violins the dread enigma was solved. But there were few other instruments on the leaf except the harp. Pooh! The harp was innocent enough with its fantastic spray of arpeggios; it was used only as gilding to warm the bitter, wiry tone of the fiddles. No, it was not the harp, Pobloff decided. The tam-tam, a pulsatile instrument! Perhaps its mordant sound coupled to the hissing of the fiddles, the cheeping of the wood-wind, and the roll of the harp; perhaps — and then he was gripped by a thrilling thought.

He paced the length of the empty hall talking aloud. What an idea! Why not put it into execution at once? But how? Pobloff moaned as he realized its futility. He could secure no other musicians because every one that once resided in Balak had disappeared; there was no hope for their recrudescence. He tramped the parquet like a savage hyena. To play the symphonic poem again, to rescue from eternity his lost Luga, his lost comrades, to hear their extraordinary stories! . . . Trembling seized him. If the work could by any possibility be played again would not the same awful fate overtake the new men and perhaps himself? Decidedly that way would be courting disaster.

As he strode desperately toward the stage, staring at its polished boards as if to extort their secret, he discerned the shining pipes of the monster mechanical organ that Balakian municipal pride had imported and installed there. Pobloff was a man of fertile invention: the organ might serve his purpose. But then came the discouraging knowledge that he could not play it well enough. No matter; he would make the attempt. He clambered over the stage, reached the instrument, threw open the case and inspected the manuals. By pulling out various stops he soon had a fair reproduction of the instrumental effects of his score. Trembling, he placed the music upon the rack, tremblingly he touched the button that set in movement the automatic motor. Forgetting the danger of detection, he set pealing in all its diapasonic majesty this Synthesis of Instruments. He reached the enchanted passage, he played it, his knees knocking like an undertaker's hammer, his fingers glued to the keys by moisty fear. The abysm was easily traversed; nothing occurred. Despair crowned

340

the head of Pobloff, pressing spikes of remorse into his sweating brow. What could be the reason? Ah, there was no tam-tam! He rushed into the music-room and soon returned with an old, rusty Chinese gong. Again the page was played, the tam-tam's thin edge set shivering with mournful resonance. And again there was no result. Pobloff cursed the organ, cursed the gong, cursed his life, cursed the universe.

The door opened and the stage carpenter peeped in. "Say, Mr. Pobloff, do come and have your coffee! The coast's clear. All the women have gone away to the country on a wild goose chase." His voice was kind though his expression was one of suspicion. Pobloff did seem a trifle mad. He went into the property room. As he drank his coffee the other watched him. Suddenly Pobloff let out a huge cry of satisfaction. "Fool! Dolt! Idiot that I am! Of course the passage will have to be played backward to get them to return, to disenchant the symphony!" He leaped with joy. "Yes, governor, but you've upset your coffee," said the carpenter warningly. Pobloff heard nothing. The problem now was to play that vile passage backward. The organ — there stood the organ but, musician as he was, he could not play his score in reverse fashion. The thing was a manifest impossibility. Then a light beat in upon his tortured brain. The carpenter trembled for the conductor's reason.

"Look here, my boy," Pobloff blurted, "will you do me a favor? Just take this music — these two pages to the organ factory. You know the address. Tell the superintendent it is a matter of life or death to me. Promise him money, opera tickets for the season, for two seasons, if he will have this music reproduced, cut out, perforated, whatever it is — on a roll that I can use in this organ. I must have it within an hour — or soon as he can. Hurry him, stand over him, threaten him, curse him, beat him, give him anything he asks — anything, do you hear?" Thrusting the astonished fellow out of the room into the entry, into the street, Pobloff barred the door and standing on one leg he hopped along the hall like a gay frog, lustily trolling all the while a melancholy Russian folk-song. Then throwing himself prostrate on the floor he spread out his arms cruciform fashion and with a Slavic apathy that was fatalistic awaited the return of the messenger.

The deadly solemnity of the affair had robbed it for him of its strangeness, its abnormality; even his sense of its ludicrousness had fled. He was consumed by a desire to see Luga once more. She had been a burden: she was waspish of tongue and given to seeking the admiration of others, notably that of the damnable horn-player — Pobloff clenched his fists — but she was his wife, Luga, and could tell him what he wished most to know. . . .

He seemed to have spent a week, his face pressed to the boards, his eyes concentrated on the uneven progress of a file of ants in a crack. The cautious tap at the stage door had not ceased before he was there seizing in a clutch of iron the carpenter. "The rolls! Have you got them with you?" he gasped. A cylinder was shoved into his eager hand and with it he fled to the auditorium, not even shutting the doors behind him. What did he care now? He was sure of victory. Placing the roll in reverse order in the cylinder he started the mechanism of the organ. Slowly, as if the grave were unwilling to give up its prey the music began to whimper, wheeze and squeak. It was sounding backward and it sounded three times before the unhappy man saw failure once more blinking at him mockingly. But he was not to be denied. He re-read the score, set it going on the organ, then picked up the tam-tam. "These old Chinese ghosts caused the trouble once and they can cause it again," he muttered; and striking the instrument softly, the music for the fourth time went on its way quivering, its rear entering the world first. . . .

The terrified carpenter, in relating the affair later swore that the darkness was black as the wings of Satan. A lightning flash had ended the music; then he heard feet pausing in the gloom, and from his position in the doorway he saw the stage crowded with men, the musicians of the Balakian orchestra, all scraping, blaring and pounding away at the symphony, Pobloff, stick in hand, beating time, his eyes closed in bliss, his back arched like a cat's.

When they had finished playing, Pobloff wiped his forehead and said, "Thank you, gentlemen. That will do for to-day." They immediately began to gabble, hastily putting away their instruments; while from without entered a crazy stream of women weeping, laughing, and scolding. In five minutes the hall was emptied of them all. Pobloff turned to Luga. She eyed him demurely, as she covered with historic green baize her brave harp.

"Well," she said, joining him, "well! Give an account of yourself, sir!" Pobloff watched her, completely stupefied. Only his discipline, his routine had carried him through this tremendous resurrection: he had beaten time from a sense of duty — why he found himself at the head of his band he understood not. He only knew that the experiment of playing the enchanted symphony backward was a success: that it had become disenchanted; that Luga, his violet, his harpist, his wife was restored to him to bring him the wonderful tidings. He put his arms around her. She drew back in her primmest attitude.

" No, not yet, Pobloff. Not until you tell me where you have been all day." He sat down and wept, wept as if his heart would strain and crack; and then the situation poking him in the risible rib he laughed until Luga herself relaxed.

" It may be very funny to you, husband, and no doubt you 've had a jolly time, but you 've not told where or with whom." Pobloff seized her by the wrists.

"Where were *you ?* What have you been doing, woman? What was it like, that strange country which you visited, and from which you are so marvellously returned to me like a stone upcast by a crater? " She lifted her eyebrows in astonishment.

" You know, Pobloff, I have warned you about your tendency to apoplexy. You bother your brain, such as it is, too much with figures. Stick to your last, Mr. Shoemaker, and don't eat so much. When you fell off the stage this morning I was sure you were killed, and we were all very much alarmed. But after the hornist told us you would be all right in a few hours, we — "
"Whom do you mean by *we,* Luga? " " The men, of course." " And you saw me faint?"
" Certainly, Pobloff."

"Where did you go, wife? " "Go? Nowhere. We remained here. Besides, the doors were locked, and the men could n't get away."
" And you saw nothing strange, did not notice

that you were out of my sight, out of the town's sight, for over thirty hours?" "Pobloff," she vixenishly declared, "you've been at the vodka."

"And so there is no true perception of time in the fourth dimension of space," he sadly reflected. His brows became dark with jealousy: "What did you do all the time?" That accursed horn-player in her company for over a day!

"Do?" "Yes," he repeated, "do? Were there no wonderful sights? Didn't you catch a glimpse, as through an open door, of rare planetary vistas, of a remoter plane of existence? Were there no grandiose and untrodden stars? O Luga, tell me! — you are a woman of imagination — what did you see, hear, feel in that many-colored land, out of time, out of space?"

"See?" she echoed irritably, for she was annoyed by her husband's poetic foolery, "what could I see in this hall? When the men weren't grumbling at having nothing to drink, they were playing *pinochle*."

"They played cards in the fourth dimension of space!" Pobloff boomed out reproachfully, sorrowfully. Then he went meekly to his home with Luga, the harpist.

MUSIC THE CONQUEROR

THE hot hush of noon was stirred into uneasy billows by the shuffling of sandals over marble porches; all Rome sped to the spectacle in the circus. A brave day, the wind perfumed, a hard blue sky, the dark shadows cool and caressing and in the breeze a thousand-colored canopies fainted and fluttered. The hearts of the people on the benches were gay, for Diocletian, their master, had baited the trap with Christians; living, palpitating human flesh was to be sacrificed and the gossips spoke in clear, crisp sentences as they enumerated the deadly list, dwelling upon certain names with significant emphasis. This multitude followed with languid interest the gladiatorial displays, the chariot races; even a fierce duel between two yellow-haired barbarians evoked not a single cry. Rome was in a killing mood: thumbs were not often upturned. The imperial one gloomed as he sat high in his gold and ivory tribune. His eyes were sullen with satiety, his heart flinty.

As the afternoon waned the murmurs modulated clamorously and a voice shrilled forth, "Give us the Christians !" The cry was taken 'up by a thundrous chorus which chaunted alternately the antiphonies of hate and desire until the earth trembled. And Diocletian smiled.

The low doors of the iron cages adjoining the animals opened, and a dreary group of men, women, children were pushed to the centre of the arena; a half million of eyes, burning with anticipation, watched them. Shouts of disappointment, yells of disgust arose. To the experts the Christians did not present promise of a lasting fight with the lions. The sorry crew huddled with downcast looks and lips moving in silent prayer as they awaited the animals. In the onslaught nothing could be heard but the snarls and growls of the beasts. A whirlwind of dust and blood, a brief savage attack of keepers armed with metal bars heated white, and the lions went to their cages, jaws dripping and bellies gorged. The sand was dug, the bored spectators listlessly viewing the burial of the martyrs' mangled bones; it was all over within the hour.

Rome was not yet satisfied and Diocletian made no sign. Woefully had the massacre of the saints failed to please the palate of the populace. So often had it been glutted with butcheries that it longed for more delicate devilries, new depths of death. Then a slim figure clad in clinging garments of pure white was led to the imperial tribune and those near the Emperor saw him start as if from a wan dream. Her bronze-hued hair fell about her shoulders, her eyes recalled the odor of violets; and they beheld the vision of the Crucified One. She was a fair child, her brow a tablet untouched by the stylus of sin.

The populace hungered. Fresh incense was thrown on the brazier of coals glowing before the garlanded statue of Venus as flutes intoned a languorous measure. A man of impassive priestly countenance addressed her thrice, yet her eyes never wandered, neither did she speak. She thus refused to worship Venus, and angered at the insult offered to the beautiful foe of chastity, Rome screamed and hooted, demanding that she be given over to the torture. Diocletian watched.

A blare of trumpets like a brazen imprecation and the public pulse furiously pounded, for a young man was dragged near the Venus. About his loins a strip of linen, and he was goodly to see — slender, olive-skinned, with curls clustering over a stubborn brow; but his eyes were blood-streaked and his mouth made a blue mark across his face. He stared threateningly at Diocletian, at the multitude cynically anticipating the punishment of the contumacious Christians.

Sturdy brutes seized the pair, but they stood unabashed, for they saw open wide the gates of Paradise. And Diocletian's eyes were a deep black. Urged by rude hands maid and youth were bound truss-wise with cords. Then the subtile cruelty caught the mob's fancy. This couple, once betrothed, had been separated by their love for the Son of Galilee. She looked into his eyes and saw there the image of Jesus Christ and Him crucified. He moistened his parched lips. The sun blistered their naked skins and seemed to laugh at their God, while the Venus in her cool grot sent them wreathéd smiles, bidding them worship her and forget their pale faith. And the two flutes made dreamy music that sent into the porches of the ear a silvery, feverish mist. Breathless the lovers gazed at the shimmering goddess. The vast, silent throng questioned them with its glance. Suddenly they were seen to shudder, and Diocletian rose to his feet rending his garments. In the purple shadows of the amphitheatre a harsh, prolonged shout went up.

That night at his palace the Master of the World would not be comforted. And the Venus was carried about Rome; great was the homage accorded her. In their homes the two flute players, who were Christians, wept unceasingly; well they knew music and its conquering power for evil.

By JAMES HUNEKER

MEZZOTINTS IN MODERN MUSIC

Opinions of the Press:

Mr. Huneker is, in the best sense, a critic; he listens to the music and gives you his impressions as rapidly and in as few words as possible; or he sketches the composers in fine, broad, sweeping strokes with a magnificent disregard for unimportant details. And as Mr. Huneker is, as I have said, a powerful personality, a man of quick brain and an energetic imagination, a man of moods and temperament — a string that vibrates and sings in response to music — we get in these essays of his a distinctly original and very valuable contribution to the world's tiny musical literature. — *London Saturday Review.*

❦❦❦

The most valuable treatise ever written on pianoforte studies is incorporated in Mr. Huneker's recent volume, "Mezzotints in Modern Music." — *New York Evening Post.*

❦❦❦

It is rare indeed to find a critic on music who can in his criticisms combine German accuracy with French grace, and above all with American independence and freedom of speech. — *Musical Courier.*

❦❦❦

Mr. Huneker's book is a series of essays filled with literary charm and individuality, not self-willed or over-assertive, but gracious and winning, sometimes profoundly contemplative, and anon frolicsome and more inclined to chaff than to instruct — but interesting and suggestive always. — *New York Tribune.*

By JAMES HUNEKER

CHOPIN
THE MAN AND HIS MUSIC

With etched Portrait. 12mo, $2.00

Part I. The Man

I. POLAND: YOUTHFUL IDEALS. II. PARIS: IN THE MAËLSTROM. III. ENGLAND, SCOTLAND, AND PÈRE LA CHAISE. IV. THE ARTIST. V. POET AND PSYCHOLOGIST.

Part II. His Music

VI. THE STUDIES: TITANIC EXPERIMENTS. VII. MOODS IN MINIATURE: THE PRELUDES. VIII. IMPROMPTUS AND VALSES. IX. NIGHT AND ITS MELANCHOLY MYSTERIES: THE NOCTURNES. X. THE BALLADES: FAËRY DRAMAS. XI. CLASSICAL CURRENTS. XII. THE POLONAISES: HEROIC HYMNS OF BATTLE. XIII. MAZURKAS: DANCES OF THE SOUL. XIV. CHOPIN THE CONQUEROR. BIBLIOGRAPHY.

Opinions of the Press :

No pianist, amateur or professional, can rise from the perusal of his pages without a deeper appreciation of the new forms of beauty which Chopin has added, like so many species of orchids, to the musical flora of the nineteenth century. — *The Nation.*

🐝🐝🐝

We have not space to follow him through his luxurious jungle of interpretations, explanations, and suggestions; but we cordially invite our readers, especially our piano-playing readers, to do so. — *The Saturday Review.*

By JAMES HUNEKER

Chopin: The Man and his Music

Opinions of the Press:

It is written at white heat from beginning to end; the furnace of the author's enthusiasm never abates its flame for a moment. . . . I ransack my memory in vain for another instance of such unflagging fervor in literature. . . . I think it not too much to predict that Mr. Huneker's estimate of Chopin and his works is destined to be the permanent one. He gives the reader the cream of the cream of all noteworthy previous commentators, beside much that is wholly his own. He speaks at once with modesty and authority, always with personal charm. . . . Mr. Huneker's business was to show the world Chopin as he, after years of study and spiritual communion, had come to see him; and this he has done with a brilliancy and vividness that leave nothing to be desired. — *Boston Transcript.*

❧❧❧

It is a work of unique merit, of distinguished style, of profound insight and sympathy, and the most brilliant literary quality. — *New York Times Review.*

❧❧❧

We have received from the Messrs. Scribner an admirable account of Chopin, considered both as a man and an artist, by James Huneker. There is no doubt that this volume embodies the most adequate treatment of the subject that has yet appeared. — *New York Sun.*

CHARLES SCRIBNER'S SONS
NEW YORK